PAUL BUCHANAN

CITY OF FALLEN ANGELS

Legend Press Ltd, 51 Gower Street, London, WC1E 6HJ
info@legend-paperbooks.co.uk | www.legendpress.co.uk

Contents © Paul Buchanan 2020
The right of the above author to be identified as the author of this work has
been asserted in accordance with the Copyright, Designs and Patents Act
1988. British Library Cataloguing in Publication Data available.

Print ISBN 978-1-78955-9-811
Ebook ISBN 978-1-78955-9-804
Set in Times. Printing Managed by Jellyfish Solutions Ltd
Cover design by Simon Levy | www.simonlevyassociates.co.uk

Paul Buchanan earned a Master of Professional Writing degree from the University of Southern California and an MFA in Fiction Writing from Chapman University. He teaches and writes in the Los Angeles area. The second PI Jim Keegan novel *Valley of Shadows* will be published in 2021.

*For the illustrious Jim Blaylock,
the most generous of writer-friends*

CHAPTER ONE

Monday, August 13, 1962

IT WAS BARELY dawn when the little dog's yapping put an end to Jim Keegan's restless night of ankle-deep sleep. He pulled himself up to a sitting position on the sofa. The dog, his late mother's Welsh Terrier, barked at him again from the living-room floor, her stubby tail wagging madly. It was time to let her out.

Keegan's mouth tasted of Irish whiskey and stale graham crackers, a vile residue of the morning's sleepless wee hours. He'd bought the whiskey—a fifth of Jameson—last night at a liquor store on Sunset on his way up to his mother's hilltop cottage. He'd hoped a shot of it might help him sleep once the August daytime heat finally loosened its grip. But one shot wouldn't do it. The crackers he'd found around 2:00 a.m., rummaging in his mother's kitchen pantry. They were behind a can of Del Monte peaches.

Keegan ignored the barking dog and looked around the cottage's small den, working the kinks out of his neck. The room was crowded with the worldly belongings of a very old woman who had spent too many years holed up here with no one but a dog for company—silver-framed photographs and delft figurines, lace doilies and countless yellowing Zane Grey pulps. The place smelled of old laundry and Luden's cough drops, which the old lady had eaten as if it was candy. The cottage was bigger than Keegan's own apartment down in Mid-Wilshire, but sleeping here amid his late mother's belongings made him feel claustrophobic just the same.

His mother's terrier—the dog answered to Nora—now crouched in the center of an oval braided rug, aquiver with excitement to see Keegan finally rousing himself. She crouched low to the rug with her rump raised high, and barked at him twice more, a pair of strident, high-pitched yelps.

The sound cut through Keegan's skull like a rusty saw. "I heard you the first time," he groaned. He rubbed his forehead and stretched his legs out under the coffee table. A twinge of pain rippled across his lower back. That's what he got for falling asleep on his mother's wood-framed Victorian settee again. At fifty-three, you'd think he would know better.

Keegan found his Timex on the coffee table and squinted at the smudged crystal: 8:15. In her last few years, his mother had kept old-lady hours—dinner at five and bed by nine. Now, with full daylight shining behind the curtains, her dog expected to be let out. The poor thing should have been taken out hours ago. He buckled the watch on his wrist.

Keegan stood—too fast—and he clutched the arm of the settee when he felt like he might black out. The heat and the whiskey and the sleepless nights were wearing him down. The Jameson bottle on the coffee table was more than half empty; he'd meant to have only a shot—two at the most—to help him sleep. He scratched the stubble on his cheek. A half of a fifth. How much was that? He couldn't do math in his head in the best of conditions. Fractions least of all. But half of a fifth was too much, and now he was hungover. He straightened up gingerly and tested his footing. The dizziness had passed.

The dog darted around the coffee table and tugged playfully at Keegan's trouser leg.

Keegan cursed and shook his leg free. "Nobody likes a morning person," he told the dog, then he shuffled in the direction of the back door, working the aches out of his legs and willing his blood to circulate. What day was it, anyway?

The dog sprinted ahead of him, claws skittering on the oak floorboards, and disappeared into the kitchen.

Keegan plodded after her. The dog had been his mother's constant companion in her final years, but his own apartment quad had rules against pets. Eventually he'd have to take out an ad in *The Times* classifieds or cart the poor mutt down to the Eagle Rock pound—but, hell, there were so many other raveled strands of his mother's life left for him to knot up. Her dog would have to wait.

When Keegan got to the kitchen doorway, Nora pressed her nose to the crack beneath the back door and pawed at the weather stripping. He unlocked the deadbolt and pulled the door open for her, and she rocketed down the back steps, scattering finches from the rosemary hedge. Keegan left the door standing wide and went over to rinse his face at the kitchen sink. If the forecast was right, it would be another brutally hot day, but for now the breeze that seeped in through the door felt cool.

Keegan had been in a funk an entire week now. It started last Monday morning when he heard, over KNX, that Marilyn Monroe had died. He'd been sitting in the chair at The Owl Barber Shop when the announcement was made, and the news hit him like a sucker punch. He looked down at the silvery clippings gathering on the lap of the barber's cape and felt something like a swelling in his throat. He hadn't particularly liked the woman—in truth, he'd only seen two or three of her movies—but he'd glimpsed her once, or so he thought, getting out of a black Fleetwood in the alley behind the Formosa Café. He'd been waiting in a line of cars to turn onto Santa Monica Boulevard when she caught his eye. She wore beige slacks and a black turtleneck. He caught sight of her face, then, with the turn of her head, that platinum sweep of hair. She disappeared inside, followed by an older man in a pinstripe suit, and the door had closed behind them. That perfect face. Just the briefest glimpse of it. Keegan didn't tell a soul, but he'd felt oddly buoyant the rest of that day.

The news that Marilyn was gone—and, a day or two later, that she'd likely taken her own life—was a trapdoor he'd fallen through. He wasn't stupid. He knew, on some level, that it was his own mother he was grieving; she'd died the Tuesday before, and it had taken him a while to get clear of the numb, mechanical days leading up to her funeral—days full of phone calls and visits and countless small decisions about what the old woman would have wanted. The grief had hit him late, he supposed, in the form of a movie star and a bottle of Nembutal—like the sonic boom that rattled the windowpanes after the jet was already out of sight.

Keegan dried his face on a dish towel and went to his mother's wall phone by the refrigerator—*his* phone now, he reminded himself. He dialed the number of his office downtown. While the phone rang, he pulled a chair from the kitchen table and dropped into it, taking the weight off his knees. Mrs. Dodd, his secretary, had kept the office open all last week while Keegan crisscrossed the city, running down all his mother's lapses and loose ends. Shit. He still hadn't ordered a headstone.

The phone rang six times before Mrs. Dodd picked up.

"Any point in coming in today?" Keegan asked.

"You don't sound so good, boss," Mrs. Dodd informed him in that nasally Queens accent she had somehow picked up from her husband. "You hanging in there?"

Keegan kneaded his temples. *Hanging*. A hang*over*. There was probably a quip to be made, but it was too much effort, and he wasn't up to it. "Any business I need to worry about?"

"One new call," Mrs. Dodd said. "It came in early. Almost missed it. I told him you were taking a few days off, but he was very—"

"He *who*?"

"Simon something," she said. "Let me look."

Keegan heard the creak of her office chair, the shuffle of

papers. He pinched the bridge of his nose and tried to wish away the blunt ache gathering behind his eyebrows.

"*Catling*," Mrs. Dodd said at last. "Simon Catling. Not sure if there's two Ts or one. You know him?"

"Never heard of him. What does he want?"

"Wouldn't say," she said. "Real tight-lipped. Said he wanted you to track someone down. Wouldn't tell me why."

A skip trace. There was no easier paycheck, and he'd have to get back to work sometime, anyway. "Did he tell you who?"

"Wouldn't tell me a *thing*," she said. "No contact number *or* address. I was lucky to drag his name out of him."

Keegan glanced at his watch. He was a good half-hour from the office, if he hit nothing but green lights. He'd need a shower and a change of clothes, so he'd have to swing by his apartment. And what about Nora? He rubbed the sweaty stubble on his cheeks again. "How am I supposed to get hold of the guy?" he said into the phone.

"You're not," she said. "He wants you to meet him this afternoon."

"Where?"

"Grand Central Market," she told him. "Said you should be on the farthest stool at the pizza place at three o'clock sharp." Her tone dropped, as if she were about to say something confidential, though he knew she had to be sitting alone in his sixth-floor office. "He sounded foreign," she informed him.

"Foreign how?"

"Just *foreign*," she said, with a kind of verbal shrug. "Not from around here. How do *I* know?"

A shadow passed the kitchen window, and Nora set to barking outside.

Keegan stood, but from his angle he couldn't see anything through the window over the sink except eucalyptus limbs and a patch of cumulus clouds beyond the mountains to the east. Outside the kitchen door, the dog kept up her insistent yapping while a deep, burbling voice tried to soothe her.

Keegan plugged one ear with a finger. "You think it's on the level?" he said.

"I just sit here and answer the phones," Mrs. Dodd told him. *"You're* the big detective."

When Keegan hung up, he headed out the back door to see what the commotion was about. There, on the edge of the hill, a man stood among his mother's bedraggled Snowbird rose bushes, taking in the view, his broad back turned to Keegan. He wore linen trousers and an expansive white shirt with the sleeves rolled up. The updraft breeze stirred his mane of white hair. He stood with his arms akimbo, and his boat shoes planted a couple of feet apart—it was a pose that suggested he might just own everything he could see.

This hilltop cottage had been in Keegan's mother's family for three generations. First as a modest hunting lodge in the days when herds of mule deer still trampled the hills above Los Angeles. Keegan had only seen sepia-toned photographs of the original lodge in his mother's biscuit tin of old family photos. Before he was born, his mother and her two older brothers had torn the cabin down and built a weekend cottage. His mother had only moved here permanently when she got into her eighties and no longer felt safe negotiating the stairs in the old family place down in Melrose.

In the decades since his grandfather had first cleared away the scrub brush and sumac, Hollywood had arrived down in the valley in all its key-lit glory. The empty hills of Keegan's boyhood holidays were carved up now to make room for miniature estates that crowded these hillsides cheek by jowl. Each terraced lot down below now hosted a Tudor- or Greek-revival mansion, with a circular driveway in front and a glittering, robin's-egg pool in back. Flowers bloomed year-round inside the cinnamon-bricked garden walls, and verdant lawns blanketed the flat lots cut into the hillside. Keegan's mother, a pipe-fitter's widow, had spent her final years looking down on moguls and movie stars from her modest, three-room cottage.

"Can I help you?" Keegan said.

The man turned to face him.

Keegan was caught up short. He'd lived in LA his whole life, but these disconcerting moments of almost-recognition still had a way of knocking him off balance.

The man who now faced Keegan was a character actor, the kind of man whose face everyone recognized but whose name no one looked for when the credits rolled. He'd been the hero's sidekick in a string of Republic westerns from Keegan's twenties. Later, he was the avuncular next-door neighbor on some short-lived sitcom. Now, older, he seemed always to be the silver-haired professor or the pompous art collector on those Sunday night made-for-TV mysteries.

Though the two of them had never met, a bleached smile broke across the man's tanned face, as if he were genuinely thrilled to see Keegan, his old friend. Keegan couldn't remember the man's name, but he had heard stories about him. Over the years, his mother had kept him abreast of this man's excesses: the boozy soirées, the midnight skinny-dips, the string of leggy 'nieces' who stayed with him while his long-suffering wife shopped her way across Europe. The man's exploits seemed to shock Keegan's devoutly Catholic mother, but she never tired of describing them, each time Keegan paid her a visit, in a wide-eyed, scandalized whisper.

The actor held out his hand for Keegan to shake. "Nigel Ormsby," he said, more loudly than seemed necessary among the birdsongs and slight breeze. That name meant nothing to Keegan, but his voice—a reedy baritone—felt as familiar and soothing as warm Ovaltine.

Keegan shook the man's hand. "Jim Keegan," he said. The handshake left a floral-scented residue on Keegan's fingers, which he subtly wiped on his trouser leg.

"I was so sorry to hear about your mother," Ormsby said. Again, he spoke thunderously, from the diaphragm, as if projecting to the back row of the house. "She was a fine woman. Heartbreaking."

If Keegan were a gambling man—and he *was* when he could afford to be—he'd have bet a lobster dinner at Dal Rae that Ormsby had never actually spoken to his mother in all the years they'd shared this hilltop.

Ormsby glanced over at the cottage. "Will you be moving in?" he wanted to know. "Or are you planning to sell the place?"

Keegan flexed his jaw. The family cottage, and the rocky acre of hollyhock and poison oak outside the garden fence, was now prime real estate, and this actor clearly had designs on it. His mother's grave did not yet have a tombstone, but here Ormsby was, already picturing a guesthouse or stable or solarium where her cottage stood.

"I'm sorting things at this point," Keegan said coolly. "No firm plans as yet."

Ormsby looked down at his own hillside mansion and the sprawling city beyond. "It's a beautiful spot," he conceded. "But much too far from town to be practical."

It might have been Keegan's hangover, but the man's unctuous smile and booming voice grated on him in a way he couldn't account for. He worked his jaw from side to side and tried to tamp down his rising anger. Better to bite his tongue. He might, after all, want to sell the place once he'd sorted things out.

Ormsby turned back to Keegan and regarded him with an air of world-weary wisdom. "Well," he said, offering a slick smile, "if you *do* decide to sell. Please let me know." He bowed with an odd, stately flourish. Without another word, he crossed to the front garden, glided through the gate in the white picket fence, and strode down the road towards his own back gate.

AT A QUARTER to three, Keegan parked his MG in the lot on Spring and Third Street and got his ticket from the attendant. He walked up to Broadway, past the Currier and the Bradbury, feeling the sun bounce up at him off the sidewalk. The heat today had turned clammy—like a barber's hot towel—and Keegan felt like he might drown in it.

He'd shaved and changed clothes at his apartment, but now—not even a block from his car—he could feel the clean shirt clinging to his back under his twill blazer. He'd left Nora in his apartment with all the windows open and a saucepan of tap water on the kitchen floor. He hoped she wouldn't get hold of any of his shoes before he made it back to her.

Keegan crossed Broadway and passed the old Grauman theater. He paused on the sidewalk in front of the Grand Central Market's open entryway, with the stinging-hot afternoon traffic at his back. He stepped into the entryway and let his eyes adjust into the dim, neon-punctuated gloom. The old open-air arcade smelled of sea bass, old fruit and sawdust—a cocktail of scents that, with his hangover, was almost too much to bear.

He went in past the empty breakfast counter and the tobacco booth and headed deep into the arcade, on the lookout for the pizza place and the tight-lipped Simon Catling. Exotic spices and unfamiliar languages crowded the air. He stepped into a Chinese medicine booth to let a burly man roll a handcart past in the aisle. The woman there took him by the sleeve and tried to lead him back to her acupuncture table, but Keegan just shook his head and mimed his apologies. Time was the only reliable treatment for a hangover.

Keegan hadn't been inside the market in years—not since they opened the gleaming, fluorescent-lit Alpha Beta two blocks from his apartment. The market was shabbier and more cheerless than he remembered it in decades past. He wandered back up the aisle feeling queasy and wishing he'd just stayed in his mother's kitchen.

His kitchen.

Papa's Pizza turned out to be on the market's south side, across from a cinder-block wall where a row of step-up shoeshine stands loomed empty, like abdicated thrones. A bored teenager sat by the stands on a low stool with a shoe rag slung across his knees. His name tag bore a strip of masking tape, on which LUIS was printed in shaky ballpoint. The boy perked up when he saw Keegan coming towards him, but Keegan shook his head at him and sat down at the end stool at Papa's counter—as instructed. The kid quickly sank back into lethargy.

It took a minute or two for the white-haired man behind Papa's counter to look up from his *Press-Telegram* and realize he had a customer. Three o'clock on a sweltering Monday was clearly not the lunch rush. The man folded up his paper and set it beside the register. He came down to Keegan's end of the counter and asked him what he wanted.

Keegan knew he ought to buy something if he was going to occupy the man's stool. He looked at the chalked daily menu mounted on the back of the stall. A good, greasy meal would probably help settle his stomach, but pizza seemed like a bad idea. He didn't want to be caught—mouth full, slick-chinned—when Catling, whoever he was, showed up. Keegan just asked for a Bubble Up, lots of ice, and then looked at his wristwatch, so the man knew he didn't plan to stay.

It was three o'clock exactly.

Papa set Keegan's drink in front of him, in a waxy paper cup without a lid, and gave the counter a cursory wipe-down with a damp rag. He went back to his stool and his newspaper. For a while, a couple of women behind a knock-off perfume counter argued stridently in a language Keegan couldn't identify. By the time his watch read 3:07, he was feeling antsy. How long was it proper to wait for a man who wouldn't even leave you his phone number? How much longer would his Florsheims be safe in a hot apartment with a bored terrier?

By 3:10, Keegan's soda cup held nothing but melting ice and a chewed straw. He'd come all the way downtown on a sweltering Monday for a no-show. Welcome back to work. He took a single from his wallet, smoothed it on Papa's counter and pinned it down with a parmesan shaker. He rose to his feet, and a phone rang aggressively behind him, making him jump. He turned to find a battered payphone mounted on the cinder-block wall in a dim corner beside the shoeshine stands. He hadn't noticed it before, but its shrill ringing now set his nerves jangling.

Luis, shiner of shoes, swiveled his head from the phone to Keegan and back again. He shrugged and grinned, and showed no inclination to get up off his stool and answer it.

Keegan went over and picked up the receiver halfway through the fourth ring.

"Mr. Keegan?" a man's voice asked before Keegan could say a word.

"Who's *this*?" Keegan said. He turned his back to the wall, so he could see the rest of the arcade. None of the dozens of people he could see took any notice of him there in the corner.

"Be out on Broadway in two minutes," the voice told him. "Be discreet." The line clicked. The phone went dead. Keegan hung it back in its cradle. When he turned around, Luis was watching him, as if something in the situation had piqued his curiosity.

Keegan nodded at the kid. "Curiouser and curiouser," he told him.

KEEGAN BARELY MADE it to the sidewalk before a gleaming Fleetwood limo pulled up on the far side of the cars parked along the curb. Keegan shaded his eyes in the blinding daylight. The big car was glossy black with whitewall tires and shark-like fins on either side of the trunk. The windows were tinted so dark, Keegan might as well have been looking into the mirror above his bathroom sink. A couple of young guys came out to the market's entryway to get a better look at the car. If this was Simon Catling's version of being discreet, Keegan could have worn a bridesmaid's dress.

A driver in a black suit came around the back of the idling car to open the curbside door, unfazed by the blocked cars that had started up honking all the way back to the corner. From inside the open door, a manicured hand waved lazily for Keegan to climb inside. Keegan did, and the driver shut the door behind him. The car's air-conditioned interior felt like a plunge into a swimming pool; it had to be thirty degrees colder than the heat on the sidewalk, and the effect was jarring. Keegan's scalp tightened, which did nothing to help his aching head.

Keegan hadn't quite taken a seat before the limo lurched ahead. Not wanting to tumble forward onto a stranger, he sat down hard on the black leather seat, feeling the impact in his lower back and his knees. It took him a stunned second to catch his breath and gather himself.

The man who now sat facing Keegan was small, clean-shaven and well kept. He wore a pressed seersucker suit, with a blue bow tie and a red carnation on the lapel. His attire seemed designed to create an effect—more costume than mere clothing—though what effect was intended, Keegan couldn't guess. The man looked at Keegan wryly but didn't speak.

Keegan settled back into his seat and looked the man over some more. What else was there to do? The car was smooth and silent as it moved. The tinted windows made the street passing outside look like it was dusk.

The little man nodded almost imperceptibly. A small, smug smile tugged up the corners of his mouth. "I am Simon Catling," he said. This was not the broad American voice Keegan had heard a moment ago on the payphone. Catling's speech was soft and precise, with a hint of something exotic, the accent of a man who had wandered the world but put down no roots.

"I'm Jim Keegan," Keegan said. "Though I'm guessing you already know that."

Catling's features were delicate, pale and perfectly symmetrical, except for a small vertical scar etched on his left cheekbone. The parting in his coppery hair was steel-edge straight. Gold rings glimmered on both his pinkies. His smooth skin was the blue-white hue of fish bellies—like the man had remained forever untouched by the searing sun outside his car. Mrs. Dodd was right: he *was* foreign, alien in some conspicuous but unclassifiable way. Then again, there was something altogether contrived about the man, Keegan thought. Even his scar seemed too perfectly placed on his cheek—like a starlet's penciled-in beauty mark.

Without changing position, Catling held out his hand, and, with effort, Keegan leaned forward far enough to shake it. The hand was dry and quick to pull away. The ring on his pinky felt unnaturally cold.

Keegan settled back in his seat and let Catling study him. Despite the man's small-boned frame, Catling had the air of someone whose power was in no way limited by his physique. The universe, he made it clear, could wait for him to speak—and so, apparently, could Keegan. The limo slowed to a stop at a light.

"I used to read your articles in *The Times,*" Catling finally said, when the car moved forward again. He gazed out the window at the passing gray buildings. The sunlight—glinting dimly off passing cars—played upon his pale face. "I admired your technique," he said airily. "You always unearthed some curious—what is it you newsmen say? Angle? Slant? You knew how to shape mere events into a true story."

Almost every private detective in the Los Angeles Yellow Pages was a retired cop. They signed on with the LAPD or the Sheriff's Department and worked their beat while their pensions ripened. Then they retired and ran out the clock, double-dipping as bodyguards or PIs.

Keegan was the rare exception. For twenty years, he'd covered crime for *The Los Angeles Times.* But the paper had cut him loose a few days before his forty-fifth birthday. It was the old hack-writer cliché: the bottle of whiskey in a desk drawer; the missed deadlines; the angry, ill-chosen words to the wrong people.

The Seattle Post Intelligencer had offered him a job the moment word got out that he'd been fired, but Keegan couldn't bring himself to get on a plane. What was there for him in Seattle? Ferries and fish markets, and all that dismal rain. Not even any decent crime to speak of. LA averaged thirty-five days of measurable rain a year, and eighty homicides. It had the Black Dahlia, Mickey Cohen and Johnny Stompanato. And now it had brought out the Brooklyn Dodgers. Better a hungry PI in the City of Angels than a well-fed newsman somewhere else.

"I'm a private eye now," he told Catling. "I quit the news game. But I'm guessing you already know that, too."

Catling waved the information away. Of course, he knew it. "And you are a most capable detective, I am told," he said. He pulled a silver cigarette case from somewhere inside his trim suit and clicked it open with his thumb. "We have some acquaintances in common," he said. He held the cigarette case out to Keegan. It contained a neat row of short, unfiltered cigarettes in hazel wrappers. They infused the air with a peculiar scent, something like raisins and orange rind. These were not Lucky Strikes.

Keegan shook his head. "No thanks," he said. He didn't want to add nicotine to the chemical mayhem that was only now beginning to settle in his gut. "Sounds like you've been talking to Louis Moore," Keegan said.

Louis Moore—now *Lieutenant* Moore—was a cop Keegan had championed in the pages of *The Times*. He was one of the few black beat cops on the force in the old days, and Keegan gave him regular appearances in the Cityside column. Over the years, they'd traded favors and helped each other along in their respective careers. Moore had made lieutenant, around the time Keegan lost his job, and he had greased some gears to get Keegan his PI license without the typical rigmarole. There wasn't a whole lot either could do for the other after that, except to buy a round every now and again or to put in few kind words when they counted.

But the wily smile on Simon Catling's face slipped at the mention of Moore's name. The man took a cigarette for himself and snapped the silver case shut. He gave the cigarette three smart taps on the case and then tucked the case inside his suit again. "*He* was not the acquaintance who endorsed you," Catling said frostily. "I can assure you of that."

Keegan shrugged. So, it wasn't the lieutenant.

Catling lit his cigarette with a sleek-looking silver lighter and looked out the window again while he took a few slow drags. It was like the cameras were rolling, and he knew his lines, but he was just waiting for someone to say "action". In fact, the whole situation—the nonsense about the payphone; the man in the natty summer suit; the odd, hazel cigarettes— struck Keegan as made for TV.

Keegan wasn't in the mood to play along. He glanced at his wristwatch and then folded his arms in front of him. "I'm not sure what you want from me, Mr. Catling, but I'm a busy man."

Catling nodded, still facing the window, and blew out a stream of cigarette smoke. If Keegan was busy, it was no concern of his. "I need your utter and absolute confidence," he announced in precise, unhurried syllables. He turned to Keegan and eyed him imperially.

"Copy that," Keegan said. "Confidence is what they pay me for."

Catling raised his eyebrows in acknowledgment and took another pensive draw on his cigarette. "I find myself in a most delicate situation," he said, "the exact details of which I cannot divulge." He leaned to one side and pulled a black leather folio from a flap in the car door. He propped it on his knees, holding his cigarette in his lips. He opened the folio and pulled out a plump brown letter-sized envelope, encircled with a twice-wrapped beige rubber band. He held it out to Keegan and gave it a little wave in the air between them. Keegan didn't move to take it, so Catling tossed it across the gap onto the seat beside him.

Keegan didn't acknowledge the envelope in any way. It was clearly stuffed with cash—yet another TV cliché—but Keegan wasn't ready to talk about payment. He had no idea what this man was about, and it would be a mistake to even hint that he was agreeing to anything.

"In that envelope is ten thousand US dollars," Catling said. The cigarette bobbed in his lips as he spoke around it. "One hundred hundred-dollar bills. A down payment of one-third of the total fee I propose."

Ten thousand dollars riding on the seat beside him. Keegan resisted the temptation to glance over at the envelope. Thirty thousand total. It was a hell of an offer—more than Keegan could expect to make in a couple of busy years, and the last few years had not been busy. "That's a hell of a paycheck," Keegan admitted. "It makes me worry what you'd want me to do for it."

"I just need you to locate someone," Catling said. "I need you to find a young woman."

It sounded so easy, uncomplicated, which only made Keegan warier. "What's her name?"

"Alas, I don't know," Catling said. "Which is one of the reasons I am willing to pay so handsomely." He crushed out his cigarette in an armrest ashtray and pulled a large manila envelope from the leather portfolio that still rode atop his knees. He unbent the envelope's clasp and pulled out some eight-by-ten photographs. He held them out to Keegan.

Keegan hesitated. Nothing about this situation felt right.

"Please, Mr. Keegan," Catling said. "I only ask that you look at them. You may refuse to help me if you wish."

Keegan reached for the photographs. There were three eight-by-tens: black-and-white close-ups of the same young woman's face. Keegan recognized the flat, grainy distortion of a long telephoto lens. He'd shot hundreds of photos just like these—parked outside motel rooms and far-flung nightspots—with the pricey Nikon he kept locked in his office.

In the photos, the woman's dark, curly hair was cut short—stylishly, Keegan guessed. Her face was lean and angular. The photos seemed to have been taken on the same day: she wore the same pearl earrings and scalloped lace collar. They were cropped close. Only her face showed, not her surroundings or her companions, if there were any. In the last photograph, her head was bent down a little. A shadow, slanted across her shoulder, suggested someone had been sitting across from her.

The woman was primly pretty, Keegan thought—a Vanessa Redgrave type. Her eyes glistened as though she'd finished a good cry and was vulnerable and unguarded in its aftermath. She seemed completely unaware of the photographer, and Keegan felt the guilty twinge of a voyeur just holding the photos. He never felt quite clean looking through the viewfinder, but it was part of the job.

He sat back in his seat. "What do you want with her?"

"I'm afraid you will have to refrain from questions," Catling said. He nodded at the plump envelope beside Keegan. "You will be paid amply to keep your curiosity in check."

Keegan looked down at the top photo again. He tilted it to catch the gray daylight filtering in through the tinted window. How old was the girl? Certainly not much over thirty, maybe younger. He thought suddenly—and for no worldly reason he could name—of Marilyn Monroe's bright face as she turned and vanished through the back door of the Formosa Café. Some unspeakable emotion stirred in him. "What can you tell me about her?"

"Only that she's somewhere in Los Angeles," Catling said. "At least, that is what my sources suggest." Catling crossed his legs the other way and leaned forward a little over the folio in his lap. "She had an association with a gentleman in whom I had an interest."

"Had?"

"That particular gentleman is deceased."

Of course, he was. Keegan sighed and looked down at the photo again. "And if I don't take the job?" he asked.

"It will be offered to one of your less-capable competitors, and you will never hear from me again," Catling said. "I only ask that you keep our meeting in the utmost confidence."

Keegan imagined it: some other schmo sent to Papa's

Pizza and treated to the limo ride. Some other hungry flatfoot slipping the fat envelope of cash into an inner jacket pocket.

He leaned over and looked out the side window. The neon sign for Cole's swept past. They must have turned down Sixth Street. It would be a hot fifteen-minute slog back to his car in the worst of the afternoon heat, but what choice did he have? "This is my stop," he said when the car pulled up at the light on South Los Angeles. "I'm not your man."

KEEGAN WALKED A block out of his way up to Hill Street, keeping on the south side of Sixth, so he'd be out of the sun.

Lusk's newsstand, on the eastern corner of Pershing Square, was like any other sidewalk rag-rack in town: a stall where you could pick up *The Times* or *Herald Examiner* or maybe a pulp novel, if your tastes weren't too highbrow. You could get a Baby Ruth or some breath mints for a dime—even a bottle of aspirin, if your bus was due and you didn't have time to cross Fifth Street to the drugstore.

There weren't many people on the Square for a weekday. Empty park benches baked in the sun. Even the pigeons flocked by the fountain. A couple of teen girls stood in front of the newsstand in short-sleeved blouses and pedal pushers, taking chatty inventory of the candy rack.

While Keegan waited for them to make up their minds, he glanced at *The Times*' headline. TWO SOVIET SPACESHIPS ORBIT EARTH. Great. Just when his Monday was going so well.

Keegan wondered who might be sitting at his old desk right now in the southwest corner of *The Times*' newsroom. He could hear the clatter of typewriters, smell the ink. Part of him missed the hubbub and commotion, the hive-like feeling of so many people swarming around him in common pursuit. He thought of Judy Reynolds, down in the archives room, chain-smoking her Winstons and scissoring up the morning edition. He made a guilty mental note to give her a call, maybe meet her at some air-conditioned bar later on in the week to finally pay out on all the drinks he owed her for favors.

"Seeing how much you can read free without me catching you?"

Keegan looked up from the headlines.

The two girls were now loping down the sidewalk after their bus, and Kipper Lusk sat watching Keegan from inside the booth, behind the tiers of Lifesavers and Good & Plenty. The man had a way of hunching over in his folding chair like an old man, though he was probably in his mid-forties. His hair, still black, was thinning on top now. Sweat beaded his forehead and his ample upper lip. A barely audible radio, somewhere out of sight in his lair, was tuned to a baseball game.

"How's business?" Keegan asked.

"Lousy," Lusk told him. "Nobody comes out in this heat, and I'm sweating like a sumo in here."

In his younger days, Lusk had been a B-list hood. He'd moved cigarettes, run a few numbers, never scored a lot of money, but never really pulled any serious time in lockup. Now he eked out a living selling news and sundries to passing Angelinos. As far as Keegan could tell, Lusk was on the up-and-up these days—but he still had a good sense of what was going on on the streets, and he was always willing to shoot the breeze with a paying customer.

"Say, you know everybody in this town," Keegan said.

Lusk shrugged; maybe he did.

"You ever come across a guy called Catling?" Keegan plucked a pack of Juicy Fruit from the rack and set it on Lusk's counter. He jingled in his pocket, brought out a nickel and set it beside the gum. "Might not be his real name. Little guy. Real fastidious. Got a scar right here." Keegan ran his finger in a vertical line down his own left cheekbone.

Lusk made a face like he had smelled something foul. "Fas*tid*ious?"

"You know," Keegan said. "Real neat. Snappy dresser."

Lusk shook his head and picked up Keegan's nickel. "I'm

25

familiar with the word," he said. "But a guy who throws out fancy words like 'fastidious' should maybe buy a nice five-buck cigar, not some five-cent pack of Wrigley's." He tossed the coin into his strongbox.

"The guy I'm asking about is foreign," Keegan pressed on. "Got some kind of accent—could be from anywhere. Rides around in a limo."

"Not anybody I know," Lusk said. "Not around here."

A bus shuddered to a stop at the corner, and Keegan felt the gritty heat of the exhaust on the side of his face. "Keep an ear out for me?" he said. "Ask around. Let me know if you hear anything about him?"

"Yeah, sure," Lusk said sulkily. "Whatever you want. Maybe you'll toss me another nickel."

Keegan grinned. "You're a prince, Kipper," he said. "A true gent. A throwback to a nobler era."

"And you're a cheap son of a bitch," Lusk said. "Still, we somehow manage to get along."

Keegan turned to leave, but Lusk called after him.

"You forgot your gum, big shot."

KEEGAN HAD JUST got his keys out, when the door of the apartment next to his opened a crack. Mr. Soto squinted out at him. The man's plump, hairless head hovered above the brass chain that kept the door from opening farther. Keegan sighed and squeezed his keys in his fist.

The neighbor's door dipped shut, the chain unlatched, and Soto stepped out on the walkway, rubbing his hands on his trouser legs. He was a tiny man whose round bald head seemed too large for his body—a bobblehead doll. A retired county librarian, Soto had already been living in 203 a decade when Keegan moved in next door three years ago.

"Mr. Keegan," the little man said breathlessly, as if he'd run there from somewhere distant. "Mr. Keegan, you're keeping a dog in your apartment." Soto had a habit of staring at Keegan's right shoulder any time the two of them talked, which was infrequently.

"It's my mom's dog," Keegan said.

As if on cue, a scratching started up on the other side of Keegan's door. Nora had heard his voice.

"It's temporary," Keegan said. "I'm trying to find her a place."

"Our rental agreement is very clear on pets, Mr. Keegan," Soto said. It was easy to imagine the man, years ago, roaming the basement library stacks, shushing anyone with a heartbeat. "I'm afraid this won't do at all," Mr. Soto went on. He paused a moment and seemed to be inspecting the stitching on the shoulder of Keegan's jacket. "I don't want to have to call the landlord."

This, Keegan knew, was a lie. Soto called the landlord at every opportunity. It was a hobby he'd picked up in retirement, the way another man might do crosswords or plant tea roses.

"Look, Mr. Soto, I'll have her out of here in three minutes," Keegan assured him. "I just need to pick up some clothes." He slipped the key into the lock of 205 and could feel the tiny man's eyes glaring at him. "Three minutes," Keegan said. "Go set your egg timer."

NEAR MIDNIGHT, KEEGAN stood in his mother's back garden. The teacup he held was Royal Dalton, from his mother's best set. The liquor in it was the usual Jameson. The one ice cube he'd dropped in a minute ago had already melted away.

The lights of the valley below spread out in a sprawling grid of streets: the bright slash of Sunset Boulevard; the line of ruby brake lights moving along North Highland; and, further east, the 101. Blinking red beacons topped radio towers, and the dark obelisk of city hall, miniaturized, was barely visible way out on the southeast side. It was a view he never tired of. He should have come up here more often while his mother was still alive. Why had he not?

The breeze coming in off the far ocean was slight and tepid, but it was a welcome break from the prickly-hot Santa Ana winds that blew in from the desert. For that, Keegan was grateful.

Nora finished sniffing about in the stunted rose bushes and trotted towards the light of the open kitchen door. She hopped up the back steps and disappeared into the cottage. She'd no doubt jog, yet again, from room to room, looking for an old woman. How long would a dog remember the dead?

Alone, Keegan took another sip of whiskey and tried to ignore the gloom that seemed to have taken root in him. He wondered if his mother ever came out into her garden this late on a hot, sleepless night with her terrier at her heels. What did she think of when she looked down on the vast city she had watched, through a lifetime, spread out to every horizon?

Widowed, by a suicide, in her twenties, she'd raised her son in her own parents' house. Her father was a dour and aloof old man, always sunburned, exuding the scents of soil and orange blossom. He had little time for anything but citrus science and acreage. When he died, they'd moved to the house in Melrose, and Keegan had lived with his mother and grandmother, relying on avuncular charity. His uncles had even paid his way through college at USC—one last act of munificence before they were done with him.

But his mother must have had chances to start over again, Keegan reasoned. She could have made her own life, if that idea had appealed to her. His boyhood photos showed her as a smiling and pretty woman—not someone who would catch a director's eye at Schwab's perhaps, but attractive. In his earliest memories, she was all winsome smiles and playfulness, if a little timid. Why hadn't she remarried, even with a child in tow?

But no, she'd spent her youth doting on her son—and for what? He'd never had his grandfather's visionary drive. He even lacked whatever sad, headlong passions had led his own father to suicide. What promise had she seen in him? He'd led an insular life at best: a failed career, a failed marriage—an uninterrupted cycle of half-hearted striving undone by self-destruction.

Yes, the old woman had deserved better—a more fruitful life, a more attentive son. Since she'd given up driving, she'd been pretty much stranded on this hilltop. Keegan had visited her faithfully a couple of afternoons a week, but it was hard to put aside the daily hustle of survival to come up here and listen to an old woman's woes. The scope of her complaints ranged from air quality to arthritis, nothing could be fixed, and Keegan's biggest challenge was to refrain from checking his watch too often.

Still, he had taken care of her—or at least seen her taken care of. Mrs. Dodd was always happy to fetch her groceries or ferry her to appointments if it meant an early afternoon. So, yes, Keegan had nothing to regret. He had been a dutiful son—but now duty felt like the bare minimum. He could have done more. As her only child—her only remaining relation—he could have gone out of his way for her more often.

Down the hill, light from Nigel Ormsby's swimming pool shimmered like a nest of bright snakes against the mansion's stucco walls. Somewhere, way out to the west, in that milky sea of lights, was the Brentwood bungalow where a famous actress had put herself to sleep with pills, wanting never to wake again. Up above, among the once-inviolable stars, two Russian spaceships circled the earth—which proved, to Keegan's way of thinking, that nothing could remain unspoiled.

CHAPTER TWO

Tuesday, August 14, 1962

WHEN HIS MUG of instant Folgers was ready, Keegan put the tin kettle on the stove's back burner and took his coffee outside to where he'd stood the night before, looking down on the city lights. The temperature had to be in the eighties already, and it would be climbing fast, but at least there was still a slight updraft breeze. He stood barefoot on the lawn in the wrinkled clothes he'd slept in. The grass underfoot felt brittle.

In the harsh light of a new day, the gray city already lay under a sepia blanket of haze. The view was nothing like the black-felt jeweler's tray he'd seen glimmering in the thick of the night. This daylight vista looked tragic and tawdry—like seeing the weary starlet, sans makeup, away from the studio lights.

Keegan lingered at least a minute, blowing on his coffee and taking in the view, before he noticed the woman down below him. She sat near the edge of Ormsby's glassy swimming pool. Her back was to the water, and she bent over some sort of wooden table painting in watercolors. She was young and slender and wore what looked like beige riding pants and a tailored white blouse—clothes that evoked a kind of old-family, patrician wealth. She sat with her knees together and her legs tucked under her chair, like someone trained to ride sidesaddle.

The young woman faced a terrace of magenta bougainvillea

vines that framed one corner of Ormsby's garden. In the early light, the blooms were the color of cranberry juice held to the light. She studied the scene, then bent over her work again, presenting Keegan with the top of her head; a mop of dark curls, cut short. Her right hand darted like a Singer needle, dotting her work with a fine brush. When she looked up again at her subject, Keegan held still, so he wouldn't draw her attention.

Her face—angular and intent, with dark eyes and a narrow mouth—strummed a chord of recognition in Keegan. It was another of those Hollywood sightings, where the commonplace and the celebrated could sometimes be hard to distinguish. He'd seen this woman before, he knew, but he couldn't say when or where. He might have sat across from her at the bar at Jacob's or she might play Opie Taylor's schoolmarm on channel two. There was no way to know who she was, only that he knew her face from somewhere.

While the young woman painted, Keegan stretched out his back and took in Ormsby's elaborate garden: the box-edged flower beds, the emerald lawn, the sculpted hedges. Water burbled from a mossy, brick-skirted fountain. The whole scene seemed overly vivid and contrived—like a garishly colored antique postcard.

Keegan swirled the cooling Folgers in his mug and took another sip.

The woman below him dabbed at a tray of paints with her brush, blending the colors, and then she tried a small daub on the paper's edge to test the color. Satisfied, she went about streaking long horizontal lines of verdant green down near the bottom of the paper. From what Keegan could see, she'd mixed the right shade for Ormsby's vigorously fertilized lawn.

The woman was so intent, so unaware, that Keegan felt a stab of voyeuristic guilt for standing there. How long should he linger without announcing his presence? He cleared his throat and called down to her. "If I stand here long enough, will I end up in the picture?"

At the sound of his voice, the woman jumped, streaking a

green diagonal across her painting. She looked up wide-eyed at Keegan and then down at her ruined work. Her reaction was so overwrought—like some silent-movie damsel—that Keegan didn't know whether to laugh at her or pelt her with apologies.

"I'm sorry," he told her. "I didn't mean to startle you."

"No, no," the woman said in a good-natured fluster. She pressed her left hand below her throat and laughed raggedly while she caught her breath. With her right hand, she held the paintbrush off to one side, where it wouldn't drip pigment on her painting or on her clothes. "It's okay," she said. "I just wasn't expecting…" She let the sentence trail off and looked up at Keegan more keenly. "I'm a little jumpy these days."

"It's the weather," Keegan told her. "Everybody's jumpy. It's not just you." He took a step closer to the edge, so he'd be more visible to her, in all his harmlessness. "I'm staying in the cottage up here," he told her. "Just for a few days."

The young woman nodded eagerly, as if what he'd said were somehow noteworthy. Her bright face, now that she was smiling, struck Keegan as a few cuts above merely pretty; she might well *be* an actress—and a famous one for all Keegan knew. He didn't own a television and seldom went to the movies anymore—there was something too dismal about going to a movie alone—but he remembered his mother's stories about Ormsby's bevy of young starlets, and the thought that this lovely young woman might be the old man's latest conquest pained him in a way he wasn't expecting. He felt a flush of something like righteous anger. "You must be one of the nieces I keep hearing about," he said.

The young woman's brow furrowed. "I'm *the* niece," she said. "The only one there is, as far as I know."

"Not from what I hear," Keegan said. He had no idea why he wanted, suddenly, to be unpleasant, but he did. He allowed himself a sly smile.

The woman regarded him seriously for a few seconds, her head tilted to one side, and then her mouth dropped open. She blushed. "Oh," she said. "You think I'm one of Uncle Nigel's girls. I'm not, you know. I'm his actual niece."

Keegan felt his face grow hot. In his line of work, he was supposed to be tight-lipped, careful with words, slow to leap to conclusions. "I'm sorry," he managed to say. "I spoke out of turn."

The young woman shook her head. "Nothing to worry about," she told him, her voice going softer. "Really. I've heard all the gossip, too. My uncle is not very good at keeping secrets."

Keegan felt scolded. It *was* gossip. He thought of Mr. Soto peeking out from behind his blinds and dialing the landlord. "You live here with your uncle?" he offered lamely, trying to push the conversation on, away from this awkward moment he'd thrust them into.

"I got sent here to recuperate," the young woman said with a precision that made her words sound rehearsed. "Like you, I'm only a temporary resident." She shaded her eyes with one hand and looked up at him. "I'm Eve Ormsby-Cutler. Uncle Nigel is my mother's elder brother."

"My name's Jim Keegan. I hope I didn't ruin your picture."

She looked down at her work, and then smiled up at him again. "It's more of a sketch, really. And you've managed to give it its only daring feature."

In that instant, with her face turned up to him—earnest and attentive—it struck Keegan where he'd seen her before. She was the woman in the photographs, the woman Simon Catling was willing to pay a small fortune to find. The realization rocked him back on his heels. He almost spilled what little coffee was left in his mug. Was it even possible? What were the chances, in a city of two and a half million, that the woman he'd refused to find would turn up, unbidden, outside his kitchen door?

The young woman shaded her eyes with one hand again. "Would you like to join me for some coffee, Mr. Keegan?" she called up to him. "Or perhaps some orange juice?"

Keegan stared down at her upturned face. The more he looked, the more certain he was that this Eve Ormsby-Cutler was Catling's woman. But how could that be? The odds were astronomical. He tried to remember the photographs clearly, but all he could think about was the fat envelope of money beside him on the empty seat. Who might Catling have called once Keegan had turned him down? What men were now scouring the city for the face that was—inexplicably—turned up at him at this very moment?

He poured his instant coffee into the rose bushes at his feet. "Yes," he told her. "I could use a decent cup of coffee."

KEEGAN HAD NEVER seen a dog in his office building before, so he carried Nora under one arm, like a parcel he'd been sent to deliver. He strode across the marbled lobby floor, past the row of payphones and the cigarette machines, to the bank of elevators, trying not to look conspicuous. There were Mr. Sotos everywhere.

Up on the sixth floor, he found the outer door to his office unlocked. Inside, Mrs. Dodd sat at her desk reading a P.G. Wodehouse novel. A transistor radio was tuned to Joe Yocam and his *Fabulous Forty*. Seeing him in the doorway, Mrs. Dodd switched the radio off and slipped it into her desk's file drawer, along with her paperback. She had obviously not been expecting Keegan to come in, but she looked not at all abashed for being caught with office contraband.

"Long time no see, boss," she said cheerily, sliding the drawer shut. Her face lit up when she saw the dog. "Oh! Who's *this* you've got with you?" Her voice went all singsong, like when she talked to one of her grandkids over the office phone.

"Her name's Nora," Keegan said, looking down at the terrier under his arm. "She belonged to my mother. I don't have anywhere to leave her." He wasn't sure what to do with the dog, so he set her down atop Mrs. Dodd's big oak desk.

The dog sniffed at the blotter under her paws and then nosed Mrs. Dodd's Swingline stapler, her stubby tail wagging.

"She's darling," Mrs. Dodd said. She scrunched up her nose and pulled the resisting dog towards her across the desk

34

blotter. "Aren't you a darling? Aren't you a sweetheart?" The dog sniffed at her breath and then lunged in her direction, and Mrs. Dodd had to hold her back to keep her face from being licked. "She'll be fine right here," Mrs. Dodd said, rubbing the dog behind the ear. "She can help me answer the phones."

Keegan nodded. Problem solved. "Anything come in?"

"Not a thing," Mrs. Dodd said, still in her baby-talk voice, still seeming to address the terrier. "Nobody's called all morning. Have they, pumpkin?" She looked up at Keegan then, and her voice fell to its natural register. "What about that thing yesterday?"

"Turned it down," Keegan said. "He hasn't called back, has he?"

"Like I said, no calls all morning," Mrs. Dodd said. "You sure you're ready to be back at the office? You don't look so good."

He opened his inner office door. "Haven't been sleeping," he said.

"Who *can* in this heat?"

THAT AFTERNOON, KEEGAN made some phone calls and went through the stack of mail he'd been ignoring. He called his mother's lawyers again and phoned in a new order of business cards: *Discreet, Affordable, Dependable, Efficient.* (The initials wouldn't spell out *DEAD* this time.) What with his abandoned career in journalism and his unlisted phone number, business cards were about the only place he saw his name in print these days. He called around to see how much a window AC unit would cost for the office. It was hard to get much done in this weather. The whole city, he felt sure, was slowing to a crawl under the brambly heat.

When the clock told him it was after five, it felt seemly to call it a day, despite how little he'd accomplished. There wasn't much to do, it was true, but at least he was back at work. That counted for something. He closed the windows and was drawing the venetian blinds when Mrs. Dodd buzzed the intercom.

"There's an Eve Ormsby-Cutler here to see you," Mrs. Dodd announced. "Says you two are neighbors."

It took him a beat to realize who Mrs. Dodd meant. Eve being here seemed so out of context. Keegan switched on the fluorescent lights overhead; the tall downtown buildings made for gloomy afternoons of shadow and smog. He slid the window back up and then opened the inner office door. Out in the waiting area, Eve sat at the dead center of the big leather sofa. She held a black clutch on her knees with both hands. The dog was sniffing at her ankles, but Eve seemed not to notice her at all. When Eve saw Keegan, she rose and smiled at him nervously, biting her lower lip.

Mrs. Dodd had already smoothed the canvas cover over her typewriter and had drawn the outer office blinds for the day. Who knew how early she'd been going home while Keegan was out of the office? She stood now with her back to the desk, leaning in, waiting to see what Keegan expected from her.

"Give us a few minutes?" Keegan asked her. He nodded down at the dog. "And keep an eye on this one?"

Keegan ushered Eve into the inner office and gestured for her to take one of the two oak chairs that faced his desk. He went around the desk to his own, and it groaned when he sat down. What the hell was she doing there?

Eve was dressed in a different outfit than the one she'd had on that morning: she now wore a butterfly-print blouse and a pleated tweed skirt—nothing glamorous, but probably hand-tailored at some shop that required an appointment. She seemed adept at choosing clothes that spoke of both plainness and privilege. She set her clutch on the empty chair next to her, crossed her legs and flattened down her skirt.

"Social or professional?" Keegan asked. "This meeting, I mean."

"Professional," Eve told him. "I'd like to hire you. Or at least ask you for advice."

She folded her small hands in her lap and pivoted so her knees pointed off to one side, a pose suitable for a portrait in oils. Her easy elegance made Keegan a little self-conscious. What might she see in his spartan office, with its clunky steel desk, its bare walls and its dusty oscillating fan perched atop the row of beige file cabinets?

Eve smiled at him, but it seemed forced. "Mrs. Dodd was not what I was expecting," she told him. "I thought all private eyes had blonde bombshells for receptionists."

"Only in the movies," Keegan said. He pulled open a desk drawer and stirred about for his new box of ballpoints. "Who would you guess my average client is?" He found a loose Bic and slid the drawer shut.

Eve frowned and then looked at the desk between them, hands still folded in her lap, thinking his question over. "A woman," she said. "A housewife with suspicions." She looked down at her hands and then back up at Keegan. "I don't like to think about it."

Keegan nodded. He didn't like to think about it either. "And who would that housewife rather meet coming through my door?" he said. "A woman who looks like her mother—or one who looks like her husband's new steno girl?"

Eve sat straighter. "I see your point," she said. There was a cool edge to her voice now. "Only—" But she didn't finish the thought.

Keegan scribbled on the back of an envelope to get the pen's ink flowing. Why did blue ink clot so easily? He jotted the date at the top of a pad of paper. "So, what brings you here, Miss Ormsby-Cutler?" he said.

She shook her head at him. "Please," she said. "I asked you to call me Eve."

"That's for when we're neighbors," he said. "You're in my office now, and you want my services. Best we keep it professional."

Eve nodded without putting up a fight and slumped a little in her chair. She seemed both weary and wary. There was something haunted about her, Keegan thought, something that went deeper than this insomniac heat they'd all been enduring. Maybe it was the slant of light coming through the blinds, but she looked worn and tired now—nothing like the woman he'd sat across from in the shadow of Ormsby's cypress trees, chatting over coffee and pastries.

"I think someone's been lurking around my uncle's house," she told him. "I hear things out in the garden at night. I've found footprints in the flower beds." She fixed Keegan with a questioning look, as if she was trying to gauge his reaction. "Uncle Nigel thinks I'm imagining things," she said. "Perhaps he's right."

Keegan thought of Catling's dark limousine slipping away from him as he stood on the baking Sixth Street sidewalk. "Perhaps he isn't," he said. "Tell me what you've seen."

"*Seen*?" she said, as though he'd used the wrong word. "Nothing really." She looked at the window blinds. "It's just a feeling I get. And with Uncle Nigel going out of town—"

Keegan sat forward. Someone out there had Catling's envelope of cash and the set of photographs—that much was certain. What might it mean for Eve to be left alone in that big house? "Where's Nigel going?"

Eve gave Keegan a look, like she'd heard something worrisome in his tone. "Up to the mountains somewhere," she said. "Some detective show they're shooting. Why?"

"You'll be alone in the house?"

Again, she seemed to pick up something in his tone. She sat straighter. "Only a few days," she said. "I know I shouldn't be so—" Again she let the sentence trail off. She looked across the desk at Keegan with her brow furrowed.

Keegan thought of the small woman who had brought them coffee that morning. "No staff?"

She shook her head. "Not after six."

Keegan nodded. He jotted *Catling* on the pad of paper and then crossed it out. Honestly, how long had he looked at those photographs he'd been handed in the limo? How well had he studied the face in them? How astronomical were the odds that Eve was actually the woman Catling wanted to find? The possibility seemed too unlikely to entertain under these harsh fluorescent office lights; it was a late-night hilltop fantasy, a chimera of sleeplessness and flickering lights spread out to the horizon. It didn't warrant ink on paper. She couldn't be the woman Catling wanted.

"There's more," Eve said. "It's actually why I came to see you." She stopped speaking and worried her lower lip with her teeth again, like she was stitching a sentence together in her mind. "Since you left this morning, the phone has kept ringing. When I pick up, the person on the other end hangs up." Then, as a kind of afterthought: "Uncle Nigel was at the studio today—he usually answers the phone." Her hands, still in her lap, tugged at each other nervously. "It just kept happening," she said, "and it frightened me. It shouldn't have, but it did. I know what you do for a living, so I looked you up in the phone book and came down." She glanced at Keegan pleadingly and then looked away. "You must think me a fool."

Keegan rubbed the back of his neck. If he had to guess, the hang-up calls were from the latest of Uncle Nigel's 'nieces'. Whoever she was, she was probably miffed to hear another young female voice on the line and kept calling back to confront the old man about it. If that were the case, Uncle Nigel was in more immediate danger than the young woman who sat across the desk from him.

Still.

Eve tilted her head up, as if she was steeling herself against Keegan's skepticism. "I think I'm right, you know," she said. "Paranoid as it sounds, I think someone is watching the house."

Keegan leaned back in his chair and lined his fingers up along the desk's edge. "Ever hear of a man named Simon Catling?"

Eve looked genuinely confused. "No," she said. "Maybe." She shook her head. "Oh, I don't know. *Should* I? The name sounds familiar."

"Where might you have heard it before?" Keegan said. He was careful to keep his voice even.

"*Cat*ling?"

Keegan nodded. "*Simon* Catling."

Eve frowned down at his desk a few seconds—she seemed to be studying the battered phone book, the stolen Denny's ashtray, his unrinsed coffee mug—and then she laughed, quick and silvery. The sound took Keegan by surprise. He leaned forward.

Eve smiled and shook her head again. Then she tucked her chin and spoke in a voice that was unnaturally deep: "'*What say you, Simon Catling?*'"

Keegan stared at her, his mouth open a little.

Eve seemed amused at his expression and fanned her smiling face with one hand. "It's from *Romeo and Juliet*," she said, laughing. "I *knew* I'd heard the name. It's a bit part. Simon Catling only has one line."

KEEGAN'S MG WAS a two-seater convertible, and he couldn't remember the last time he'd had a passenger beside him. Maybe it was Judy on one of their on-again, off-again dates—the cocktails, the promenade, the climb up the stairs to her cramped apartment two floors above a liquor store.

He looked over at Eve now in the passenger seat. She held Nora in her lap, while the dog strained to get her nose out the open window to gulp at the hot wind.

"Sorry about the dog," Keegan said.

"Nonsense," Eve told him. "She's darling."

A jewel dangled on a chain in front of Eve's blouse. It was a clumsy gold setting with a pale blue stone shaped like a teardrop. The gem was large and luminous, though the chain it hung on was a simple gold serpentine. It must have fallen out of her blouse when she was tussling with the squirming dog. The necklace didn't seem in keeping with Eve's austere taste in clothes. It was bulky and vulgar—the kind of clunky costume jewelry his late mother would have favored.

Eve seemed to catch him looking and tucked it quickly inside her blouse, out of sight. "It's just a rhinestone," she told him, as if he had asked a question. And a few seconds later, as if he had asked a follow-up: "It has sentimental value."

KEEGAN ALMOST MISSED the turnoff to Ormsby's place; he'd never actually taken it before. He coasted up the single-lane drive to the estate's front gates. The gates were closed, and beyond them Ormsby's circular brick driveway lay empty. The gloom of early evening had set in, but there were no lights on in the big house. All that was lit were the twin carriage lamps, set into the broad brickwork entryway.

Keegan idled in front of the gates.

Eve stroked the dog's head and looked out through the windshield. Keegan could feel her tensing up at the prospect of being left alone in that big house with night coming on. In the silence, Keegan reached over to scratch the dog's head, and their fingers brushed. Eve pulled her hand away.

"I've got an idea," Keegan said jovially. "Let's drop this one off at the cottage and go get some dinner. We'll come back when your uncle's home."

He heard Eve let out the breath she was holding. "Yes, let's," she said, a clear note of relief in her voice.

KEEGAN TOOK EVE to the Regency Café. Back when he was covering crime for *The Times*, this was where the day-shift LAPD detectives went after work for drinks or to smoke those Upmann cigars that were a cop-house fad then. It had been a few years since Keegan had been there. The new hostess was a young redhead with her hair in a ponytail and a lofty, distant stare that seemed to be expecting someone more important coming through the door behind them.

As she led them to a table, menus in the crook of her arm, Keegan looked around the room for any familiar face. The place was nearly full—at least for a Tuesday night—but the only person he recognized was the bartender, who had grown plump and bald in the intervening years. He gave Keegan a vague, noncommittal nod as he passed, as if not quite sure how to place him. Perhaps *he* wondered if *Keegan* were famous.

The hostess led them past two empty tables to a dark corner booth away from the bar's cheerful hubbub. Keegan wanted to ask her for another table, but he couldn't seem to catch her eye. She scurried away as soon as the menus hit the table—off, no doubt, to more momentous tasks.

While Eve read the menu, Keegan tried to account for the sense of disappointment he felt that there was no one in the restaurant he knew. Why had he thought to bring Eve here, a place he hadn't been to in years? The answer was both obvious and pathetic: he wanted to be seen with her. The realization rocked him back in his chair. He thought of Ormsby and his bevy of young 'nieces', and the comparison made him squirm.

He ordered a Jameson, neat, to wash away the sour taste in his mouth, and sipped it, watching Eve pore over the menu. The dim tabletop lamp bathed the smooth contours of her face and glinted in her eyes as they roamed back and forth across her menu. He cringed. Who was he kidding? This woman was too young and beautiful for anyone who glanced at them from another table to think there might be anything romantic between them.

"You know," Keegan said when the waiter had taken their orders, "there isn't really a job in all this for me."

Eve nodded and realigned the silverware on the tablecloth in front of her. "I didn't think you'd believe me."

"That's not what I'm saying," Keegan said. "I *do* believe you. It's just there's nothing here for a private detective to do. What you need is a watchful neighbor. That, I'm happy to do for free." He turned his whiskey glass—his second round—on the tabletop and watched the resistance in her face soften into a demure smile. "And maybe you'd feel better with a little protection tomorrow night when Uncle Nigel goes out of town," he said. "I can help you there, too."

Eve raised her eyebrows. "Protection?" she said. "How do you mean?"

"A gun," Keegan told her. Even though he'd only had two drinks, he heard the machismo in his own voice, and willed it away. "I've got one you can borrow. I can show you how to use it. It's against the law to carry it around in your bag, but

42

you can keep it with you in the house or on the grounds. It'll calm your nerves just to know you have it."

She bit her lower lip and then shook her head. "I don't know," she said. "I think I'd be *more* nervous to have a gun lying around. What if it went off?"

Keegan laughed. "That's from the movies, too," he told her. "It doesn't really happen. Not with a revolver, anyway. It takes twelve pounds of pressure to pull the trigger. There's no way it goes off unless you want it to." He could feel his words wearing down her resistance—and that sense of persuasiveness, along with the Irish whiskey, had him feeling good about himself again. "You could hammer nails with the thing and it wouldn't fire a round."

That got another smile from her. She fingered the gold chain that disappeared down into her blouse. "Oh, I don't know," she said, but her theatrical tone of resignation hinted that she was allowing herself to be convinced.

"I'll pick it up, and I'll give you a lesson first thing tomorrow," Keegan said firmly. He'd have to swing by his apartment for it, either tonight after he dropped Eve off or early in the morning. But what did it matter? In this heat, he wouldn't be sleeping anyway. "You'll feel better having it with you if you're alone," he said. And then he thought—again, without any good reason—about Marilyn Monroe in her empty bedroom in a big darkened house. "And I'll feel better knowing you've got it."

NEAR MIDNIGHT, KEEGAN thought he'd let Nora out one last time before they settled in. Without turning on the light, he went through the kitchen to the back door and called the dog's name. She jumped up from where she'd been sprawled drowsing on the cool oak floor and trotted over to him. He opened the back door for her, and she hopped down the steps into the dark garden.

Keegan stood in the open doorway and looked down at Ormsby's mansion, wondering which of the many dark windows might be Eve's bedroom. He imagined her decorously reclined on a canopied bed, lovely and alone. He scolded himself and sat down on the top step, his bare feet on the prickly, dying lawn. He'd always felt a deep disdain for those gray-haired men who ogled every passing young waitress and cigarette girl—and it irked him to think he might be in danger of joining their ranks.

But it wasn't like that, he told himself. Not in the least. Sure, Eve was young, and she was pretty. What was the point of pretending she was neither? But his interest in her didn't reflect poorly on his character. It was a natural human appreciation for youth and beauty. It was like appreciating an oil painting hanging in a wealthy client's home without wanting to possess it. He could *find* Eve interesting without *being* interested in her. But as he reasoned this way, he knew he was splitting hairs to ease his conscience. He tugged up a blade of long grass from between his feet and wound it around his finger. The lawn was dying. He needed to water it.

Somewhere, deep in the hills above him, a coyote yipped forlornly. Another coyote, somewhere farther away, joined the feral chorus. This was their hour. They were out hunting; it was time to get the dog back inside.

Keegan flicked the blade of dry grass away and stood.

Before he could call Nora's name, he noticed a dark sedan pulled to the side of his own road where the gravel cutoff led down to Ormsby's back gate. The car was parked facing the mansion. A cigarette glowed in the driver's-side window, and someone sat in the passenger seat as well. A couple of teens, Keegan told himself. They must have driven up from Sunset for a romantic tryst and a pack of Camels—but he knew that was unlikely on a Tuesday night.

Keegan slipped across the lawn, still barefoot. He kept close to the side of the house as he made his way around to the cottage's front gate. He pulled it open quietly, passed through and latched it behind him, so Nora wouldn't follow. He stood a few seconds at the edge of the still-warm asphalt, looking down the road at the dark car. Crickets throbbed around him in the darkness. He could make out two bulky forms sitting side by side in the sedan. These were no teenagers.

As he watched, the car's driver-side window rolled down, and a cigarette dropped with a splash of sparks to the gravel drive. A match flared and, for a brief second, it lit up a craggy face. The match went out, and a new cigarette glowed in the darkness. The window rolled back up.

Keegan wished he'd already gone back to his apartment to pick up his .38 Special, and then he scolded himself for letting his imagination run rampant. There were any number of harmless reasons why a car would be parked along a dark road at this hour—especially *this* road, with the lights of the city spread out below.

Keegan dug his hands deep in his trouser pockets and slowly walked down the center of the road, towards the car. He didn't want to catch anyone off guard. He wanted whoever was parked there—whatever their purpose—to see him coming and to know he posed no threat.

He'd only made it a few yards closer when the car's brake lights splashed a pool of crimson on the gravel drive. The engine cranked to life.

Keegan stepped to the road's edge.

The car's reverse lights came on, and, before Keegan could get a decent look at it, it rolled back onto the asphalt and skidded down the road, away from him, without turning on its headlamps.

Keegan watched the dark shape slip down the road. Its brake lights flared as it went around the first bend. A few seconds later, the headlights came on, lighting up a stand of eucalyptus trees farther down the hill.

Keegan stood barefoot among the roadside weeds and watched the car's taillights diminish until they vanished among the innumerable city lights below.

CHAPTER THREE

Wednesday, August 15, 1962

KEEGAN STOOD BEHIND Eve, watching over her shoulder. She lined up the pistol's sights with the old tree stump at the far side of the ravine and held her breath. The morning slant of the sun lit her like studio lights. Keegan studied the light brown hairs that tapered down the back of her neck and the soft hollow between her jawline and throat. Her features were fine and delicate in the golden early sun.

She squinted a little as she pulled the trigger. The old revolver jumped in her hand, but her grip on it was firm. The shot kicked up some dirt behind the stump and rattled the coyote brush across the ravine. The sound echoed down through the empty canyon. Nora, who had been sniffing around underfoot, rocketed into the bushes behind them with her rump tucked low and then looked out at them warily from the undergrowth.

"Did I hit anything?" Eve asked. Her voice was pitched high, flushed with excitement.

"Sure," Keegan said. "Just not anything you were aiming at." He straightened her shoulders with both hands and felt lingerie straps under the fine silk of her blouse. Her body was lithe and narrow in his hands. When was the last time he'd actually held a woman? He thought of Judy, with her dry lips and her smoker's breath, and her sudden sullen moods.

Even back in college, he'd had a way of undermining every romance with petty jealousies and manufactured slights. An English major at USC, he'd been surrounded by countless, fiercely intelligent girls. He'd dated several, gotten serious with two. One — a bright, bohemian who wrote strange poems on a portable Royal Signet she lugged everywhere — he'd been with for six months, only to end it in a fiery, jealous argument because of her infatuation with a young professor.

The other had been more serious. Over two years, they'd talked of marriage and grad school and dreamt about a bookish, academic life in some bosky New England college town. He'd given her a ring. She'd been accepted to Dartmouth. They were to be married before the move. It was only after graduation that he let her know he'd been applying for jobs all over LA, and, come July, he'd be a cub reporter for the *Long Beach Press-Telegram*.

They'd been riding a Red Car back from the beach when he told her. He'd worried about fireworks and anger, tears and begging, but she had just nodded while he broke the news. She looked past him, out the window, at the passing palm trees. No anger. No weeping. It was as if, somewhere deep down, she'd been expecting this from him all along.

"Line up the sights this time," he told Eve. "Get the gun up high, so you don't have to duck down to see. Focus on the front sight. Let the target be blurry."

Eve took a deep breath and held it. She fired again. Missed again. "Smells like the Fourth of July," she said.

Keegan grinned. He was enjoying her playful mood. "Same stuff," he said. "It's all gunpowder."

Eve lowered the gun and pointed at the ground a few yards in front of her, holding it with both hands, the way he had shown her, finger outside the trigger guard. She looked back at him with a curious smile. "Funny that," she said. "How it's the same stuff in guns and fireworks."

"Funny?" he said. "Funny how?"

"You know," she said. "Ironic, I guess." She shrugged. "It's so innocent—yet so lethal, depending on how you look at it." She raised the gun again, held it steady, aimed it and fired. This time, the bullet splintered the top corner of the stump, revealing the light fleshy wood beneath the bark.

"Nice," Keegan told her. "You didn't kill the guy, but he's going to need stitches."

Keegan looked around for Nora, to be sure she was somewhere safe. The dog was behind them still, up where the dirt path from the cottage dropped down into the ravine. She stood watching them, glancing behind herself now and again, as if needing reassurance that the old cottage was still in sight.

Eve held the pistol straight out in front of her again with both hands. She bit her lip and squeezed the trigger. The bullet hit the trunk dead center with a solid crack, like a banged gavel.

"That's the way," Keegan told her. "Through the heart. He's on his way to the morgue this time."

She looked back at him, pleased, and that made him smile. It had been months—years, perhaps?—since he'd felt so at ease with someone.

"Do that again," he said.

She did. A small explosion of bark erupted on the right side of the trunk. She grinned, happy with the results. "Shouldn't we try from farther away?" she asked him. She nodded behind them, where the flatter ground banked up into the wall of the ravine.

Keegan shook his head. "It's a two-inch barrel. And you're no sniper," he said. "How many rounds do you have left?"

She turned to face him, keeping the gun pointed forward. "I forgot to count."

"You've still got one," he told her. "Try to keep track while you're shooting. You should always know how many rounds you have left. It could save your life." Again, he heard the machismo in his voice; again, he willed it away.

She raised the gun, but then pointed it back down at the ground. "Can't I just *try* it from farther away?" She seemed amused and eager, like a kid showing off, and Keegan grinned at her but shook his head.

"A snub nose is for protection," he said. "Strictly close quarters. If your target is more than a few yards away, it's always better to make a run for it."

Eve gave him a pouty look, then grinned and put the tree stump in her sights again. The next shot shattered the wood at the center of the stump.

"Not bad," Keegan told her. "Hard to believe this is your first time."

She shrugged, keeping the gun pointed at the stump. "Maybe I'm a natural," she said.

THE TWO OF them came up out of the ravine into the full sunlight, glowing with perspiration. Nora trotted down from her post to meet them. The dog quivered all over with excitement, her head ducked close to the ground. She jumped up on Keegan's legs when he got to her. He bent and scratched her ear. "Atta girl," he said brightly. "Way to be brave." The dog dropped down and tugged at the hem of his trousers as they climbed the last of the hill.

When they reached the crest of the ravine, the din of the gardener's big mower got louder. It had been running on Ormsby's place since just after dawn, and the pungent scent of clipped grass rode on the updraft wind.

The two of them headed down the trail to the cottage, Nora at their heels. They had to shout to each other to be heard over the mower. The handful of unused .38 cartridges jingled, like spare change, in Keegan's trouser pocket. He looked down at the cottage and Ormsby's place and then stopped in his tracks.

Eve stopped beside him. "What?" she said. "What is it?"

Keegan pointed. Down below them, a cop car rounded a big hairpin turn and kept coming up the hill fast. Keegan couldn't hear the siren—it was too far away, and the mower drowned it out—but he could see the red lights flashing. The car passed the turnoff to Ormsby's place and climbed the last few switchbacks. There was no doubt it was coming for them.

"Someone called the cops on us," Keegan said. "They must have heard us shooting."

Eve moved a few inches closer to him and shaded her eyes with one hand. "What do we do?" Her trim body grazed the length of his arm.

Keegan watched the car make its way up along the final curve. "Shooting out here is technically illegal," he told her. "But it shouldn't be a problem. I'll talk to him."

Eve frowned and blinked up at him in the sunlight. "You sure?" she said. "We're not going to get in trouble?"

The light caught her brown eyes, and Keegan felt another twinge of masculine vanity. The police car disappeared into the last bend in the road. "Look," he told Eve. "You wait back up there." He nodded up the path towards the crest of the hill. "Keep out of sight. I'll take care of this."

"Certain?" She looked relieved, and Keegan bit the inside of his lip so as not to smile.

"Yeah," he said, feeling good. "Just stay low a few minutes. Nothing to worry about."

He watched Eve hurry back up the trail among the scrub brush, her elbows churning in their white sleeves as she scurried along. He took in her slender waist, her tapered shoulders under her white blouse, her narrow hips.

Nora lifted her head up and sniffed the air. She looked back at Eve and then at Keegan, as if deciding whom she should follow.

"Believe me," Keegan told her. "I wouldn't blame you." He turned and headed down the trail towards the cottage, and, after a few seconds of reckoning, Nora trotted up beside him.

The police car pulled up at the side of the road, just past his mother's place, a few yards beyond the carport and Keegan's MG. Keegan waved to the car as he walked around the wooden, reflector-studded barrier that marked the end of the road. He wanted to look both harmless and confident. He smiled and tried to affect a Nigel Ormsby swagger. He wanted to look like he owned the place—which, he had to remind himself yet again, he actually did.

Nora paused to sniff among the dry patch of weeds around the wooden posts of the barricade. She squatted at the concrete foundation to mark her territory, and then happily scampered after Keegan, all memory of gunfire apparently forgotten.

As soon as he stepped on the paved road, Keegan could feel the heat radiate up at him. The asphalt had baked in the brutal sun for so many days, it still simmered at daybreak. He could feel the warmth on the soles of his feet through his shoes.

Atop the squad car, the bright red light spun lazily, as if to add some small increment to the morning's heat. Through the cruiser's windshield glare, Keegan could make out a single occupant—a bareheaded man with close-cropped blond hair. He held the radio microphone to the side of his mouth, speaking into it while he watched Keegan approach.

Keegan's old .38 was stashed safely in its zippered canvas pouch, and he held it out before him, where the cop could see it plainly. A 417 call on the radio—a report of shots fired— was nothing a lone patrolman ever liked to roll up on, and a jumpy cop could be a dangerous thing. The cop hung the radio mouthpiece back on the dashboard and watched Keegan through the windshield.

"I was just doing some target practice," Keegan called, but he knew he couldn't be heard over the din of the mower still running down on Ormsby's place.

The squad car's door opened, and the young policeman stepped out, glossy black boots first. He stood, pulled on his blue peaked cap over his buzz cut and adjusted it. He couldn't have been more than twenty-five, lean and lanky, with dark oval stains under the arms of his short-sleeved uniform shirt. He pulled himself up to his full height—six one, at least. He was so skinny, so pole-like, his bulky utility belt looked like it might drop to his ankles at any moment.

The kid was trying to look solid, but his right hand kept patting the grip of his service revolver, as if reassuring himself that it was still there, should he need it. He couldn't be long out of the academy, Keegan guessed, a rookie in the locker room, still the butt of everyone's jokes—a kid with everything to prove.

The young officer hiked up his utility belt with a clatter and then planted his hands on his hips, affecting a pose he might have picked up from TV. Maybe Eve should have been here to do the talking after all; a pretty girl would have this kid cowed and tongue-tied in seconds. He'd flee down the hill, lights and siren going, before she could bat her eyelashes.

"If you got a call about gunshots," Keegan shouted over the lawnmower's racket, "it was just some practice shooting. An old tree stump over the hill." He gestured around with his empty hand at both sides of the road. "This is all my land," he said. The words, though technically true, still tasted like a lie.

The cop eyed the canvas pouch in Keegan's hand. "That gun registered to you?"

"Sure is," Keegan said. He was close enough now to speak without shouting. "I've had it since I was your age." It was a white lie designed to give himself the upper hand. He had, in fact, bought the gun in a San Pedro pawnshop when he was first cut from *The Times* and had to move into a neighborhood that worried him.

The cop held out one hand, index finger raised, indicating that Keegan shouldn't come any closer.

Keegan humored him and stopped where he was. He held out the pouch with the revolver in it.

The cop stepped up and took it from him and then stepped back again. He unzipped the pouch, pulled out the gun by its wooden grips and swung the empty cylinder open. With his eyes still on Keegan, he held the gun to his nose. It had clearly been fired. Even Keegan, a good two yards away, could taste the cordite in the air. *Smells like the Fourth of July.*

Nora came out from behind Keegan's legs and edged

closer to the cop. She sniffed at the round toes of his black leather shoes.

The cop ignored her. "Ever hear of unlawful discharge?" he said. He flipped the cylinder shut again. "Doesn't matter if you own the land, you're still inside city limits." He zipped the pistol back in its pouch but made no move to hand it back to Keegan.

The mower down below sputtered and stopped. In the sudden quiet, birds sang and parched brush rattled in the hot breeze. Nora trotted over to the cottage's white picket fence and lay down in the shade of a rosemary bush, panting.

"There shouldn't be a problem," Keegan said, adjusting his voice to the hush. "Just get on the radio. Call in for Lieutenant Moore." Keegan thought he caught a reaction in the boy cop at the mention of the lieutenant's name. "Louis Moore. You know him?"

The cop offered a slanted smile. "I know the man," he said, "but we don't exactly swim in the same pond."

"The lieutenant's an old friend of mine," Keegan said. It was gratifying to see that Louis Moore's name still opened doors. "He'll vouch. Just tell him you're with Jim Keegan."

The cop looked Keegan over, sizing him up—just so they both knew who was still in charge here, friend of Louis Moore or not. Keegan just smiled back at him, and the kid went to the open squad car door, still holding Keegan's gun. The cop leaned in the cruiser's doorway, elbows on the car roof and talked into the radio's microphone.

Keegan crossed the road and opened the front gate in the picket fence to let the dog through. She trotted up the shady porch steps to her water bowl and started lapping it up. Keegan closed the gate behind her. He stood with his arms crossed and watched a couple of finches hop and flit among the rosemary bushes. He could feel the sun on his shoulders through his last clean button-up shirt. He put his hand in his pocket and felt the blunt weight of the six bullets he'd saved from the ammo box—just enough to fully load the gun for Eve.

The kid cop finally signed off the radio and hung the microphone back on the dash. He waved Keegan over and offered him a conciliatory nod. "The L.T. says I should tell you you're a dumbass," he said, clearly uneasy with his role as messenger. "Said to remind you that your astonishing lack of common sense is not an excuse in a court of law."

Keegan grinned. He was a little impressed that the kid seemed to be using Lieutenant Moore's exact words. He'd have to buy the lieutenant a beer sometime soon. It had been too long. "Copy that," he told the kid cop.

The cop nodded and handed the gun pouch back to Keegan, but he made no move to get back in his squad car. "That thing's department-issue for detectives," the kid said. He folded his arms so that his hands were tucked into the ovals of sweat at his armpits. "Were you a jack?"

Keegan shook his head and smiled. "Not in any official capacity," he said. "Just one of the lieutenant's many well-wishers."

KEEGAN WALKED EVE past the cottage and down to the gravel drive behind her uncle's spread. He let her carry the gun pouch. He counted three cigarette butts lying in the gravel outside Ormsby's back gate. Keegan took that to be a good sign. The sedan he'd seen last night hadn't stayed very long, and it probably hadn't returned later when he was back in the cottage trying to sleep.

"So, he just turned around and left?" she said.

He liked that she seemed so impressed with how easily he'd handled the cop. "I have friends in lofty places," he said. "You're new in town, so you don't know the kind of clout I have."

Eve stopped at the gate and turned to him, smiling.

He dug in his pockets for the loose bullets he'd put aside. He held them out. "Six rounds," he told her. He dropped them in her open palm and closed her fingers over them. "That's all you need. Load it up when you get home. Put it on your nightstand and forget about it." He looked through the chain-link gate at the great house that shimmered in light reflected from the swimming pool. The heat seemed to intensify the smell of cut grass and new fertilizer. "You *do* have a nightstand in that dump, don't you?" he asked.

Eve smiled coyly. She slipped the bullets into the pocket of her slacks. "Eighteenth-century Italian walnut, if you must know."

Keegan liked the tone she'd taken on today in his company. It felt impish and intimate—maybe even flirtatious, if he looked at it a certain way. It had been years since a woman had spoken to him the way she did, and he felt rusty, keeping up with her banter.

"Don't worry," Keegan told her. "It may be old, but it'll work just as well as the new plywood model I got at Sears."

They then stood a few awkward seconds, both of them smiling, neither speaking, as if unsure how to end this outing. Eve shaded her eyes with her hand. A hot breeze tousled her dark curls. "And I don't have to worry?" she said. The gleam in her eyes seemed anything but worried just then, but Keegan knew what she meant. She had a dark night ahead of her in a big empty house.

"About the gun?" he said. He shook his head and smiled at her. "That thing is as safe as an eighteenth-century Italian paperweight," he told her. "It'll only shoot when you want it to."

Eve nodded again. She gathered her hair at the back of her head with one hand. With that one simple gesture, her face took on a new angle of light. Her hazel eyes glowed. Her smile—even with a smudge of lipstick on her front teeth—warmed him. And then, with what seemed to be reluctance, she slipped through the gate into Ormsby's garden.

Keegan watched her cross the lawn to the French doors on the side of the mansion. She turned to look back at him, once, over her shoulder, and that was enough to keep him rooted to the spot until she disappeared inside.

THAT DAY AT the office, Keegan had a couple of men come out from GE to install an air-conditioning box in the window of the outer office. The hustle and hubbub, after his morning with Eve, kept his spirits high.

Mrs. Dodd fussed happily and ordered the workmen about. "Are you sure it won't fall out the window?" she kept asking them. "A thing like that could kill a person." Something in her excited, fretful tone reminded Keegan of Eve, and that made him smile.

The men packed up and were gone. They left the unit humming in the window, blowing out a half-dozen red ribbons tied to the front grill for no purpose but show. The cooler office air seemed to fill Mrs. Dodd with energy, and all morning she kept checking in with Keegan, pouring him coffee and sorting out the old files she'd been neglecting for months.

Even Nora, whom he'd lugged to the office again, seemed caught up in the celebratory mood. The dog kept running back and forth between the outer and inner offices, her claws scuttling over the hardwood floor, as if afraid she'd miss out on something. By noon, when Mrs. Dodd went on her lunch break, the dog had tired herself out and fallen asleep under Keegan's desk, curled up at his feet in the dark.

WHEN HE'D EATEN his own lunch at a Fifth Street diner, Keegan walked across Pershing Square to check in with Kipper Lusk. The row of flags in front of the Biltmore Hotel hung leaden in the scorched windless air. Again, the park felt eerily underpopulated for a weekday. A fat man on a shady bench tossed seeds to a mass of pigeons that had gathered around him. Another man pedaled an ice cream cart along the concrete walkway, calling out for customers. Somewhere, a transistor radio played The Marvelettes: *Mister postman, look and see if there's a letter in your bag for me*.

Lusk's newsstand basked in the full sun. The man, himself, sat hunkered in the shadows, droop-shouldered, his face slick with sweat. He nodded to Keegan as he approached and then shook his head. He was fumbling, trying to fit new batteries into a tiny handheld fan—powder-blue plastic with white blades. It would be a psychological prop at best; nothing so small would be any match for this heavy, sluggish air.

Keegan grinned down at him. "Nice weather we're having," he said.

Lusk made a sour face. "*Herald Examiner* says the heat's gonna stick around another week," he said. "Humidity through the roof. Good times will be had by all." He screwed the bottom back on the little fan.

"What does *The Times* say?"

"Cough up a dime and find out for yourself," Lusk replied. He flicked the fan's switch with his thumb, but nothing happened. He unscrewed the bottom again and shook out the batteries.

"You shouldn't complain," Keegan said. "Weather like this is always good for newspaper sales. Crazy stuff happens in heatwaves. Big headlines." He looked across the park. The fat man had run out of seeds and was crumpling up his paper bag while the birds still swarmed at his feet. He wore a shabby suit and tie, despite the heat. "I could count on at least a triple homicide on a day like this when I had the crime beat."

Lusk gave the fan a shake. "Tell me about it," he said. He leaned forward and pointed across the park, tucking his head low, like he was sighting along his index finger. "Guy got knifed right over there by the fountain yesterday. Big fight. Broad daylight." He leaned back in his chair and tried the fan again. It didn't work. "Cops all over the place," he went on. "An ambulance." He gestured around at the racks of local newspapers. "Didn't even make the sports section, there's so much other shit going on. I checked every one of them." He unscrewed the fan and went back to fumbling with the batteries. "This town is one big bar brawl just waiting to happen," he said.

A yellow cab at the corner took up honking at a group of teen greasers crossing Hill Street too slowly. One of them gave the cabbie the finger, and the others laughed. Where was the world headed?

Keegan looked back down at Lusk. "You ask around about my Catling guy?"

"In fact, I did," Lusk said. He looked up from the fan. "Though why I go out of my way for you, I don't know." He'd got the batteries back in the fan, turned the opposite way. He screwed the bottom on again and tried the switch. Nothing. "Dammit."

"And?"

Lusk banged the fan on his counter a couple of times and tried the switch again, to no avail. "The consensus is that no such man exists," he said. "Maybe it was some kind of mirage you saw. Some high-temperature hallucination." He shrugged. "'Crazy stuff happens in heatwaves,' right?"

Keegan shook his head. Despite the heat, Catling's image came over him like a shiver: the cheekbone scar, the manicured hands, the bluish tint of the man's skin in the long car's icy interior. "The guy was no mirage," Keegan said. He thought of Eve and the gun, and how playful she'd been. Could she really use it if she needed to? "He was as real as you and me," Keegan said. He rubbed the stubble on his chin. "Well, as real as me, anyway."

"Well, nobody's ever heard of the guy," Lusk said. "Or his fastidious limo." He held up the plastic fan and turned it in the sunlight, to make it look enticing. "You want to buy a fan? I can let you have it cheap. Got a whole goddamn box of them in Chinatown last night." He shook his head and tossed the fan into a dark corner of his lair. "Seemed like a good idea at the time."

Keegan grinned. "Don't need a fan," he said. "Just put in air conditioning. My office will be cold as a Baskin Robbins when I get back in."

Lusk made a hissing sound and leaned back in his folding chair. "Couldn't happen to a nicer asshole," he said.

THE SUN HAD not yet set, but the cottage had begun to cool a little. The first whispers of crisper air slipped down the hillside and seeped in through Keegan's front screen door. He sat on the sofa in his mother's small living room, half listening to the Giants play the Cubs on the radio and half reading a hardback Shakespeare anthology he'd found among his mother's paperback westerns. *Romeo and Juliet*. He hadn't looked at it since college. Eve was right. Simon Catling had just one line: "Marry sir, because silver hath a sweet sound." Not a highlight for anyone's demo reel.

It was Keegan, not the dog, who noticed the shadow first—a subtle change of light beyond the front doorway, and then the clack of the front gate latch drawn back and the quiet creak of hinges. Keegan hadn't heard a car pull up.

The dog had been asleep with her chin on Keegan's thigh. She lifted her head suddenly, then scrambled to her feet, jumped down and ran to the screen door. She stood there wagging her stubby tail. Keegan stood and followed her.

Outside, in the long blue shadows of sunset, Eve mounted the porch steps. She wore blue capri slacks and a white blouse—though it was a different one than she'd worn that morning. This one was armless. It had lacework on the collar and silver buttons—a much more expensive-looking style. Something she might wear to go out. When she rapped on the screen door, the aluminum frame hissed like a snare drum.

"Jim?" she said. "Are you in there?" She cupped one hand to the screen and peered inside, but it was clear she couldn't see anything with the last daylight behind her. In one hand, she held a dark bottle of wine by the neck. Her forehead was nearly touching the screen now, but she still couldn't see in. "Hello?" she said. There was a pleasing wind-chime musical quality to her voice. "Knock knock?"

Keegan went to the door. "If that's the set-up for a joke," he said, "I'm pretty sure I've heard it." He unlatched the screen door and pushed it open for her.

Eve seemed happy to see him. It could have been the

angle of dusky light, but she looked like she might be blushing. "Is this a bad time?" she asked.

"Never better," Keegan told her. He stepped back, so she could come inside.

"It's not even eight," Eve said as she stepped past him. "But I didn't want to spend hours and hours alone in that house. All those big empty rooms."

"You're in luck," Keegan said. "You won't find any big rooms here, empty or otherwise."

Eve looked around the small living room. Keegan's mother had had a penchant for clutter—for doilies and figurines and tacky snowstorm paperweights. The basket on the end table held six or seven pairs of reading glasses, tangled by their lanyards. A wooden rack, hung on the wall next to the kitchen doorway, held her spoon collection—tiny tarnished souvenirs collected on her humdrum travels to places like Dayton and Winnipeg and St. Joseph, Michigan.

"It's lovely," Eve said, without a trace of irony in her voice. She held the wine bottle out to him with both hands, label up, like a sommelier. "I come bearing a gift."

Keegan took the bottle by the base, his thumb in the deep hollow. It was broad-shouldered and dusty. The label was gold: French words with an etching of a chateau. 1938. The first year of Keegan's failed marriage. He held the bottle up between them. "Did you steal this from Uncle Nigel?"

Eve smiled conspiratorially. "Steal?" she said. "You make it sound so felonious." She took the bottle from him. "Let's say I acquired it without his consent." She tilted her head to look at the label. "I'm guessing it's a good one," she said. "I had to stand on a chair."

"You don't think he'll mind?"

"I don't think he'll even notice," she said. "It's a big cellar. And, besides, I have as much right to it as he does."

Keegan led her to the kitchen doorway and stopped. His mother had never condoned alcohol. There would be no corkscrew in her kitchen. "Did you bring something to open it? I don't think—"

Eve stopped short. "Oh, no," she said. "I never thought to." Then she smiled archly and swept past him into the kitchen. She set the bottle on the table. "I'm going to need a shoelace and a small screwdriver," she told him.

There was that playful tone in her voice again—impish and musical. It loosened the tension Keegan had been holding in his shoulders all day. He pulled open his mother's kitchen junk drawer and stirred through the contents. "Phillips or flat blade?"

"I don't know what you mean," Eve said. She came and stood behind him.

"The screwdriver," he said. "You know. A plus or a minus?"

"Oh, I see," she said. "It doesn't really matter, but smaller is better."

She was standing very close to him. He could feel her body radiate warmth along his right arm. He sensed her soft breathing. She had shampooed her hair before she came over, and it smelled of lavender. Keegan closed the drawer and pulled open another.

"That one will do," Eve said. She reached around him and plucked out a small Phillips screwdriver with a blue rubber grip. She brandished it like a scalpel. "Now all we need is a shoelace."

Keegan pushed the drawer shut and went out to the living room. He considered pulling the laces from his own shoes, but they had lost their aglets and their ends were unraveling. He found two pairs of brown Kiwi laces in his mother's cantilevered sewing box, still wrapped in cellophane. He brought one of them back to the kitchen.

Eve shook out one of the laces to its full length, and as she did, Keegan noticed the way her crimson nail polish caught the overhead light. She hadn't been wearing polish that morning; he would have noticed it as he was showing her how to hold the gun. She had taken time to get herself ready for this visit. Keegan wasn't sure what that might mean, but the idea of it pleased him.

Eve made a show of clapping dust from her hands. "You might want to stand back," she said. "This can get messy." She braced herself against the kitchen counter and worked the screwdriver deep into the cork, twisting and pushing, until it broke through the bottom side. She pulled the screwdriver back out and handed the bottle to Keegan. She tied a knot in one end of the shoelace and cinched it tight. She took the bottle back and used the screwdriver to push the knotted end of the shoelace down through the hole she'd made in the cork. As she worked, Keegan admired the long, lean muscles in her bare arms. "This I learned in the most exclusive all-girl boarding school in the Bay Area," she said. She wrapped the loose end of the shoelace around her fist, bit her lower lip and began to tug. "Do *not* try this at home," she said, a little out of breath. "I've had plenty of practice."

The cord whitened the skin of her fist, but, pulling it firmly, relentlessly, the cork edged up and then slid out with a pop. A splash of red wine splattered the kitchen floor. "Sorry about that," she said, looking down at the tiles. She held up the shoelace between them. The cork bobbed at the end. "You might want to keep this shoelace handy in case you ever throw a formal dinner party."

That made him smile. This one was quick-witted. He hoped he could keep up. He took down two of his mother's best Royal Dalton teacups and set them on the table. Eve poured formally, her thumb in the hollowed bottom of the bottle, while Keegan dabbed the wine-splashed floor tiles with a paper towel.

They raised their teacups and clinked them. Eve took a sip and looked up at the ceiling. She swallowed and smiled. "Very good," she said. "I believe I made an excellent selection. And, do you know, I think it tastes better out of a teacup." She smiled again.

Keegan thought of what his mother would have made of

this sight—stolen wine sipped from her best teacups, her son alone in her house with a woman nearly half his age. He took a sip. The wine was tart and mellow on his tongue, and it warmed his throat when he swallowed. He'd never had an appreciation for wine before, but now he wondered if he'd just never been able to afford the kind of wine worth appreciating. This was good. "Not bad," he said.

He followed Eve into the living room, studying her every lissome movement as she crossed to the armchair facing the sofa and sat. Keegan abandoned the baseball game and tuned his mother's old RCA radio to some big-band music. 'Sleep Lagoon'. Perfect. He turned the volume loud enough to be a presence in the room without demanding attention.

The wine seemed to make conversation easy, a teasing banter about tastes and diversions and penchants—though he wasn't quite sure how to hold the teacup. That tiny handle just got in the way. They had almost nothing in common, but that somehow gave them everything to talk about. The table lamp next to Eve lit her cheek softly and seemed to imbue her features with a lovely pensiveness as the darkness outside deepened. The cut of her armless blouse made her bare arms look soft but toned. Keegan could imagine the warmth and smoothness of her pale skin under his hand.

"I do like travel," she said at one point. She was looking down into her teacup, her knees drawn up to her side in the big armchair.

Keegan thought of his mother's humdrum spoon collection on the wall behind him. San Antonio. Yellowstone. "Where's your favorite place?" he asked Eve. "If you could be anywhere right now?"

She kept gazing down into her teacup, but she tilted her head a little, like she was giving it more thought than his offhand question deserved. "Everyone always says Paris," she said. "And they're right. It's beautiful." She looked up at Keegan and then looked away. "But right now, I think I'd like to be in Cologne."

"Why Cologne?"

She gazed down into her cup again. "The Germans always keep to themselves," she said. "And I don't know a soul there. I wouldn't have to talk to anybody. I could just be by myself awhile." She shrugged and looked up at him. "And I like the way the cathedral looks at night from across the river."

She fell silent and looked at the floor, and Keegan sensed that his question had shooed her down some melancholy trail of thought. He tried to lift the mood. "What else do you like to do?" he asked brightly. "What makes you happy?"

She pulled her knees up closer to her chin. "I like horses," she said. "I know it must sound awful, but it's very nice to be—well—*rich*." She slid sideways on the armchair, and set her cup, very gently, on the table beside her. "But there are disadvantages to it, too," she said.

"Poor thing," he told her, and hoped it didn't sound cruel or insulting.

She smiled back at him. "Don't mock me," she said. "I'm being serious."

He took a sip from his cup. "And what might those disadvantages be?"

She looked at him and then looked beyond him, as if she was peering through the kitchen doorway. "There are always people around," she said, pulling back one finger, like she was counting off items. "Even when you're in your own house. Everyone is always watching you." She pulled back another finger. "No one *ever* tells you the truth. Only what they think you want to hear." She smiled and directed her gaze at him again. "At my mother's house, I could put on one red shoe and one black shoe and go about all day without anyone daring to point out my mistake." She shook her head and reached for her teacup on the table at her elbow. When she spoke again, the playfulness seemed to have vanished from her voice. She wasn't keeping count anymore. "Once you have enough money," she said, "you can never really have any friends."

Keegan thought about his own solitary life: lonely meals

taken in diners and drugstores, long evenings in an empty apartment with coffee mugs and whiskey glasses piling up in the sink. He'd let any semblance of a social life fade away years ago, along with his prospects and any hope of a steady income. Living hand-to-mouth didn't foster friendships, either.

"I know what you're thinking," Eve said. "'Poor little rich girl hasn't lived a minute in the real world.' And I can't really argue. It's true. My life has been free of the problems most people face. But wealth *does* have its own set of challenges."

Keegan wasn't in the mood to argue, and he didn't want to disrupt the easy, unhurried conversation he found himself in. He'd been drinking too much whiskey lately, just to hammer himself to sleep, but this wine—whatever its subtle chemistry—had given him a languorous, lazy buzz that felt comfortable and mellow, like a Sunday afternoon on a porch swing. "So, what's the biggest drawback about being rich?" he asked.

"Romance," Eve said plainly, as though she'd already given it a good deal of thought. "That's the hardest thing of all, isn't it? For everyone, I suppose. But when you're rich, it's impossible to know if someone loves you or just the things your money can bring him." She held the teacup by its handle, giving it a gentle swirl. "Most men find a woman's money bewitching or emasculating. It's like there's no in between." She'd been looking down into her teacup, but she lifted her head and seemed to focus on him. "Not you, though, Jim Keegan," she said. "It doesn't seem to faze you at all."

He wasn't sure what to do with that observation, though it felt like a compliment.

"Money turns most men into boys," she said. "So, there it is. Problem number one: money makes true love difficult. Poor me."

She was making light of herself now, but Keegan could sense he'd drawn out something serious—something true in her she kept from others. He didn't want to slight her with what he said next, but he also didn't want to shrug off the heady ease he was feeling in her company. He chose his words carefully. "You're young yet," he told her. "Nobody your age has really known love. It'll happen."

"Oh, it happened," she said. "Once…" Her words trailed off. Then—like a poorly edited movie scene—her mood changed abruptly. Some spell was broken. She dropped her feet to the floor and sat upright in her chair, smiling playfully. "And this is where that particular line of conversation comes to an end." She stood and swept past him towards the kitchen. "And where our next round of Bordeaux begins."

EVE WAS CLOSE by as they headed down the hill towards Ormsby's back gate. He could feel her body lean into him as they walked. When they passed through the gate into the darkly scented garden, she took his arm and rested her head against his shoulder. Keegan wanted that to mean something, but they'd both had a half-bottle of wine and that was as good a reason for the closeness as any other. But, God, that lavender smell of her hair—it belonged in this garden on this balmy August night. Moonlight played upon the groomed hedges and shimmered on the surface of the swimming pool. Far behind them, up in the cottage, the radio was playing 'Stardust', and the tinny sound of it carried down to them. *Beside a garden wall…*

Keegan stood in the brickwork front entryway while Eve found her key in the back pocket of her capri slacks. A moth circled and bumped one of the coachman lamps. She unlocked the deadbolt and pushed the door open a crack.

"Shall I bring Italian wine tomorrow?" she said. "Or is there something else you'd prefer?" She must have caught some unintended reaction in his expression because she said, "I hope you don't mind me coming by again. He won't be back until Friday."

"Italian is good," Keegan said. "Maybe I can run by the Farmers' Market and we can make some—" but before he

66

could finish the sentence, she stepped forward, kissed him on the lips and rushed inside, closing the door behind her.

KEEGAN WOKE WITH a start even before the dog began barking. He had no idea what had jolted him from sleep.

Nora bounded into the kitchen. Keegan followed her, trying to clear his head of the last vestiges of the dream he'd been having. He switched on the kitchen light and found Nora barking at the screen door. He'd left the back and front doors wide open. Nora clawed at the aluminum frame of the screen and then backed away. She tipped her head up and sniffed at the night air coming in and then set to barking again.

Keegan picked the dog up, to quiet her, but she fought him and kept twisting her head to look at the screen door. "Shhhh," he told her. "It's okay." He backed up a few steps and switched off the light, so no one could see him from outside. He crept back to the screen door and listened for anything moving outside in the garden. He could see nothing beyond the back steps, which were lit dimly by the outside lamp.

He carried Nora back to the bedroom, which was hot and stuffy, closed up for more than a week. He set her down and blocked the doorway with his leg until he could get the door shut without her slipping past him.

In the kitchen, he turned off the outdoor lamp and waited, listening, before he opened the screen door. The garden was empty. He slipped out to the edge of the lawn and looked down at Ormsby's place. The grass was cool and brittle under his bare feet. A light came on in a downstairs window, and then switched off again.

Keegan crouched low and crept past the rose bushes, until he could see Ormsby's back gate. There was no sedan in the gravel drive tonight, and the back gate was still closed.

He slipped back towards the kitchen door so he'd have a better view of Ormsby's house. Light glinted as a French door along the side of the house opened and closed. A shadow slipped between the house and the dark garden hedges. The shape finally emerged from the shadows and rushed across the lawn towards the back gate. It was Eve. He was certain. But she moved with a strange excess of energy, like she was flushed with panic.

Keegan rushed along the side of the cottage to the front gate and trotted down the hill towards Ormsby's back drive. The blacktop was still warm underfoot and grit bit at his bare soles as he ran. He heard the chain-link gate thrown back and a flurry of light footsteps across the gravel, and then she was on the road, rushing up the hill towards him. She wore a light-colored robe and fleece slippers. Her face, lit by moonlight, was damp and terrified. Keegan stopped running, and she rushed up towards him.

"I shot him," she managed to say when she was a few steps away. "I think he's dead."

She was in his arms then, and he felt her heart racing and her damp face against his chest. She sobbed convulsively.

"Who?" he said, holding her close, feeling her ragged breaths. "Who did you shoot?"

It took a moment for her to choke the words out: "Uncle Nigel," she said. "I think I killed him."

He put an arm around her shoulder and led her up to the cottage.

CHAPTER FOUR

Thursday, August 16, 1962

ORMSBY'S HOUSE LAY just the way Eve had told him it would. The south-facing French door stood wide open, the glass panes reflecting a murky sheen of moonlight.

Keegan slipped inside the house, turning sideways and holding up his hands, careful not to touch the door frame or any of the glass as he did. He found himself in a vast, high-ceilinged room. It was dark, but what moonlight came in through the tall windows suggested a world of polish and glass: wall panels of burnished wood, dangling crystal lamps, glass-encased paintings. He moved quietly, but the squeak of his rubber-soled shoes on the marble floor echoed in the cavernous space.

He passed a small table that sat beside a wingback chair. A black phone was sat on a lace doily. If he made the call—and he wasn't sure yet whether he would—it would be better made from his own kitchen.

Keegan crossed the room to a wide arched entryway. Beyond it was a formal dining room, with a ship-like table and a tiered chandelier. This single room was easily as large as his mother's entire cottage. On the opposite wall, a large antique mantle clock tick-tocked softly above a gaping black fireplace.

At the other end of the room, Keegan shouldered through a

large swinging door, careful not to brush it with his hands. The roomy kitchen was all sinks and racks, scoured steel surfaces and dangling copper pots. Keegan made his way around an island stovetop, straining to see in the dark. He stopped short when he saw the body.

Ormsby lay slumped in the far doorway, back to the doorjamb. One leg was bent under him and the other stretched out into the hallway beyond. His chin was tucked down against his chest and his white mane of hair had fallen forward into his eyes. Keegan had seen his share of crime scenes, and it always struck him—as it did now—how tawdry and commonplace they seemed: the slack limbs, the crumpled posture, the whiff of urine in the air.

Keegan slipped closer and stood over the body. Ormsby's linen shirt, which still had light-colored sleeves, was stained dark everywhere else. One hand was balled into a fist at his side. The other was caught among the buttons of his shirt.

Keegan dropped to one knee, careful to avoid the slick oval of blood that lay congealing around the corpse, half on the kitchen tile and half on the parquet floor of the hallway. He bent close to the old man's face. Even in the dim moonlight coming through the kitchen blinds, Keegan could tell the coloring of his skin was all wrong. His cheeks sagged like warmed wax. His empty eyes stared blindly down the empty hallway.

Judging by the small tear in the front of his blood-soaked collar, the bullet had entered at the base of his throat. The old man hadn't died instantly, Keegan guessed, but he wouldn't have suffered long.

Keegan stood, feeling the ache in his knees. The body at his feet seemed so small and inconsequential now— nothing like the big, blustering man who had stood among his mother's roses.

Keegan stepped over Ormsby's outstretched leg, again careful to avoid the pooled blood, and made his way down the hallway, scanning the floor for his revolver. He found it at the hall's far end, half hidden under a tea cart that had been pushed against the wall. He looked back down the hall to where Ormsby's leg jutted out from the doorway. It had to be a good thirty feet—probably more—quite a shot for a snub nose in a dark hallway. She'd wanted to shoot at the stump from farther away. Hadn't he told her it would be better to run?

He stood looking down the dim hallway as the precious seconds ticked away. He thought of Eve, crumpled in the big armchair up in the cottage. How would she stand up to the scrutiny, the ham-fisted sleuthing of the LAPD? He'd lived in that world for decades and he knew its cruel machinations. He'd seen the corruption, the railroading, the hunger for accolades. A celebrity killing, with a speedy conviction? It was any junior DA's wet dream. A man could ride a case like that up South Broadway—like a Rose Parade float—to a better office, a household name, a shot at something bigger. Justice be damned. It was all about the headlines. Keegan knew; he'd written enough of them.

Keegan glanced back down the hallway at his dead neighbor. He could imagine the crime-scene photo enlargements from this very angle, set on an easel where the jury would have to ponder them. He thought of Eve, small and pale behind the big oak table flanked by men his own age. Innocence might make it harder to get a conviction. Money would be even more of an obstacle. But in the cold calculus of legal guilt and innocence, of petty politics and careerism, Eve wouldn't stand a chance. They'd dig up a motive—any loose words or reports of raised voices would do—and the rest would be taken care of. Prints on the gun. Powder residue. A cooling body slumped in a doorway. All in a big house locked tight with top-of-the-line deadbolts.

His best move seemed obvious. He reached down and picked up the revolver, feeling a twinge in the small of his back. He didn't even have to raise it to his nose to smell the gunpowder. *So innocent, yet so lethal*. He flipped it open and tilted it to catch what little light there was. Six brass cartridges, one dimpled by the revolver's hammer. A single shot was all it took. One twelve-pound pull on the trigger. He tucked the gun into his waistband. He'd have to move fast, but he couldn't make mistakes.

He slipped farther down the hall to the front foyer, and crept up the curved staircase, careful not to touch the bannister. Only one door was ajar in the second-floor hallway: that would be Eve's bedroom. He slipped past the other doors and looked inside. The sheets on the king-sized bed were rumpled on one side where she had been sleeping. A few books were scattered on the undisturbed side, along with an unbuckled wristwatch and a manicure set. The window next to the bed was wide open and the drapes pulled back to let the cool night air in.

He found the zippered pouch for his gun on the ornate nightstand, next to a glass of water that was covered with a postcard, and, of all things, an antique silver inkwell with a goose quill. He flattened the pouch, folded it the best he could, and stuffed it into his back pocket. He pulled one hand up into his shirtsleeve and nudged the things on the nightstand together, so there wouldn't be an obvious space, like a chalk outline, where the gun had lain.

Behind the electric alarm clock on the dresser, not hidden, but tucked away, he found a couple of amber prescription bottles. With his hand still in his sleeve, he picked one of the bottles up. *Meprobamate*. He'd never heard of it. He set it carefully down and picked up the other. *Nembutal*. He thought of Marilyn, lying naked in her bedroom, emptied of life — even smaller and less consequential than the body he'd left downstairs.

He tugged out the front of his shirttails and held the medicine bottle carefully folded in the cloth. He unscrewed the cap, keeping his fingers inside his sleeve. He shook a few yellow capsules into his palm. Six. He slipped them into his pocket and tightened the lid again.

Downstairs, he went through the main entryway to the living room, so he wouldn't have to step over Ormsby's body again. He inspected the French door Eve had fled through. The cops would need a point of entry. The door opened onto a concrete walkway. That would work. He wouldn't have to worry about footprints. He looked at the door's brass handle. There was no lock on the inside. It was just a plain handle. He found the latch, a brass slide bolt, mounted on the door up above eye level. He stepped outside and pulled the door closed behind him, holding the handle with his shirttails.

He pulled the gun out of his waistband and swung it like a hammer. The noise of the glass splintering surprised him—a loud crack, like a gunshot, and then the splash of glass falling on the tile floor inside. At the sound, the crickets around him broke off their chorus. He stood breathlessly in the ensuing silence, waiting for something to happen. But not even Nora, up in the cottage, barked. Ormsby's spread was too big for the sound to have carried much beyond its garden walls.

Keegan looked down at the concrete beneath his shoes. The broken glass had all fallen to the inside of the door, which is what he wanted. He pushed open the door now, and let it sweep the shards of glass aside in an arc, as if someone had broken in. He slipped back inside, careful to step around the broken glass; he didn't want any of it embedded in the rubber soles of his shoes.

He slipped through the dark living room again and out to the front foyer. He unlocked the front door and slipped out onto the brick entryway.

Ormsby's black Fleetwood was parked in an open garage just off the circular driveway. He looked up at the dark house. Ormsby had to have driven right under Eve's open bedroom window. How had she missed hearing him come home?

BACK IN THE cottage, the lights were still out. He'd told Eve to keep them that way. He came through the kitchen door and found her sleeping in the armchair, with the dog curled at her feet. Eve lay sideways, her knees tucked up to her chest and her hands to her face, innocent and vulnerable. Keegan watched her breathing softly, noting the small, quick flutter to her eyelids. He felt suddenly heart-pierced and protective. She seemed lost in a shallow sleep. She must have taken one of the sleeping pills when she'd gone to bed. That would explain how she'd missed the rumble of Ormsby's big Lincoln driving right beneath her open window.

Back in the kitchen, Keegan put the gun and its pouch in a brown paper grocery bag and hid it under the sink. He'd take them to his office in the morning and lock them in his desk. Or maybe he'd pack them away in his apartment somewhere.

In the living room, he sat down on the sofa, exhausted but buzzing with adrenaline, calculating his next move. He watched Eve sleep and tried to collect his thoughts before he woke her and had to navigate her through the ordeal the two of them would have to face. It was like he was in the driver's seat and Eve was his passenger, sleeping beside him, her face lit soft by the oncoming cars, her fate entirely in his keeping. There was something intimate that he didn't want to hurry. He had the impulse to get up, to go over and touch her hair, but he sat still, simply watching, simply trying to get a fix on this moment and what it might mean. Here the two of them were, bound together in misadventure, and this coupling would be permanent, he sensed, for better or for worse. For richer or for poorer.

Keegan would have sat like this as long as he could, but the sun would soon rise on a dead man. An arriving cook or a housekeeper would stumble upon him; there'd be screams and sirens and all hell would break loose. He went to Eve and shook her gently.

He watched her face move from sleep to confusion to panic as she remembered where she was and why she was here. Her glassy eyes went wide. She gasped and sat up quickly, gripping the arms of the chair.

He put a hand on her shoulder. The muscles there were tensed. "Easy," he told her. "I'm taking care of it."

"Oh, God, oh, God," she said—she might have been either cursing or praying—and her breathing turned quick and shallow. She sat forward and pressed her palm to her breastbone. "Oh, God. I killed him."

She stood, and Keegan took her by the shoulders. She felt wild and edgy between his palms.

"I did, didn't I?" she said. "I killed him."

"Easy," he told her. "It's going to be okay."

Nora, sensing alarm in the air, scampered around them in a circle. She barked twice and then prodded Keegan's ankles with her nose.

Still holding Eve's shoulders, Keegan pushed her towards the kitchen. Nora scampered underfoot, threatening to trip him. "This way," he told Eve. "Come on. It's okay. You can do this."

Eve's gait was unsteady, like a cruise ship passenger on rolling seas. He slid his forearm under her arm to steady her. He steered her to the kitchen counter, and she slumped forward against it, propped on her elbows. He rummaged in the cupboard under the sink and found a can of Comet. That would be abrasive enough to do the job. He ran the faucet until the water got hot and then physically moved Eve in front of the sink to scrub her hands of gunpowder.

She tried to pull away from the hot running water, but Keegan held her wrists firmly.

"It's not that hot," he told her, though steam was beginning to coat the bottom half of the kitchen window. "We need to scrub you down," he said. "We're not taking any chances."

"What?" she said. "Why?" But she didn't resist him. She leaned against him drunkenly while the water coursed through her fingers.

He gently scrubbed her hand and wrist. When her right hand looked pink and raw, he went to work on the other. Her fingers were slim and pale, and the scarlet, glistening nail polish she wore made him think of Ormsby's pool of blood. How many hours before they found him?

Eve rested her whole weight against him now, breathing softly. It made it difficult to finish scouring down her hands, but he pressed on.

He steadied her against the counter with his body and wiped his damp hands on his trouser legs, then he took her by the shoulders again and shook her awake. "How many pills did you take?" he asked her. And again: "How many pills?"

Eve sucked in a sudden breath. "Two," she said.

"And how many are you supposed to take?"

"Just one," she said. Her head drooped forward.

Again, he thought of Marilyn. Was that how it went? One pill, until that no longer worked? Then another and another? And then the coroner's van and the headlines and all the speculation?

He pulled back the sleeve of Eve's robe and scoured her right arm all the way up to her elbow. He scrubbed her other arm, too. He looked at the dim clock on the oven. It was just coming up on two o'clock. He turned off the faucet. The whole kitchen window was fogged over now.

He pulled a chair from the kitchen table, and Eve slumped down on it. She put her elbows on the table and covered her face with her hands.

"Jesus," she said. "What have I done?" Again, she might have been praying or cursing—but what did it matter?

Keegan got a glass from the cupboard and turned on the faucet to let the water run cold. He filled the glass and felt around in his trouser pocket for one of the sleeping pills he'd taken from her bedroom. He held it in his palm. She had to be deeply asleep when they found Ormsby. They had to climb the stairs and find her there and shake her awake. She had to have an excuse for why she knew nothing about what happened. If they tested her blood, they'd know she had too much Nembutal in her system. Enough to have slept through a Sousa concert in the front row. It was the best excuse he could think of on the fly—but were three pills too many?

He sat down in the chair beside Eve's and put his arm around her. "Here," he told her. "Take this." He put the pill in her hand. "Just gulp it down with some water."

Eve looked down at the pink tablet uncertainly, as if she couldn't fathom what it was.

"It won't hurt you," Keegan promised her. "It's okay. You'll be fine." He held his breath and hoped to God he was telling the truth.

Eve shook her head groggily, as if she'd finally deciphered his meaning. "I already took them," she said.

"I know," Keegan told her, his face close to hers, trying to hold her attention. "But you need to take another. They have to believe you slept through the whole thing." He thought of the big sedan driving under her window. He thought of Ormsby's booming voice. He thought of the gunshot echo in the ravine up the hill. "If they ask, you're going to tell them you took three pills. Do you understand? Tell them the heat was making it impossible to sleep."

Eve shook her head, weary of this argument they seemed to be having.

He jolted her by the shoulders again. "Listen to me," he said. "You need to do this. You need to take the pill."

Eve's eyes roamed across his face, like she was trying to place him, but she finally sighed, defeated. She took the pill and put it on her tongue. He helped her raise the glass to her lips, and she swallowed it down.

As he walked with her down the road from the cottage, she kept lagging. He pulled one of her arms across his shoulders and led her across the gravel to the back gate with the other arm around her waist. He carried most of her weight while her small, slippered feet stumbled and dragged. What if Catling's men were watching tonight from the dark perimeter? What would they make of this scene?

He'd left Ormsby's front door unlocked, and now he helped Eve negotiate the front steps. In the entryway, he propped her against the brickwork while he reached for the doorknob, hand in his sleeve. He twisted it and then pushed the door open with his foot. He needed her to hear him, and he shook her by the shoulders until her eyes opened wide. "Listen," he told her, holding his face close to hers. "When you get inside, just lock the door and go back to bed. Sleep until they wake you."

She lifted her head, with apparent effort, and looked at him unsteadily. "What do I do about—?" Another sentence left unfinished.

"You don't do anything about anything," he said. "You lock the front door. You go upstairs. You go to sleep. Understand?"

It was hard to know if he was getting through to her. Her head lolled on her neck as he shook her again.

"Here's your story," he told her when her eyes met his. "The sleeping pills knocked you out, and you didn't hear a thing. You slept through the whole ordeal, and you have no idea what happened. Okay?"

She nodded limply, her eyelids heavy, her gaze going vacant again. Would she even make it up the stairs? Or would some early-morning maid find her snoring on the marble foyer, blocking the front door? Maybe the third pill was a bad idea. But it was too late to wonder about that now.

"When you get inside, close the door and lock it," Keegan told her again.

He steered her in through the open door. The big front hallway was dark, but a chandelier loomed, ghostly and cold, high in the open space. She began to close the door on him.

"Lock it and go up to bed," he told her.

"Yes. Yes," she said wearily. "I know. I know." The door clunked shut.

Keegan waited a beat, holding his breath and listening. The deadbolt scraped into place. He slipped down the steps and back into the garden.

KEEGAN LEFT THE dog shut up in the house and drove to his apartment with the windows of his car rolled down. The wind chilled him through his damp shirt. His head hurt and his whole body ached with a kind of fever. It felt like the flu, but he knew it was just fatigue. How long could the human body survive without real sleep?

There was some kind of overnight construction going on along Fairfax. Orange pylons crowded traffic down into a single dusty lane. The line of cars crept between klieg lights and dump trucks and heavy machinery. Eventually, Keegan had to stop completely, and for a few maddening minutes, his headlights lit up the back of a Helms bakery truck that idled inches from his front grille. Only in LA could you find a traffic jam at 3:00 a.m. on a Thursday. The stench of diesel and fresh asphalt made him roll his windows up and suffer the airless heat. He tried the radio, but all the stations he knew had signed off the air an hour or two ago.

It was nearly four when he finally pulled into his reserved space in the carport outside his apartment quad and cut the engine. He opened the car door and climbed out. He felt the ache in his knees and back. His damp shirt clung to him. Standing on the concrete walkway between his car and the Pontiac in the next space, he felt like he was still moving. He looked both ways along the line of cars and then slipped the gun back in its zippered pouch. He tucked them into the waistband at the back of his trousers and tugged his shirttails down to cover them. He pushed down the car's door lock and then closed the door as quietly as he could.

The apartment quad was quiet when he came in through the front gate. Bone-white moonlight shimmered on the central swimming pool and dusted the bushy palm fronds. The shamble of his footsteps on the concrete stairs to the second level seemed impossibly loud in the balmy stillness. In a far corner apartment, the nervy blue light of a television rose and fell behind the drawn curtains. Someone must have fallen asleep watching. At least he hoped they were sleeping.

As he crept past apartment 203, Mr. Soto's place, he thought he saw the blinds stir in the corner of his eye—but it had to be just nerves, a trick of the light, a shimmer from off the pool. Even Mr. Soto would have abandoned his lonely vigil at this hour. Keegan's keys jingled softly, as he fumbled, numb-fingered, to unlock his deadbolt as quietly as he was able.

In the dark kitchen, he washed his face with cold water. Water hissed in the pipes, but it was okay now if someone heard him and knew he was there. He'd claim to have been here all night. He dug two tablets out of his trouser pocket and drizzled more faucet water into a glass from the cupboard. The sleeping pills were bitter and bulky on his tongue. He knocked them back with a swig and left the glass on the kitchen counter.

In the bedroom, he lay on top of the covers with the windows still closed. He shut his eyes and lay his head on the pillow, but his body was still strumming with energy. He stared up at the dark popcorn ceiling, trying not to think, waiting for the pills to pull him down. He thought of Marilyn and that deep sadness of not caring she must have felt. He waited on the Nembutal, indifferent, in that moment, as to whether he slept or died.

KEEGAN WOKE WITH a start before nine. The room was hot and stuffy and now smelled of him. He still wore the clothes from the night before, and they were already soaked through with sweat in the early heat. He'd slept atop the covers, but for some reason the sheets were tangled in a heap on the floor beside the bed.

Despite the two sleeping pills, his sleep had been fitful and crowded with half-formed dreams, a jumble of nonsensical snippets—of Lusk and Marilyn and the fat man in the park with his birdseed. At one point, he was standing on a sidewalk waiting for someone important—even in the dream, he didn't know who it was—and an old woman had tugged at his sleeve and asked him if he wanted to buy a dog. The dog on the woman's leash was a German Shepherd, but it was Nora as well—and he had felt a deep, unsettling dread.

He pulled his shirt off over his head and spread it out, still buttoned, on the bare mattress under the hanging ceiling lamp. He did the same with his trousers, smoothing them out flat on the bed. He'd been careful last night, and he could see no traces of Ormsby's blood on his clothes. On the cuff of his trousers, he found a small splatter of scarlet, but it was the wrong shade—clearly wine from when Eve had yanked the cork free with the shoelace. He crumpled the clothes up, took them to the closet, and wedged them down in the bottom of his laundry hamper, below the others.

In the bathroom, Keegan considered his face in the mirror above the sink, side-lit by the small window above the shower stall. It was amazing what a little August insomnia could do to a man. His eyes looked sunken and glassy. The stubble on his face seemed to be growing in unevenly, thicker on the cheeks than on the chin, which added to the general impression that his face might be a work in progress—a sketchy second draft of something that might someday pass for handsome.

Keegan showered in tepid water, taking his time, letting the cool water wake him up, feeling it sweep away both his sweat and misgivings. Then he shaved and pulled on clean slacks and took down a new blue shirt that was still wrapped in Bullock's paper. He made no effort to be quiet. Better if Soto heard him there, documenting Keegan's morning routine, in case he was ever asked. He'd locked the poor dog in the cottage overnight, but with most of the windows open and her water bowl full. She'd probably torn the place apart and barked all night, maybe pissed all over the living-room rug— but what could he do?

HE LISTENED TO the news on KNX while he drove—Russians rejoiced at the safe return of their spacemen; a US fighter plane was shot down over Laos; all of LA was gearing up for a visit by the Kennedys. *Happy Birthday, Mister President*.

There was nothing on the news yet about Ormsby.

Keegan drove, with his arm on the open windowsill of his car, conscious of looking like any other man heading to work on a Thursday morning. He stopped for yellow lights and cruised well under the speed limit. Whatever work they'd been doing on Fairfax the night before had been packed up and cleared. The only evidence he could see now was a single pylon wedged under a newspaper machine and the pungent smell of tar coming in through the dashboard vents.

It was a little before eleven when he turned off the main road and headed up Skyline Drive.

Near the crest of the hill, where the road split in two, a couple of LAPD cruisers blocked Ormsby's half of the intersection. Keegan braked and turned down the radio. A cop stood leaning against the front grille of one of the squad cars. His arms were folded, and he smoked a cigarette. He turned his head as Keegan slowly passed, watching from behind a pair of dark aviator glasses. Keegan nodded to him, got no response, and continued up the hill to the cottage. At least he'd been seen returning to his cottage and his dog. If anyone wanted to know, he'd been away all night. Sad business about the old man, but he had nothing to say, no leads to offer.

When Keegan came in through the front door, Nora trotted out from the kitchen, yawning. She stopped and stretched, sticking her rump up in the air. The fur on one side of her face was flattened down. It gave her the comical appearance of a confused old woman. At least someone seemed to have got some sleep. She nuzzled his pant leg and then trotted back towards the kitchen and her food bowl, wagging her tail.

Keegan looked around the cramped front room. Nothing seemed amiss. Nothing was chewed up. No doilies had been tugged down from their tables. No paperback books lay tattered on the rug. Good girl.

He went through to the kitchen to let the dog out into the yard. When he saw the empty wine bottle there on the counter, his heart sped up. He'd been so focused on leaving no traces of himself in Ormsby's place, he'd forgotten to check his own place for signs that Eve had been there. He pushed the bottle to the bottom of the trash bin under the sink, arranging paper towels and tin cans on top. He'd get rid of it altogether when he got the chance. The shoelace, sans cork, lay neatly coiled on the counter, next to the tiny screwdriver. He slipped both into the junk drawer.

Keegan followed the dog out into the garden and found her

standing at the edge of the lawn, barking down at Ormsby's place. He went and stood beside her.

Below them, a knot of vehicles crowded Ormsby's circular drive—two more squad cars, an unmarked gray sedan and a white crime-scene van. Another squad car was parked diagonally outside the open front gate, which was now laced with crime-scene tape. A few years ago, he would have ducked under the yellow tape and been welcomed with slaps on the back and a tour of the gore. Everyone he met would spell out their names for him to jot into his notebook, hoping they'd make it into the story. He wasn't sure if he missed those days or not.

Another unmarked sedan pulled up at the gate and got waved through. Two men got out and walked up to the front door, buttoning their suit coats. There was no coroner's van— those, Keegan knew, were black and had no windows in the back—so it was likely that Ormsby, or what was left of him, was already on the cold steel table down at the morgue.

A woman in a white smock kneeled by the French door, dusting for prints, or maybe documenting the pattern of fallen glass. She was too far away to be sure what she was up to. A couple of uniformed officers crept across the lawn behind her, walking slowly, hands on their utility belts, staring down at the ground at their feet—a sweep for evidence that might be overlooked.

Keegan had been careful—he knew how a crime scene was processed—but it had been very dark down there last night. He'd been sleep-deprived and running on adrenaline.

And Eve? She'd been barely conscious when he'd steered her through the garden, across the lawn to the front door. She could easily have dropped something—a hairpin, an earring, a tissue tucked in the sleeve of her dressing gown. What story might it tell?

Nora finally let up her barking and approached Keegan, bent low, as if she thought she might have done something wrong. She sniffed at his shoes, and he bent and scratched her behind the ears. The dog looked up at him and pressed her head into his scratching. "That's a good girl," he assured her. "You're doing your job."

"*Jimmy?*" The man's voice was clear.

Keegan straightened up quickly, heart racing. The blood seemed to flee from his fingertips. He looked down at Ormsby's place, where the voice had come from. The two cops had halted their progress across the lawn. One was kneeling now, and the other was bent over him, watching. The kneeling man stood, and they started their slow progress again.

"Keegan!" the voice called again.

Keegan glanced down and found the man directly below him. Only his head and shoulders were visible above Ormsby's back wall. He was a black man, and he wore a white Panama hat with a black band. It was Lieutenant Louis Moore—Keegan's last, best friend on the force. The shock of recognition brought a rush of heat to his face. Shouldn't a lieutenant be downtown behind a desk?

Keegan studied the smiling face looking up at him. Moore still had the lean look and the penetrating eyes of the young beat cop Keegan had championed in *The Times* all those years ago. The pressures of the job hadn't fattened him up or whitened his hair like they might do lesser men. Moore had always been smart and relentless; that's why he'd made such good copy, and now Keegan tried to sort out in his mind what Moore's presence in Ormsby's garden might mean.

"Well, if it isn't Jimmy Keegan in the flesh," Moore called up, grinning.

Keegan forced a smile. "Louis Moore," he said. "Long time no see. It was nice while it lasted."

"What are *you* doing in this neighborhood?" Moore asked. "Don't tell me you've started cleaning pools for a living." He walked along Ormsby's wall towards the back gate, looking at Keegan over his shoulder. "Or is my wife looking to divorce me?" He pulled the gate open and slipped through to the gravel drive.

Keegan tried to keep his voice glib and steady. "I always said she could find a better man in any passing Red Car," he said. "Sadly, she hasn't come around to my point of view."

Moore closed the chain-link gate behind him and strolled easily up the road towards the cottage, his hands dug deep in the pockets of his light gray summer suit. His clothes were expensive-looking, impeccably tailored. He might have stepped out of the Brooks Brothers summer catalogue. He had chosen the clothes, Keegan guessed, for the newspaper lens man who was bound to show up at Ormsby's place sooner or later. Maybe the KTLA news truck would rumble up from downtown once the story of an actor's murder broke. It would be good TV. Hell, Moore might leak the story himself, if no one showed. He'd never been camera-shy, and he'd slipped Keegan plenty of inside tips back in the day.

Keegan opened and closed his numbing hands and then dug them into his trouser pockets where he wouldn't have to think about them. He walked along the side of the cottage to the picket fence and waited for Moore inside the closed front gate.

They shook hands over the fence. The lieutenant's grip was cool and dry, despite the heat. Now that he was close, Keegan could see new lines etched into the other man's cheeks and the smudge of gray hair at his temples that showed beneath the band of his hat. He was older, but he still held himself tall, buoyed up no doubt by senior rank and sterling reputation.

Moore opened the front gate, uninvited, and stepped into the garden.

"Don't let the dog out," Keegan told him. The caution sounded fretful and old-lady-ish in his own ears. It might have been his mother's voice.

Moore closed the gate without hurry. "So how are you doing, Jimmy?" he said. "I'd say you haven't changed a bit, but to be honest you look like something a sick cat spat up."

Keegan forced another smile. "Haven't been sleeping," he said. "You know. This weather."

Moore nodded genially. "You, me and everybody else in this town," he said, though there was nothing about his manner or posture or clear-eyed gaze that hinted he'd missed a minute of shut-eye. He smiled and tilted his head, as if something funny had occurred to him. "Hell, look at us, Jimmy," he said. "That sorry day has arrived. We're two old farts standing around complaining about the weather."

Keegan, in the moment, could think of no glib comeback, so he just nodded.

The lieutenant rocked back on his heels, hands in his pockets. He looked the cottage over amiably, and then looked beyond it at the view of the city. He walked over to the edge of the hill. "So, what *are* you doing in these parts, Jimmy?" he said. "I'd never expect to find you in a neighborhood this well-to-do."

Moore's jibe stung a little, intentional or not, though Keegan couldn't have said why it bothered him. "I could say the same thing about *you*," he told the lieutenant. "These hills are white as bird shit."

Moore shot him a sharp look he couldn't interpret—it had not been in his arsenal back when they saw a lot of each other—but then the lieutenant broke into another of his big, easy smiles and jingled the coins in his pocket. "Times are changing," Moore said. "Nat King Cole lives in Hancock Park, these days." The words were neat and precise. This man would not be easily ruffled.

Keegan nodded. "'On the Sunny Side of the Street', no doubt," he said. He pulled his hands out of his pockets, and then, not knowing what to do with them, dug them back in again. He wondered if he looked nervous, and then he scolded himself for wondering.

The lieutenant looked the cottage over and then turned back to Keegan. "This *your* place?" he said. "Thought you lived down Mid-Wilshire."

"I do," he said. "This was my saintly mother's place. She died last week. I'm cleaning it out. Trying to figure out what to do with it."

Moore nodded slowly. "Sorry to hear that," he said, though there was no actual trace of regret in his voice. "Sudden?"

"Yes and no," Keegan said. This isn't what he wanted to be talking about. He'd prefer to give his alibi and be done with it. He shaded his eyes and looked down at Ormsby's place. "So, what're your people up to down there? Looks like a whole presidential motorcade." He thought of Kennedy. He thought of Marilyn.

"Old man got shot," Moore said. "Some TV actor."

"Murder? Suicide?"

"We're still working the scene," Moore said cagily, but then he seemed to relax a bit. This was Keegan he was talking to. His old friend. "But, yeah," he said. "Looks like it's probably a murder."

"Thought you got out of homicide when you made L.T."

Moore nodded. "I did," he said. "They pulled me back in for this one."

Just Keegan's luck. "So, a celebrity detective for a celebrity murder," he said. "Two famous names in one headline."

Moore grinned. "Something like that," he said. His smile faded and he focused on Keegan. "You hear anything up here last night? See anything out of the ordinary?"

"Nah," Keegan said. "I was down in Mid-Wilshire, where poor slobs like me belong. I just got up here a few minutes ago to check up on the dog." Mr. Soto could confirm when he'd left the apartment, and the cop in the aviator glasses could testify as to when he'd arrived—but it would be better to let Moore find all that out on his own.

The lieutenant tilted the hat back on his head and nodded over at the cottage. "Anybody in this place last night?"

"Just a Welsh Terrier," Keegan said, "but she's a stubborn one. I'll be impressed if you can get her to talk."

The lieutenant gave him a half-smile. "Terriers are headstrong that way."

Keegan nodded. "This one's a bitch if I ever saw one."

Moore's smile grew a little before it faded. He was all business. "But you stay up here some nights," he said. It didn't sound like a question.

Keegan felt a bead of sweat creep down his ribs under his shirt. It was just the heat, he told himself. He willed his heart to slow. "If you say so," he said.

"I came up earlier and knocked," Moore said. "Routine canvass. The dog went berserk. I thought, somebody's gotta be looking after the mutt. I saw the trash cans by the carport. Nice collection of empty bottles." He gave Keegan a knowing smile. "I'm guessing those didn't belong to your saintly mother."

Keegan wondered if he'd looked through the kitchen window and saw the wine bottle on the counter. "I've stayed here a few nights," he admitted. "Dogs aren't allowed at my apartment."

Moore nodded and looked back down the road he'd come up. "You know the girl who lives down there?"

Keegan thought of Eve's kiss at the doorway. Even now, the surprise of it left him a little unsteady. "Met her a couple of times," he said. And then, before he could stop himself: "What was her name again?" Shit.

But Moore had already reached inside his jacket to pull out a black notebook — the same kind Keegan had always carried on the crime beat. The lieutenant flipped the notebook open with a flick of the wrist. "*Eve*," he read. "Eve Ormsby-Cutler."

"Yeah, that's right," Keegan said. "The old man's niece. What did *she* say happened?"

"Says she slept through the whole thing," he said. He gave a sort of *who's-to-say* shrug. "Sleeping pills on the bedside table. Acting all groggy when we got there."

Keegan felt a warm rush of relief. Eve had done what he'd told her to do. She'd got the story straight, despite the triple dose of sleeping pills.

Moore flipped the notebook shut and slipped it back inside his jacket. "At least that's how she's playing it."

"Any reason to doubt her?" Keegan said. "Hell, they hand out Seconal in PEZ dispensers up here."

Moore looked in the direction of Ormsby's place, squinting in the sunlight, despite the Panama hat. "It's early," he said. "I don't know what I believe." Another jingle of coins in his pocket. "Something's not right down there." He looked at Keegan, serious now. "You've got that gun, right?"

"Gun?"

Moore squinted at him a few unsettling seconds. "The one you were shooting the other morning," he said. "The one I got pulled out of a meeting for."

"Oh, yeah," Keegan said. "Sorry about that." He felt the urge to talk—to just rattle out words—but he held himself together and tamped out the impulse like a spent cigarette. He'd seen a lot of police interrogations from the far side of a two-way mirror. He'd seen a lot of men talk their way into a prison cell. He measured his words before he spoke. "Some high-school kid with a badge was trying to play me, so I might have dropped your name," he said. "I owe you one for that." He hadn't answered the question, he knew. And Moore was still waiting. "It's just an old .38 revolver," he said. "Ancient, really. I keep it in my office. Locked in a file cabinet."

Moore nodded again. "Do me a favor," he said. He took out the notebook. He put his fountain pen's cap in his teeth so he could unscrew it. He scribbled something in the notebook and then screwed the top back on the pen. "Stay up here a few nights," he said. "Keep the poor dog company." He tore the page out of the notebook and handed it to Keegan. "And keep an eye on the girl for me." He slipped the pen and notebook back in his jacket.

Keegan tried to hold the page steady with his bloodless fingers. It listed Moore's phone numbers: precinct, office, home. "I usually get paid for this kind of thing," Keegan said.

Moore grinned—a set of wide, too-white teeth. "The day Jimmy Keegan won't watch a beautiful woman free of charge is the day we really *are* past it," he said. "Keep an eye out. I'll buy you a drink and we can compare notes."

IT WAS NEARLY six in the evening when Keegan climbed the front steps of the brick entryway and pressed Ormsby's doorbell. He heard the muffled two-toned chime on the other side of the thick oak door. He wondered if Eve would even hear the bell if she were deep in the house, or, more likely, locked away in that bedroom with her books and her sleeping pills. There was no rustle of life inside the house. He rang again. Again, the house was still.

He looked back at the oval driveway. There was little evidence of that morning's commotion. The lawn looked trampled down in a few places, and a yellow scrap of crime-scene tape was caught under a potted plant. Otherwise, starlings still pecked around in the flower beds, and the high cirrus clouds still scudded across the unrelenting summer sky. Time moved on, with or without Ormsby or Marilyn or his mother.

The big door swung open when Keegan wasn't expecting it. He took a step back and felt a quick jolt of adrenaline set his heart racing. Dammit! He couldn't afford to be so jumpy.

A face peered out at him blankly from the partly opened door—a plumpish woman in her forties—maybe fifties. The surprise of seeing a stranger made Keegan wonder, nonsensically, if he'd knocked on the wrong door. The woman's face was pale, but it bore a harried kind of beauty that must have served her well in her youth, with high cheekbones and heavy, inquisitive brows. Her eyes were rimmed in red and her silver-threaded brunette hair was pulled back in a hasty bun. "Flowers?" she said.

Keegan dug his hands in his pockets. His blue Arrow shirt was open at the collar, and he'd rolled up the sleeves. Even freshly shaven, he knew he didn't look like the well-bred, well-heeled men anyone would expect to come knocking on the door in this neighborhood. He *did* look like someone making a delivery.

"No," he said to the woman. "Sorry. I'm a neighbor. I'm here to see Miss Ormsby-Cutler. Is she—?"

The door opened wider, and Keegan could see the bright front entryway behind her. The woman who stood on the checkerboard tile wore a black mid-length dress with a white collar. She looked Keegan over appraisingly and seemed to shift into a more genteel mien. "Of course," she said, her voice suddenly deeper and more fluid. "How nice of you to call. Please come in, Mr.—?"

"Keegan."

"Of course, Mr. *Keegan*," she said, as though she should have known. She held her hand out, limply, for Keegan to shake, and he did. "Please do come in."

Her transatlantic accent struck Keegan as more Bryn Mawr than Brentwood. She must have grown up on the other coast.

She stepped to one side, so Keegan could enter, and then she closed the door behind him. "I didn't think Eve *knew* any of our neighbors." Her voice echoed faintly in the grand open space. "She only just arrived a few days ago. But then I've been out of town."

Keegan glanced around at the sweeping staircase, the dangling crystal chandelier, the blinding white walls and glossy tilework. A silver tray stood upon a central pedestal table, as if waiting for Edwardian calling cards. The August afternoon light shone down through a lofty atrium. In daylight, the whole scene lacked any hint of menace. It was opulent, but in the blandest, most benign and unimaginative way—all whipped cream and icing.

"You must be Mrs. Ormsby," Keegan said. "We've never met. I'm staying at my mother's place up the hill. She passed away a few weeks ago."

"Oh, dear," Mrs. Ormsby said. She pressed a palm to her breastbone. "So sorry to hear that. She lived in that little cottage, didn't she?" Despite her practiced graciousness, the woman had a flustered air about her, like a wedding planner surprised by an early guest. It was understandable. She didn't seem prepared yet for all the visitors and well-wishers who would no doubt flock to her once news about Ormsby got out. She waved for Keegan to follow her into the next room. "You might have heard what befell Mr. Ormsby," she said.

The sentence had the stilted ring of something he'd read in a Victorian poetry class he'd taken as an English undergrad at USC. *I hold it true, whate'er befall...* But it didn't seem out of place in this grand, echoing hallway. What odd anachronisms washed up on the shores of great wealth: the silver inkwell on a bedside table, the calling-card tray in the entryway, *befell*.

"Yes," Keegan said, following her towards a broad doorway. "I heard a little about it. A policeman came by my mom's place to see if I'd heard anything, but I wasn't at home last night. I wish I had been. Maybe I could have..." He let the sentence trail off. What *could* he have done? The question was a pit in his stomach.

"I was gone, too," she said. "I was in Santa Barbara for the summer regatta. Of course, I raced home the moment I heard."

The rubber soles of his department-store shoes squeaked on the tile floor as he followed Mrs. Ormsby into the next room. "Did the intruders take anything valuable?" he asked.

Without turning to him, Mrs. Ormsby waved his question away. She almost seemed irritated. Who would ask such a question at a time like this?

She led Keegan across the great room—the same room Keegan had slipped into in the dark morning hours. It was both familiar and disorienting to encounter it again in the light of day. It seemed like a week ago at least that he'd crept into this room through the open French door—a memory already beginning to fade at the edges. Was it possible that all of this had happened in just one day?

With the light streaming in from all the tall windows, and

the many lamps now lit, the paneled walls took on the warm glow of cello wood. Silver glinted from every tabletop and shelf. Each smooth surface was polished to a gleam. Even the tiled floor dimly mirrored the furniture arranged on top of it.

The pane he'd broken in the French door had already been replaced by a new rectangle of glass up next to the latch. He couldn't help but stare at it a few guilty seconds. That pane was slightly clearer than the others—but no one would notice who wasn't looking for it. The broken shards of glass he'd left behind had been swept up. Even the fingerprint technician's black smudges seemed to have been scrubbed away. How quickly things were patched and painted over in this realm of the wealthy. Was there even a chalk outline back in the kitchen doorway? Or had every trace of Ormsby's life and death already been sanitized and rinsed away?

Mrs. Ormsby took a seat in a wingback chair, and waved—a queenly, airy gesture—for Keegan to take a seat across from her on the settee. A mug of beige coffee sat next to a folded newspaper on a small table at her elbow. Keegan could tell by the typeface that it wasn't *The Times*. *The Wall Street Journal*, no doubt. A pair of tortoise-shell reading glasses balanced on the chair's arm, where she'd set them when she rose to answer the door. Mrs. Ormsby folded them shut and slipped them into the pocket of her dress. The cup she'd been drinking from was Pyrex glass in a red plastic holder—clearly not the good china—more the kind of thing Keegan's mother would have bought with those Green Stamps she was always squirreling away. He should have visited her more often.

"And how may I help you?" the widow asked Keegan, once she was settled.

Keegan crossed his legs uncomfortably. "I actually dropped by to see Eve. Is she in?"

"She hasn't come down yet," Mrs. Ormsby said. "It was all quite a shock to her, as I'm sure you can imagine." She leaned forward and dropped her voice to a whisper. "She was actually *here* in the house when it happened," she said. She shook her head with a kind of ghoulish shiver. "Imagine! Upstairs, asleep. The poor thing." She leaned back and recovered her more formal tone. "We're all hoping she'll get some rest. She's had no end of troubles recently."

Keegan thought of the Nembutal bottle on Eve's bedside table; she might still be in a fog after her triple dose. She was probably asleep right now. He'd try her again later.

The widow Ormsby had sunk into her chair now, as if she wasn't planning on moving any time soon. She gazed absently at the tall windows, her lips moving wordlessly. Was she looking at the French door? What did she know? What might Lieutenant Moore have told her?

Keegan was perched too far forward on the settee to lean back. He was unsure what to do with his hands, so he held his crossed knee. He'd pay good money for a knock on the door or a ringing telephone right now—any reason to rise and excuse himself and take his leave. After a too-long silence he cleared this throat and said: "Well, let her know I stopped by." He uncrossed his legs and stood.

The Ormsby widow looked up at him, pleadingly. "Please, Mr. Keegan," she said. She stretched out one hand as if to catch him by his rolled-up shirtsleeve, though he was a good three feet beyond her reach. "Do stay a few minutes." She waved him back into the chair. "It's good to have someone to talk to who isn't involved in all this… this—" She paused, searching for the right word. "Up*hea*val." Her tone was warmer now, less imperious.

Keegan felt trapped. What kind of a cad would make a run for it now? He nodded and sat back down.

"Could I get you some coffee?" she said. "I'm sure it's still hot."

Keegan leaned back into the settee. He folded his hands in his lap. What else would an innocent man, a good neighbor, do in a moment like this? "Thank you," he said. "Black. No sugar."

Mrs. Ormsby smiled. She looked behind her, and then it

seemed to dawn on her that she'd sent the day help home early on this dark and troubling day. She stood, took up her own cup and trod into the next room, looking impossibly small as she passed through the high doorway.

While she was gone, Keegan glanced up at the high ceiling and listened for any sign of Eve upstairs. Had she downed yet another sleeping pill to get her through the day? Perhaps some fawning doctor-to-the-rich had come by and prescribed her an even stronger sedative, some syringe of tranquility. He imagined her up there in her room, lying in bed, eyelids aflutter in some restless, drug-induced limbo.

Across the room, a black grand piano loomed near the fireplace. Its curved coffin-lid propped open. Keegan must have walked right past it this morning without noticing it in the dark—too focused on his mission to fully take in his surroundings. If he had missed a Steinway, what small details might he have overlooked in his rush to clean things up and be gone?

It was taking the widow longer than it should have to pour some coffee into a mug. Keegan looked at his watch. It was a few minutes after six now. Another hour or so of sunlight before the world began to cool a bit.

Mrs. Ormsby swept back into the room, bearing a butler's tray. She seemed relieved to have fallen into the comforting protocol of the hostess. The tray held bone-china teacups on their saucers, a silver tea set and a platter of pink wafer cookies arranged in a fan. The Pyrex cup was gone now, stowed out of sight with the everyday Fiestaware and the stainless-steel cutlery. Keegan was being entertained.

She set the tray on the table between them and perched daintily on the wingback across from him, holding herself a good five inches from the chair's back. She smoothed down her dress and offered Keegan a practiced smile.

The coffee—like the wine Eve had stolen from Ormsby's cellar—didn't taste like anything Keegan was used to. It was silky and bore the scent of blackberries. He tried a few sips, couldn't decide if he liked it or not, and then set the cup and saucer on the table between them.

For a while the widow talked, and Keegan tried to listen, though his legs itched with the urge to get up and flee. In his years writing about crime, he'd never understood the old chestnut that a criminal always returned to the scene. Nothing seemed less likely. He kept glancing at the French door, with its pane of too-clean glass. Just beyond it—through the garden, through the chain-link gate, up the hill—was the place he'd much rather be.

"I don't know what will become of me," Mrs. Ormsby was saying.

Her voice cracked as she spoke, which drew back Keegan's attention. It didn't seem to be an affectation. Keegan looked at her more keenly.

The widow worried the silver buttons on her dress with one hand and seemed to be blinking back tears. Vertical lines showed in her lips when she pursed them. She seemed on the verge of breaking down, and that possibility redoubled Keegan's need to be somewhere—anywhere—else. He was a complete stranger. It was not his place to console. There had to be someone this woman could call.

The best he could do was lighten the mood, however clumsily. "You've got a beautiful place here," he said brightly. He looked around at the splendor that surrounded them, noticing, yet again, how out of place he felt, an interloper in a too-opulent world. The gilt-framed hunting scenes, the burnished wood and glimmering crystal, the lacquered grand piano, all seemed to press in on him, an obscene clutter of riches. Keegan felt an odd, irrational pang of envy for a dead man.

Mrs. Ormsby picked up her cup and saucer and held them in front of her stiffly, trying to compose herself.

Keegan pressed on: "Why, you could sell this house and live on the Riviera for the rest of your life, if it took your fancy."

Mrs. Ormsby sat straighter. "This place?" she said. She shook her head forlornly, and the beige coffee swirled a bit in her cup. "None of this really belonged to Nigel. It's all part of the family trust. His grandfather set it up. Ironclad. Everything will go to his sister now, and her girl. I won't see a penny."

"Her *girl*?" Keegan said, a little too quickly. "You mean Eve?" What had she said about Ormsby's wine? She had as much right to it as he did?

The widow nodded and set her coffee cup back on the tray. "Nigel didn't have any *real* money," she said. "Not of his own."

Keegan felt caught off guard. The idea seemed impossible. "Wasn't he an *actor*?" he said.

"Of course, he was," the widow said. "And a very good one, too." She leaned forward, as if the conversation had veered into something confidential. "But he was no Gregory Peck, Mr. Keegan." She lifted the cup from her saucer and then put it back. "He wasn't even a Joseph Cotten." She lifted the cup again and took a fussy sip. "Poor Nigel never got his big break," she said. "He was all B-films and television. There's no real money in that."

KEEGAN WAS HEADING across the lawn to Ormsby's back gate when Eve's voice called out his name. He stopped and turned and looked for her, shading his eyes with one hand. She stood in a back portico at the far end of the pool, almost invisible in the looming late-afternoon shadows. She looked behind her at the glass-paned doors and then waved him over.

Keegan looked up at his cottage and back in the direction from which he'd come. What were the chances the police had posted someone to keep an eye on the place? It seemed unlikely—but, still, he'd best not be seen talking to Eve in any way that looked suspicious. Keegan turned and walked toward her, around the pool. He walked slowly, casually, in case there were witnesses. As he drew nearer, he worried that she'd rush to him, out in the open, and he tried to warn her away with his eyes—but she stayed where she was, pressed back against the closed door.

He slipped through the small rose garden beyond the pool and up the steps to where she waited. Eve wore a skirt and a simple pale blue blouse, both wrinkled, as though she'd slept in them. Her face was pale, her eyes red and glassy—but from crying or too much medication? Keegan couldn't guess.

Now that he was close to her, she seemed as wary as he was, which he supposed was a good sign. She kept close to the mansion, back pressed to the door, like a worried child clinging to the edge of a pool. At least no one posted to watch the place would likely see her there in the shade.

"Any cops still around?" Keegan said, when he was close enough to speak in something near a whisper.

"They're all gone," she said, keeping her own voice low. "My aunt shooed them away. She didn't want them mucking up the place."

"Great," Keegan said. He blew out a breath. "That's a good sign."

Eve seemed bewildered. "Why?" she said. Her eyes, Keegan thought, looked a bit unfocused. "What's good about it?"

He put his hands on her shoulders. She was trembling a little, but she didn't pull away from him. "It means they don't suspect anything beyond what's on the face of it," he told her. "They think the killer is long gone."

Eve bit her lip and nodded. It was hard for Keegan to read her mood. "What do we do now?" she asked.

"Now?" Keegan said. "Nothing. Nothing has changed." He was still holding her shoulders, but her breathing seemed to be gradually coming faster, clearly struggling to keep herself together.

"Easy," Keegan told her. "Everything's going to be fine. We just need to stick to the plan."

She shook her head and looked beyond him. Her eyes seemed to be searching the darkening garden for any solace it might offer. "Can't we just come clean?" she said. "It can't be too late to just tell the truth." Her voice had a slight quiver in it, and that made Keegan worry. Maybe he'd misjudged her. She could ride horses and steal wine with aplomb, but was she really up for what she'd gotten them into? It would be too much for most people.

"You shot a man," Keegan reminded her. He tried to speak evenly, reasonably—in a voice he might use to explain something to a child. "You killed him with my gun. We're stuck in this together." He searched her eyes for comprehension. "You don't know this town like I do," he told her. "Guilt or innocence mean jack squat when there are headlines to be got. I know. I used to write them." He squeezed her shoulders with both hands. "It was too late for us the moment you pulled the trigger." That much Keegan knew to be true, but was it too late when he'd handed her the gun outside Ormsby's back gate? Was it too late when Catling pulled up outside the Grand Central Market in his absurd limo? When, in a long chain of cause and effect, did a catastrophe move from possible to destined?

"It was an *accident*," Eve told him. "He wasn't supposed to be there. Why can't we just tell them that?"

He shook his head. "There's no way back," he said. But it was more than that, Keegan now knew, though this was not the time to bring it all up. This was an accident that netted Eve and her mother a fortune. It was one thing to tell the truth and another to convince a jury to disregard a few million good reasons to assume that you're lying. And then there were the headlines. With a case like this, some ambitious DA could jump up a few rungs on the career ladder. There were so many stories he could tell her, so many old clippings, under his own byline, he could give her to read. In Los Angeles, the criminal justice system was barely acquainted with justice. It couldn't pick fairness out of a lineup.

"But I didn't *want* to lie," Eve said. "I couldn't think for myself last night. It was those pills they make me take." She stirred one hand in front of her face. "I was all… all *foggy*."

She looked like she was about to cry now, and Keegan wanted to shake her hard—but how would that look through a set of binoculars or a telephoto lens?

"Stay calm," he told her. "Trust me. This is the only way to handle this. They don't have anything on us. The whole thing will blow over in a few days." He gripped her shoulders more firmly and looked steadily into her eyes. "We stick to the script," he said. "Ormsby came downstairs and confronted an intruder. One shot, and it was over. You slept through the whole thing. You didn't see anything. You didn't hear anything. You stayed in your room. End of story." He probed her eyes for any hint of what she might be thinking. "You have to be strong," he told her. "If you crack, you take me down with you."

Eve's gaze finally focused on him. She looked from one of his eyes to the other. No, Keegan thought, her eyes weren't just focused—they were *hard*. Again, she looked beyond him at Ormsby's garden. *Her* garden soon, Keegan thought. Her breathing slowed.

"You needn't worry," she said. She seemed to grow taller while he still held her by the shoulders. "You're *safe*." She injected the word with venom. "I'm not going to crack." She looked in his eyes again, and her gaze was steely. She shrugged his hands from her shoulders. "Now, please just leave me alone for a while."

Keegan stepped back from her, surprised. What inside her had turned her voice to ice and set the jut of her chin? Who *was* this woman? And how had he let himself get this deep in the shit with a woman he barely knew?

Eve turned from him and opened the door. She stepped through and shut it solidly—but quietly—behind her. Through the panes of glass, he watched her march away from him without looking back and disappear into the big house.

Keegan stood a few stunned seconds, regarding his own reflection in the door's glass panes. He knew Eve was telling the truth: she *wouldn't* crack. But he was damned if that made him feel safe.

THE GRAY SEDAN parked in front of his mother's front gate was sleek and glossy, with chrome fins that jutted owlishly above the round brake lights. Keegan didn't see it until he'd left Ormsby's gravel back drive and started up the asphalt road. There might have been a catch in his stride, but it was too late for him to turn back, so he tried to cover it. He had no idea who owned the car, but, whoever they were, there was a good chance they were watching him.

A lone tall figure stepped down from the cottage's front porch and crossed to the gate. It was Louis Moore, still in his white Panama hat. There was no mistaking the upright posture, the smooth, decisive strides. Moore carried something in one hand, but Keegan wasn't close enough to make out what it was. The lieutenant let himself out through the gate in the picket fence and went around the car to the driver's side, jingling in his trouser pocket for his keys.

Keegan slowed his pace and cursed his luck. Another few minutes sipping coffee with the widow and the lieutenant would have driven off and left him alone. But there was no turning back now, no ducking into the bushes. Keegan braced himself and kept walking. It was what an innocent man would do, wasn't it? Keep walking and wait to be noticed? Or maybe an innocent man would call out the lieutenant's name. Keegan wasn't sure. He focused on keeping his gait casual, unconcerned.

The lieutenant pulled the car's door open. He took off his hat and was about to duck inside when he straightened up. He'd spotted Keegan. He grinned and pressed the hat back on his head. He leaned down into the car to get whatever it was he'd been carrying.

Keegan gave him an awkward wave, a stiff smile. He kept his pace steady, measuring every stride. This was the way an innocent man walked.

Moore pushed the sedan's door shut and came around to the back. He leaned against the trunk, arms folded, holding a bottle by the neck in one fist, waiting for Keegan to come up the road. Another surprise visitor bearing libations, Keegan thought. Yet worlds had been born and ended in the hours since Eve had climbed this hill with her embezzled Bordeaux.

"I wondered where you'd got to," Moore called down to him. "Your car's in the carport, and the dog's in the house. I knew you couldn't have gone far."

"I was down offering condolences," Keegan said, a convenient truth. "Just being a good neighbor."

Moore smiled slyly and shook his head, arms still crossed. "You know that girl's young enough to be your daughter," he said.

"Yeah," Keegan said, "I've done the math. But I was talking about the widow, so you can wipe that asinine grin off your face."

The lieutenant uncrossed his arms and held out his big, dry hand, so Keegan shook it.

"Hell," the lieutenant said. "A girl like that? I wouldn't blame a man for being a good neighbor."

Keegan wasn't in any mood for the lieutenant's brand of manly banter. He folded his arms. "What brings you to my doorstep?" he said.

Moore held out the bottle, and Keegan took it from him. "Payment, as promised, for your assistance," he said. "It's not top shelf, but it's ninety-proof."

Keegan turned it to look at the label. Old Fitzgerald. It must have been riding in Moore's car a few hours; it felt bathwater-warm. "Bourbon," Keegan said. "How like a gentleman."

Moore nodded in the direction of the cottage. "Let's go on in and crack her open."

"You're not on duty?"

The lieutenant tugged back the sleeve of his jacket and showed Keegan a gold wristwatch. It looked expensive. "Off the clock, and driving my own wheels," Moore said. "I can do whatever the hell I want."

There was no avoiding it.

Moore followed Keegan up the porch steps and doffed his hat at the door. Keegan pushed the door open—he'd left it unlocked—and Nora darted out to jump up on his legs. When she saw Lieutenant Moore on the porch, she barked twice and backed up into the house.

Keegan stood to one side. "After you," he told the lieutenant. "There's a decent chance she won't bite."

The lieutenant glanced at Keegan warily and then stepped inside, ducking his head. He set his hat on the entry table. Nora growled at him from the center of the rug. She barked once and then scuttled back into the kitchen, out of sight.

"Not much of a guard dog," Keegan admitted, "but she's a damn good judge of character."

Moore dabbed at his forehead with a handkerchief and looked around at the dim, cramped room. It was hard to read what he was thinking.

"Make yourself at home," Keegan told him. He set the warm bottle on the coffee table. "I'll get us some glasses."

He went to the kitchen and opened the back door for Nora, who seemed only too happy to make her escape from the lieutenant. Lucky dog. She bounded down the back steps and across the dying lawn. Keegan left the door ajar for her and took down a couple of cartoon juice glasses—Henery Hawk and Daffy Duck—gas-station giveaways from a decade ago, when his mother was still driving her old Pontiac. No Royal Dalton for LA's finest. He rinsed the glasses at the sink and wiped them out with a paper towel.

"Neat or rocks?" he called into the other room.

"You're joking," the lieutenant answered. "In weather like this the whiskey should be *cold*. Ice, please."

Keegan carried the glasses into the living room and found Moore standing, looking out the side window. His jacket was draped over his arm now, and his sleeves were rolled up to his elbows. The afternoon light blanched his face.

"Some view," the lieutenant said, turning from the window. "Any idea how much this place is worth?"

Keegan shrugged, and the ice jingled in the glasses he was holding. "The land alone would probably go for fifty-large," he said—though his most interested buyer would no longer be making an offer.

The lieutenant whistled and looked up at the roof beams. "Quite a windfall for you," he said.

Keegan went over and set the glasses on the coffee table next to his mother's Shakespeare book and sat down on the settee. "Some of us loved our mothers," he said. He sliced the paper seal on the bottle with his thumbnail and pulled out the stopper. He poured a generous shot into each glass and pressed the corked top back in the bottle. When Keegan looked up, Nora was watching him from the kitchen doorway. He snapped his fingers down near the floor, but she wouldn't come to him, not with Moore in the room. Smart dog. He nudged the lieutenant's glass to the far side of the coffee table.

Moore took his time draping his jacket over the armchair's back and lowered himself heavily into the same seat Eve had fallen asleep in the night before. His tall frame made the chair look too small, a playhouse miniature. Moore lifted the glass Keegan had poured for him and held it to the light with his long fingers under it. At first, Keegan thought he was considering the whiskey's color—a connoisseur—but he was just looking at Henery the cartoon hawk. *Are you comin' quietly, or do I have to muss ya up?* The lieutenant smiled faintly.

Keegan picked up his own glass and took a generous sip. Maybe it was the heat or the food he'd neglected to eat that day, but the bourbon burned his throat like acid. Perhaps a half-bottle of fine wine and a sip of fancy coffee had ruined his palate for lesser pleasures. He set the glass down on the coffee table and licked the stinging flavor from his lips.

Nora, still eyeing the lieutenant warily, lay down in the

kitchen doorway and rested her chin on her paws. She'd wait this one out.

"So, how's it going?" Keegan said. "The investigation, I mean. What are you finding out about the old man's death?"

"It's early yet," the lieutenant said. He took a pensive sip of the bourbon, but his face didn't register an opinion of it. He, it appeared, had weightier things on his mind. "Not a whole lot to go on. Nobody in the neighborhood heard the gunshot. Your place is the only one with a view of the house, and you weren't here."

"Wish I could have helped."

The lieutenant nodded and took another sip of his drink. "All we've got is the crime scene."

Keegan thought of the swept-up main room where he'd sat with the widow. He thought of the one too-clear pane of glass in the French door. There wouldn't be much of a crime scene anymore, not with Mrs. Ormsby back in the house. "And what did the crime scene look like?"

"Broken glass in a door," the lieutenant said. He pressed the cold glass to his forehead. "No fingerprints. No footprints. No nothing."

"Sounds like a stone-cold whodunit." Keegan turned his own glass in his hands. Beads of condensation had gathered on the sides, and the coldness of it felt good on his dampening fingers. "I'm no big-city jack," Keegan said. "But maybe it's the obvious. A break-in that went awry." He turned the Daffy Duck glass in his hand again. "How many times did I type *that* sentence up for *The Times*?"

"Motive?"

Keegan shrugged. "Money," he said. "Lot of burglaries in these hills. At least according to my mother, who didn't miss much in the way of gossip." He passed the glass to his other hand and dried his fingers on his trouser leg. "Probably even more of them *this* week. People get careless in this kind of weather. All those open windows. Easy pickings for your enterprising local malefactor."

The lieutenant shook the ice in his Class—the cubes were just nubs now—and took a long last sip. He set the glass down on the table. "Could be," he said finally. "But I doubt it."

"Why's that?"

Moore eyed Keegan warily. It was clear he was holding back. "We're off the record, right?"

Keegan smiled. He let his head drop back against the settee, and then lifted it again. "Give me a break," he said, arms spread in a gesture of innocence. "I don't even *subscribe* to a newspaper these days."

Moore sat back in the armchair and plucked at the armrest covers with his long fingers, looking Keegan over. Light from the window behind him made his damp whiskey glass glow like a votive candle. "The French door," Moore said. "The supposed point of entry. The glass was broken up near the latch."

Keegan took a moment to let this information settle. The word *supposed* had put him on edge. "What about it?" he said. "What's the problem?"

"You can't *see* the latch from outside the house," Moore said. "If I were breaking in, I would have smashed the pane down by the handles. That's where I'd assume the lock would be." His face was maddeningly neutral, impossible to read. His fingers moved restlessly on the chair's arms.

"Okay," Keegan said. "So, whoever did it cased the place first. What does that tell us?" He took the last sip of whiskey in his glass and swallowed it. It was watery. "Servants. Deliveries. Pool cleaners. Hell, they probably have a topiary gardener. I'll bet a hundred people are in and out of that place every week."

Moore nodded, his face still neutral. "That's not all," he said. "Nothing was missing. Nothing was even moved. Why did our man bother to case the place and then break in if he wasn't planning on stealing something?"

Keegan looked at the bottle. He was tempted to pour himself a second shot—with or without ice cubes—but knew he shouldn't. "Okay, so somebody broke in," he said, thinking it through as he spoke. "The old guy hears the glass break and comes blustering down the stairs. He surprises the burglar and catches a slug for his troubles. Burglar hoofs it. Three-zero. End of story."

The lieutenant's face remained impassive. He nodded thoughtfully. The window behind him lit the fine sheen of sweat on his cheeks. His fingers went back to plucking at the chair's armrests.

Keegan didn't like the silence. He wanted to fill it, the way he wanted to reach out and pour himself another glass of bourbon. "It could have happened that way," he said when he could no longer resist the urge to speak.

Moore shrugged. "Could have," he said. He shook his head. "Didn't, though."

"Why not?"

"Ormsby had a Browning 1911 in his nightstand," Moore said. He began rolling down his shirtsleeves, like he was getting ready to leave. "Fully loaded with wadcutters. Seven rounds." He tugged both sleeves straight. "If I'm going downstairs in the middle of the night to check on a noise in my big empty mansion, I'm sure as hell not leaving my forty-five upstairs with my reading glasses." He buttoned his cuffs, first one, then the other.

Keegan's mind raced to catch up. "So maybe the old man *didn't* hear the intruder," Keegan said. "Maybe he just went down to the kitchen for a glass of water and surprised the guy."

Moore had started to rise, but he sank back down in his chair. He looked Keegan over. "Who said anything about a kitchen?"

Shit. "The widow told me," Keegan lied, quickly.

The lieutenant nodded. He picked up his glass and shook the remaining slivers of ice into his mouth. He crunched them up and swallowed. "How well do you know your girlfriend?"

Keegan waited a beat before he answered. Had the lieutenant seen them talking on the portico? "Just enough to speak to," he said. "Gossip over the back fence."

The lieutenant nodded. "She's got that wide-eyed Audrey Hepburn thing going," he said, rising to his feet again. "She plays a good innocent, but she's lying about something." He pulled on his jacket and turned to the door, adjusting the lapels. Then looked back at Keegan as if something had just occurred to him. "Ormsby was shot with a .38," he said. "I'm going to need to take yours with me."

This, Keegan realized, was the actual purpose of the lieutenant's visit. The bourbon, the banter, it was all foreplay. "*My* gun?" Keegan said. "What the hell for?"

"You know what for," Moore said. "I've got to clear it." He fastened the top button of his jacket and smoothed the lapels again. "The news will be all over this when the story breaks," he said. "I've got to dot every T."

"I'd love to help you out," Keegan said, "but I keep it down in my office, like I told you." It was, in fact, in the trunk of his car. He hadn't yet decided what to do with it.

The lieutenant nodded. "You still on West Sixth?" he said. "I can swing by tomorrow. Just leave it with your secretary if you're going out."

Keegan reached for the two empty glasses on the coffee table. "I've got a better idea," he said. He held up the glasses. "Come on by when you get done tomorrow, and we'll have another round."

Moore paused, and then he nodded and picked up his Panama hat. He tilted it back on his head, so his face was fully visible. "Date," he said.

As soon as the door clicked shut, Nora darted out of the kitchen and jumped up on the sofa next to Keegan.

Keegan rubbed the dome of her skull through her dense, curly fur. "Don't worry about him," he said to the dog. "He's just flexing his muscles. You and I are going to be okay."

THERE WERE MORE cars in the pier's parking lot than Keegan would have expected so close to midnight. He drove past a row of old pickups and a couple of beat-up sedans, all parked close to the pier, all facing the ocean.

He coasted down to the farthest corner of the lot, away from the boardwalk streetlamps where it would be dark. He pulled in, facing away from the shoreline, and cut the engine. He looked along the shore in both directions and in the rearview mirror, where the choppy sea glimmered out on the horizon. Satisfied that no one was watching, he reached between his feet, under the driver's seat, and pulled out the bundle he'd stowed there. It was heavy and padded, the old revolver wrapped in a shoe rag and stuffed in a liquor store bag. He'd sealed the brown-paper bag with about a yard of cellophane tape strips, clipped from the dispenser in his mother's kitchen drawer.

Out the passenger window, the line of parked cars were all rimmed in moonlight. So many cars. At least a dozen. Keegan hadn't made provision in his plan for witnesses. He hadn't even bothered to bring a jacket so he could hide the bundle he'd be carrying. He got out of the car, tucked the package into his waistband and tugged his shirt down over it. The bulge was absurd, but what could he do? He walked along the darker side of the parking lot towards the pier. The waxing moon was nearly full, but it was low over the water. It lit up the gray pylons and glinted off the lines of distant swells.

Evenly spaced lamps lined both sides of the pier, so Keegan walked straight down the center, tugging down his shirttails when they rode up.

Up ahead, just beyond the breakers, a small cluster of men tended a row of fishing rods that leaned against the rails on either side. The men were sunk in folding chairs and bundled in blankets, despite the balmy night air. A transistor radio was tuned to a Spanish-language station. On it, a man crooned, something about blossoms and a garden and first kisses. Keegan's Spanish from college was rusty at best.

Aquella tarde probé, de las cerezas la miel
En la quietud del jardín, de los cerezos en flor...

Keegan didn't look at the men as he walked past. He stared down at the splintering planks at his feet and the scuffed nailheads glinting in the lamplight. His breathing was slow and conscious. Out here on the pier, the ocean breeze was colder than he'd bargained for, and it rippled in the folds of his sweat-dampened shirt. The bulge of the gun would have been obvious if anyone looked in his direction, but soon he was beyond the fishermen and breathing easier, the dark end of the pier up ahead of him, the Mambo King music growing tinny at his back.

He passed the locked bait shop and the gutting tables and the steel pump and fire-hose station. The radio music faded into the distant din of the breakers. Soon he could hear his own footsteps on the weathered boards and the slosh of waves lapping the pylons far below.

At the farthest reach of the pier, Keegan leaned over the scarred wood railing and looked down at the inky water. He pulled the bundle from his waistband and felt the heft of it in his hand. He glanced behind him, down the length of the pier. None of the fishermen had moved from where they sat. If they'd noticed him at all, they were no longer interested.

He could see the milky glow of Avalon on Catalina Island, a smudge of light on the black horizon. A scattering of ships' lamps dotted the sea. The dim shape of the old Pacific Park amusement pier lay half a mile to the north, fenced off and falling into ruin. Its ramshackle Ferris wheel and the roller coasters and the old dance hall, all faintly dusted with moonlight. It was an eyesore. An arson job waiting to happen.

Keegan threw the package overhand, a lofty lob to get it as far away from him as he could. He watched the dark shape tumble in an arc through the moonlit sky. There was a small, silent plume of white in the distance, and it quickly vanished among the glimmering swells.

CHAPTER FIVE

Friday, August 17, 1962

KEEGAN LOITERED AT the corner of Fifth and Hill, where he could keep an eye on Lusk's newsstand over on the edge of the park. It was a little after five, and sunrise was more than an hour away. It wasn't cold out, but the streets were sunk in the color-muted gloom of the wee hours. The Pershing Square palms were dwarfed by the dark buildings that loomed all around. The early, empty MTA busses were running, but otherwise the city still slept. Keegan kept close to the building on the corner, ready to duck out of sight if need be. Someone, wrapped in a grubby newspaper, snored in the alcove of the Owl Drugs across the way, a shambled shape that was only vaguely human. Keegan wondered how many times his own writing had served as a blanket against the chill. Maybe his doomed career as a newsman had accomplished something after all.

A white box truck rumbled up Hill Street with its high beams on, and Keegan ducked closer to the corner alcove. At Lusk's corner, the truck pulled across lanes and parked, facing the wrong way. Lusk got out, jingling keys, and went to his newsstand. He unlocked the padlock on the plywood back door and went back to the truck.

Keegan looked both ways and jogged across the street against the light.

Lusk pulled on a pair of leather work gloves and wiggled his fingers to loosen them up. When he saw Keegan coming, he straightened up and grinned. "Kind of early for the likes of you," he said. He rolled up the back door of the truck.

"At least it's cool," Keegan said.

"Seventy-two degrees never felt so good," Lusk admitted. "But it's all uphill from here. They say it's going to break a hundred today." He grunted and lifted a stack of newspapers out of the truck by the twine that bound them. "What has you out and about at this ungodly hour?" Lusk lugged the papers over to the back of his stall, listing to one side with the burden, and disappeared inside.

Keegan followed him.

"Shouldn't you still be in bed?" Lusk asked. His voice was muffled by the plywood.

Keegan stood in the shed's doorway. "Kip, I need a big favor," he said, keeping his voice low.

Lusk emerged, clapping imaginary dust from his gloves. "I've done you enough favors, buddy." He brushed past Keegan and headed for the truck. "I'm starting to think you take me for granted."

"I'll pay for this one."

Lusk stopped and turned back to Keegan, his hands on his hips. "If you're paying, it's not a *favor*," Lusk said. "It's a *job*. You'd think a writer would have a better grasp of the English language." Lusk went back to the truck and lifted down another stack of newspapers—*The Daily Breeze*—and lugged them to the back of his stall. HOTTEST DAY OF YEAR SINGES LA the paper's banner headline read.

Keegan waited until Lusk was inside the booth again and spoke to him through the doorway. "Look, Kipper," he said. "I need you to find me a gun. A Smith and Wesson Model Ten."

Lusk pushed past him again. "That's a revolver, right?"

Keegan followed him to the back of the truck. "Yeah, and

it has to be a snub nose," he said. "Not nickel, either. It's gotta be blued. Original wooden grips. At least ten years old."

Lusk looked both ways along Hill Street and then down along Fifth. He waited while an empty bus slowed to make the turn onto Hill. Its hydraulic brakes hissed, and then the engine rumbled as it pulled away. "Listen, Professor," Lusk said when the bus was halfway down the block. "I can get you a real pretty Colt Python three-fifty-seven. Like new." He was using his salesman voice now. "No papers, but a price you won't believe." He tapped Keegan's chest with one gloved finger. "In your hand in twenty minutes. No questions asked."

"No," Keegan said. "You don't understand." He didn't want to raise his voice, and that required him to slow down and focus, but he could feel his frustration mounting. "Listen to me, Kip," he said. "I need a very particular gun. It's gotta be a snub-nose Smith and Wesson. Just like the ones the LAPD jacks carry. And I need it today."

Lusk looked at Keegan steadily. The morning slant of light glowed in his squinting brown eyes. "I know better than to ask why you're so particular," Lusk said. "That's your business. But such fastidious demands can run into money." He scratched the side of his head. "How much bank do I have to work with?" he said. "And I'm talking hard cash. Nobody moving guns is going to take a personal check or your solemn word as a gentleman."

Keegan gazed across the park in the direction of the Biltmore and tried to do the math in his head. There were a few twenties—maybe a hundred bucks—in his desk that Mrs. Dodd wouldn't know about. He could cash a couple of checks at the stores around town that knew him. "I think I can get maybe two or three hundred without drawing attention," he said. "If it's more than that, you'll have to front me a few days. I swear I'll make it worth your while."

"You *think* or you *can*?"

"I *can*," Keegan said. "Three hundred."

Lusk shrugged. "Three hundred ought to float it. The Model Ten is no exotic bird. I'll see what I can do."

"Thanks," Keegan said. "You're a godsend."

Lusk took down two more bundles from the truck and turned to Keegan, a bundle hanging from each hand. "None of my business, big shot," Lusk said. His face showed the effort of carrying the papers, as did the strain in his voice. "But you're not in some kind of trouble, are you? Despite the many pains you bring my ass, I'd hate to see you get hurt."

"A little trouble," Keegan admitted. "I think I can get clear of it. Shouldn't be a big deal."

Lusk pinched his lips together and nodded. He pushed past Keegan again and shuffled over to the newsstand carrying his papers. "No offense," he said over his shoulder. "But you're not really cut out to run with the criminal element in this town. If you're planning on shooting some mysterious stranger in a limo, you're going to end up on page two of the City section. HACK GETS WHACKED. No photo." Lusk disappeared into his shack.

KEEGAN DIDN'T OPEN the copy of *The Times* until he was in the cottage with the kettle set to boil. Whatever the next hours held, he had to make a run at the day without any sleep whatsoever.

Ormsby's photo was on the front page of the City section. CHARACTER ACTOR SLAIN. Art and copy. No leads. A likely break-in, the article said. Lieutenant Louis Moore heading the investigation. The splashy lead was followed up on page five after the jump. One of the photos there showed a much younger Ormsby dressed as a cowboy, standing next to Jimmy Stewart. Another, more recent, showed him sitting in some restaurant with a woman who looked to be a decade or two his junior; she was pleasant-looking, but unremarkable; a cigarette dangled from between two of her fingers. It took him a few seconds to make the connection: it was Ormsby's widow as she'd looked a decade ago.

Lower in the column was a photo of Ormsby's house, and a small oval picture of Eve. Her hair was longer in the photo, and she was smiling awkwardly, head tilted—probably a yearbook shot from whatever elite girls' school had taught her to open wine bottles in a pinch. It wasn't a large photo, and it wasn't recent, but it looked like her. If Simon Catling hadn't found her yet, he'd know where she was before he sat down to lunch.

KEEGAN SPENT THE day in and out of the office, running from Bullock's to the Thrifty to the Robinson's on West 7th, cashing small checks that wouldn't raise eyebrows or leave much of a paper trail.

In the afternoon, he went to see Lusk again for an update. It was hard to guess how the man had managed it without abandoning his newsstand, but Lusk said the light was green. He'd found what Keegan needed. He gave Keegan an address and told him to bring the money in cash.

THE MEETING WAS set for seven o'clock, but Keegan was running early. The address Lusk had given him—scrawled in dull pencil on a page torn from a paperback book—took him to a residential street on the south side of the Silver Lake reservoir. Lusk said the gun would be waiting for him. No further elaboration was offered. No hint of who or what Keegan might find there.

Keegan looked at his watch again. Six-forty. He'd be cutting it close. He'd best be back in the cottage before the lieutenant arrived in his fancy sedan for another shot of bourbon. There would be fewer questions for Keegan to answer if Moore found him at home, fewer lies to invent.

The street was steep and narrow, with parked cars crowding both sides. Nora sat beside him in the MG's passenger seat, looking out the half-open window at the bungalows set back at odd angles from the road. Each lot was a new terraced level cut into the hillside, like a great suburban staircase rising to heaven.

Around a blind curve, the road grew yet steeper, and Keegan downshifted to first. He had to drive slowly enough to keep track of the house numbers he passed—black numerals affixed to porch posts or above lintels. He rode the clutch to keep the car from stalling, one hand on the parking brake, in case he started to slip backwards. The dusky light made it easier to make out the even numbers on the east side of the road. He was looking for 65 ½. Whether that was odd or even, he had no idea.

When he got to the high fifties, he found a parking space between a Thunderbird and an old pickup that was facing the wrong direction. Better to approach the house on foot, he thought. It would give him more time to see what he was getting into.

It took him a few tries to parallel-park at such a slant, and then he let the MG roll back until the front wheel bounced against the curb, pointing out towards the middle of the street. He set the parking brake and cut the engine.

The dog looked at him now with her head cocked to one side. Keegan reached past her and cranked the window up, so it was only open a couple of inches. He did the same to his own and then scratched Nora behind the ear. "You're staying here," he told her. "Be brave. I'll be as quick as I can."

He stuffed the envelope of cash—most of it in twenties—into the inner pocket of his jacket and got out of the car, stretching out his back as he did. He turned and leaned down to speak to the dog through the open door. "If you see anything suspicious, honk three times," he told her.

He closed the door without locking it and started up the street. If, for some reason, he never returned, at least someone could rescue the dog without having to break a window.

There was no sidewalk in this neighborhood, so Keegan walked on the street-side of the parked cars, feeling absurdly conspicuous—an obvious interloper here, with a bulge in his coat pocket. But it was almost dark now, and, though the street was bustling with life at the dinner hour, no one was outside where they might see him.

Many of the houses Keegan passed were lit from within, their windows wide open against the heat. Keegan could hear voices and television programs and the clatter of silverware — the soundtrack of a domestic realm Keegan had failed to enter when he'd had the chance. His childless marriage had flamed out after barely two years. And now, a couple of decades later, it was hard to remember ever having lived with someone else. She was up in Salinas, last he'd heard. Remarried with kids. Wife of a broccoli tycoon.

Some long nights, alone in his apartment, Keegan wondered if he'd really missed out on anything. He doubted it. After all, how many happily married men his age could he name? It was even harder to imagine himself cast as a doting father. He'd never had the patience to enjoy the company of children. Just Mrs. Dodd's singsong voice on the telephone when she was talking to her grandchildren was enough to put him on edge.

It didn't help any that he had no first-hand memories of his own father, a pipe-fitter who, in photographs at least, looked ill-prepared to take on the world. His was a dour, Edwardian head in the back corner of a few formal family photos. His face, always turned a little too far from the camera, looked like it had been slapped. He'd turned up dead on the rocks beneath the Point Fermin lighthouse when Keegan was barely forming sentences, and he was quickly written out of the script. The only man in Keegan's childhood was his maternal grandfather, who had little time for anything but citrus grafting. Once his two sons were grown and out of the house, with land of their own, he had no patience for those he came home to, spending his evenings on the porch, where he could keep an eye on the hunched ranks of his orange groves, rippling out over the hilly ground.

Keegan kept his eye out for house numbers as he climbed the hill. As he passed Number 61, a studio audience burst into laughter. Out front, an unattended garden hose spun a sprinkler in the middle of a sodden lawn. Water streamed along the gutter, pushing cigarette butts and dead leaves down into lesser, lower-lying neighborhoods. At Number 63, an angelic young girl practiced a piano piece framed in a lit bay window. She stared down at her hands as she played. Her brunette hair was pulled back in a ponytail. Her smooth brow glowed in the lamp aimed down at her sheet music. Her aura of innocence gave Keegan a twinge of guilt: he'd be committing a felony, illegal purchase of a firearm, much too close to where this young girl lived.

And then there it was: number 65 ½, a small Mexican-style bungalow on the right side of the road—two lit windows, both open, on either side of a blue porch. The house stood on a triangular scrap of land between two larger homes. A tile roof awning slanted down over its doorway. A concrete pathway angled from the curb, through a small cactus garden, to the front steps. Even in the dusky light, nothing about the house looked sinister. Was this really where Lusk had meant to send him?

Keegan hesitated at the curb, getting himself ready for whatever waited behind the door. He'd spent years writing about crime, but he'd always been one healthy step removed. When he'd arrived at a crime scene, notepad in hand, the deed had already been done. The space was cordoned off and teeming with cops. If the coroner had been there, all that remained was a chalk outline on the asphalt. When he'd interviewed the accused, they were safely shackled or behind acrylic windows. Or he'd watched them being questioned from the comfortable side of a two-way mirror. But now there were no cuffs or glass to shield him. He felt edgy, scared even, but he could still hear the girl's piano in the background— she was practicing scales now—and that benign ladder of pure notes offered a level of comfort. In this middle-class neighborhood of sitcoms and sprinklers, how ruthless could the people behind this door really be? There was even a tan coir mat set out on the front doorstep. WELCOME.

Keegan walked up the path through the front yard, trying to look at ease. The aloes and prickly pears and barrel cactus he passed were arranged in a carpet of red lava rock. A garden for someone who was not inclined towards gardening.

There was no button for a bell, just a lion's head knocker in the center of the door. Keegan gave it a couple of firm clacks. A dog took up yipping inside the house. A woman's voice called out from some back room: "Could you get that, sweetie? I'm looking for my keys."

Keegan heard claws scratching down low on the door and then the sound of footsteps coming down the hall. He sucked in a breath and braced himself. The door opened a crack, and a tiny black Pomeranian darted out, yapping. It startled Keegan more than it should have. The dog quivered, sniffing at the hem of Keegan's trousers.

When Keegan looked up, Kipper Lusk was standing in the doorway, a half-smile on his face. He wore an undershirt, dungarees and a pair of moccasins. "Careful," he told Keegan. "He's likely to piss all over your shoes."

Keegan took a reflexive step back from the dog and felt a cactus spine prick his calf through his trousers. He jumped forward and squelched one foot in a puddle of fresh urine.

Lusk shook his head, wryly amused. "It's a world full of peril," he observed wryly. He stepped back into the hallway and called the dog. "Come on, Sugar Drop," he said. "It's okay. The big dope's a friend of mine." The dog hopped back up the step and darted ahead of Lusk down the hallway.

Keegan scrubbed the damp sole of his shoe on the welcome mat and stepped inside. Before he could pull the door shut behind him, a red-headed woman rushed down the hall in his direction, pinning on a pillbox hat. She kissed Lusk's cheek as she passed him.

"James," Lusk said. "This is my wife, Laura."

The woman stopped and smiled brightly at Keegan. She was pretty, in a sturdy, Midwestern sort of way, and she was a good three inches taller than her husband.

"It's very nice to meet you, Mr. James," she said, as she pivoted past him, "but I'm late for choir practice. You boys have fun. There's leftover pot roast in the refrigerator if you want sandwiches."

She pulled the door shut after her. The sound of heels on concrete faded down the walkway.

Keegan looked at the closed door a beat before he turned back to his host. For some reason, it had never occurred to him that Kipper Lusk might be a married man, or that he might have a house in the suburbs. The idea would take some getting used to. "Choir practice?" Keegan said.

Lusk shrugged. "First Methodist," he said. "Their only alto." He led Keegan to the living room. It smelled of Darjeeling tea and lemon furniture polish. One whole side of the room was a wall of built-in fish tanks, each one lit up brightly. Two easy chairs faced a fireplace. There was no television, just an old console record player with beige fabric speakers.

Keegan turned slowly, taking it all in. "You live here?" he said.

"You thought I had a cot in the newsstand?"

"No," Keegan said. "I just wasn't expecting anything so—I don't know—*domestic*. This is right out of *Father Knows Best*."

Lusk nodded; it was a fair assessment. He scratched the stubble on his cheek. "The wife," he said, by way of explanation.

Keegan wandered over to the wall of fish tanks, each of them a bright, mesmerizing window into a carefully arranged underwater world. "Why all the aquariums?"

"The word you meant to use is *aquaria*," Lusk said. "Good thing you're not a writer. And don't tap on the glass, thank you very much."

Keegan took his finger away from the tank where he'd been trying to get the attention of a long skinny fish with a bullet-like tail. "Sorry," he said. "Where did you get all this?"

"Here and there," Lusk said vaguely. "That one you're annoying is called a snakehead."

Keegan nodded. The fish nuzzled the pebbles at the bottom of the tank and then darted behind a lava rock. "But why?"

Lusk shrugged. "Am I not allowed to have a hobby?"

In another tank, a tiny zebra-striped shark seemed to be hovering in place, mesmerized, studying Keegan from the other side of the glass.

"I don't know," Keegan said. "It just seems a tame pastime for a man of your reputation."

Lusk dug his hands into his denim pockets. "If it makes you feel any better, most of them are illegal. Smuggled up from Mexico."

"Fish can be illegal?"

"Dangerous ones can," Lusk said. "I wouldn't dip my fingers in any of these tanks if I were you."

One aquarium on the far-right side held a dense mass of common goldfish—a glinting orange cloud of them. Some floated, dead, at the water's surface, bleaching to white.

"Why all the goldfish?" Keegan asked.

Lusk grinned. "Think about it," he said. He gestured at a pair of matching recliners. "Sit down and make yourself comfortable." He drifted over to a doorway. "I'm getting a beer, if you want one."

"Sure," Keegan said. He sat in one of the chairs. The table between them held a broad assortment of ladies' magazines —*Redbook*, *Good Housekeeping*, *McCall's*—all a month out of date, some sun-faded. Newsstand cast-offs.

While Lusk was in the next room, Keegan glanced over his shoulder at the writhing mass of orange fish in the single aquarium. "You use those ones to feed the others?" he called into the next room.

"Nothing gets past you," Lusk called back.

The chair Keegan sat in was peppered with dog hair. From under the coffee table, the tiny black dog looked up at Keegan with rheumy eyes. The hair on its muzzle was going white. It lifted and set down its paws in some odd, excited rhythm.

"Sugar Drop?" Keegan said.

At the sound of his name, the dog launched himself at Keegan and leaped up on his lap. Keegan stiffened. Was he about to get peed on? He tried to shoo the dog away, but the dog didn't seem to understand the gesture. He insistently sniffed at Keegan's shirt front—Nora's scent, no doubt. Keegan tried to brush him away, but the tiny thing held his ground.

In the kitchen, Lusk hummed to himself as he puttered about. He came back into the room, carrying a couple of Schlitz bottles by the neck, one in each hand. "You don't need a *glass*, do you?" he asked. The question felt like an accusation.

Keegan shook his head, and Lusk put one of the bottles on the side table by his chair. He set it on a wooden coaster inlaid with cork. "Kipper Lusk uses coasters?" Keegan said.

"Again, with the assumptions," Lusk said. "We've got silverware and indoor plumbing and everything. That's some high horse you're riding, my friend." Lusk plopped down on the other recliner and folded out the footrest. The dog jumped out of Keegan's lap, darted under the coffee table and then jumped up on Lusk's lap. Lusk took a sip from his bottle and looked across at Keegan. "So, do I need to worry about you, my friend?" he asked. "If I give you this gun, is your story going to be all over the papers I'm selling tomorrow?"

Keegan shook his head. "It's just a prop," he said. "I'm not even going to buy ammo." He could hear the bubble and hiss of fish tanks behind him.

"It's not like we're buddies or anything," Lusk clarified. "I only ask because I don't want this blowing back on me."

"Nothing's going to blow back," Keegan told him. His voice sounded unconvincing, even in his own ears. "If it does, it won't be on you."

Lusk nodded, clearly unconvinced. "Because if you need some help," he said. "I know people." He held his bottle aloft like he might be making a toast. "Whatever kind of help you need, I know a guy." He tipped back his bottle and swallowed and then wiped his lips with the back of his wrist. "And, unlike you, they're very good at what they do," he said. "They're fastidious, you might say."

Keegan sighed and shook his head. He'd come here for a gun, not a lecture. "It's fine," he said. "I know what I'm doing. Nobody's getting hurt." Nobody *else*, at least. Nobody who wasn't already dead. He thought of Ormsby's empty-eyed stare in the kitchen doorway. He thought of the goldfish behind him, floating on the water's surface.

"Does this have something to do with that Simon Catling guy you're so interested in?"

Keegan shook his head. "No," he said. But that wasn't necessarily true. "Well, sort of. Indirectly. But not really."

Lusk eyed Keegan skeptically. "That," he said, "is not the kind of decisive response that convinces me you know what you're doing."

Keegan stared at the damp-eyed dog on Lusk's lap who was staring back at him. He remembered the beer on the coaster and took a sip.

When Keegan looked at Lusk again, the man gestured at the kitchen doorway with his beer bottle. "Couple of years ago, I had this leak under the sink back there," he said. "A valve or a washer—who the hell knows what? It kept dripping. Rotted away all the woodwork down there." He took another swig from his bottle, keeping his eyes on Keegan. "I coulda called a plumber," he went on, "but I figure, why pay some schmo? I drive over to Sears. I buy myself—I don't know—a pipe wrench, some washers. Whatever."

The dog finally lost interest in Keegan and curled up on Lusk's thighs to lick his own privates.

"Long story short," Lusk went on. "A week later I'm out four hundred bucks, and I got a couple of fat Irish plumbers jackhammering the concrete slab." He finished his beer and set the empty bottle on the table next to him. That seemed to be the end of his story.

"Hell of a yarn there, Kip," Keegan told him. "Drama. Intrigue. Comedy. A little something for everyone. Had me on the edge of my seat."

Lusk gave him an easy, arch smile. "I'm just saying that a smart man knows when it's time to call in a professional," he said. "Because some jobs—the kind that require sudden firearm purchases—require a certain street-smarts. A certain finesse, which you—no offense—just don't got."

As HE DROVE back to the cottage, Keegan couldn't stop thinking about the orange cloud of doomed feeder fish biding their time, oblivious, in Lusk's tank.

THE LIEUTENANT SWUNG the gun's cylinder open and sniffed. He pointed it at the floor and looked down the two-inch barrel. "Man," he said. "When was the last time you cleaned this thing?"

"It's been a couple years," Keegan said. "How often does a guy like me need a gun?"

Keegan sat on the sofa, and the lieutenant stood on the far side of the coffee table next to the big armchair. Keegan scooted the Shakespeare book to one side with his heel and put his feet up on the table, waiting to see how this would play out.

It was clear the lieutenant didn't plan on staying long. He'd dispensed with the small talk and seemed unwilling to take a seat. He wore neither his jacket nor his Panama hat tonight, so he stood with his shirtsleeves rolled up and his loosened tie dangling. The reporters and photographers must have packed up and called it a night, Keegan thought. No need for the man to look his best. The leather shoulder holster he wore looked worn and abused, but the gun in it gleamed like a new dime.

The cottage's windows and doors were all open, and most of the lights were off to keep it cool. In the cross-ventilation that drew in the front door and out through the kitchen, the cottage was beginning to feel almost comfortable. Maybe he'd manage to get some sleep tonight. He was coming up on forty-eight hours.

The lieutenant flipped his wrist and the revolver snapped shut. He looked at Keegan. "You didn't clean this before you used it the other day?"

Keegan grinned and gestured around them at the living room. The cartoon whiskey glasses still sat on the coffee table. That morning's newspaper lay scattered across one end of the sofa. "Do I strike you as the kind of guy who cleans his gun every chance he gets?"

Moore looked around the room. "Point taken."

Keegan leaned back on the sofa and stretched his legs across the coffee table. It was important that he look at ease. He hadn't yet thought through to his next move. It was only a matter of time—a day, maybe two—before the lieutenant pulled the paperwork and realized the gun he was holding wasn't the one registered to Keegan. "What is that you're carrying these days?" Keegan said. He nodded at the lieutenant's shoulder holster.

The lieutenant patted the holster with his right hand but didn't unsnap the leather strap. Maybe he didn't want to smudge the gun's nickel finish. "Smith and Wesson. Model 39," he said. "Christmas present from the wife."

"You like it?"

"Jury's still out," he said. "It can be a little temperamental." He slipped Keegan's gun back in the canvas pouch and zipped it shut. "Thanks, Jimmy," he said. "This shouldn't take more than a couple of days. I'll get them to move it along."

"No rush," Keegan said. "It's not like I ever use the thing." He glanced over at the kitchen door. Nora was still asleep under the table on the cool kitchen tile. "You don't have time for a whiskey?" Keegan asked.

The lieutenant consulted his watch and shook his head. "Not tonight, Jimmy. I've gotta work late."

"Well, that's reassuring to hear," Keegan said. "None of us can relax up here while there's a killer still at large."

The lieutenant nodded at him knowingly. He was holding something close to his vest, and Keegan could tell he was tempted to spill it. It was an old newsman instinct he hadn't yet lost.

"Just be careful of the girl down there," Moore finally said. "She's up to something." He turned towards the door.

"Like I said, I barely know her."

The lieutenant stopped and then turned back. The motion was slow and deliberate. He worked his jaw back and forth. It was a look Keegan recognized from the old days, when he was trying to decide how much he wanted on the record. "You keep saying that," he said. "It's like you're trying to convince somebody." He looked over at the door and then back again, mulling something over. Then he turned squarely to Keegan, feet planted. "I'm just trying to help you out here, Jimmy," he said. His voice was low and even. "Don't let that one down there mix you up in anything. She's very attractive, but she's poison. You need to trust me on that."

Keegan blinked twice. "I'm not mixed up in anything," he said. "What's your problem with her, anyway?"

Moore tucked the revolver pouch under one arm and dug his hands in his trouser pockets, feet spread apart. He shook his head and smiled. He was about to spill it, whatever it was, Keegan could tell. "We got a couple of rookie detectives working down on Third Street now," he said, keeping a close eye on Keegan's reaction. "They just started in vice. They were beat cops when you were on the paper, so you wouldn't know them." He jingled coins in his pocket. It was a small, grating habit he'd picked up. "But *they* sure as hell know *you*."

"What does that mean?"

"They were at the Regency a few nights ago," he said. "Sitting at the bar, taking the edge off, the way we used to do back in the day."

The lieutenant paused. Keegan waited.

"They saw you come in with some young knockout," Moore said. "Mop of curly dark hair. Well dressed. They said you took a booth in a dark corner. Very romantic, they thought."

Keegan was about to object, but the lieutenant waved his words away.

"Don't talk, Jimmy," the lieutenant said. The tone of his voice didn't allow for rebuttal. "For now, just listen. There was a photo of Eve in the paper today. I'm sure you saw it. I showed it to them, and they're pretty damn sure she was the girl you were with."

"They're mistaken," Keegan said.

"Don't talk," he said. "Your girlfriend's also got a motive."

"And what would that be?"

"Somewhere around twenty million US dollars is the estimate they gave me," the lieutenant said. "It's a hell of a good reason to pull the trigger." He pulled his hands out of his pockets and crossed his arms, Keegan's pistol pouch still tucked under one arm. "Hell, *I've* got a couple of uncles I'd bump off for that kind of payday."

"It's in a family trust," Keegan said. "It doesn't go to Eve. It all goes to her mother."

The lieutenant looked surprised and then checked himself. He watched Keegan closely a few seconds before he spoke. "Where did you hear that?" he said. "I thought you barely knew the girl."

"The widow," he said. "She's a little worried about her prospects. I guess none of the money is coming her way." At least that part of his story would check out if the lieutenant pursued it.

The lieutenant nodded. "And what did the widow tell you about Eve's mother?"

"Nothing," Keegan said. "Why? You think she's next on the hit list?"

The lieutenant smiled. "You really don't know, do you?"

"Don't know what?"

"The mother's got a month or two left on her calendar," the lieutenant said. "Some kind of cancer. She's in a wheelchair.

Getting vitamin shots from some quack down from Montreal. She'll be lucky to see Halloween."

A dark flicker of misgiving shivered through Keegan.

Moore studied Keegan's face. He nodded, as if he'd just learned something. "Your girlfriend didn't tell you *that* detail, I take it."

Without waiting for an answer, the lieutenant turned to leave. He crossed the floor and pushed open the screen door. He turned and pressed the door shut behind him and glanced back at Keegan grimly as he did so.

"Watch your step with her," he said through the door's mesh. "She's smarter than you and me put together, Jimmy."

With a couple of steps, Moore vanished into the darkness outside.

CHAPTER SIX

Saturday, August 18, 1962

KEEGAN TOOK NORA to the office, knowing the place would be quiet and cool on a Saturday. It felt good to be alone in the nearly empty building. The dog was asleep now on the other side of his desk, curled on the leather chair reserved for clients.

The call came in just before noon. He'd had all morning to think of a story, but he'd come up with nothing that sounded right. He rested his hand on the phone a few rings before he picked it up. Without Mrs. Dodd there, he could have pretended the office was empty, but what was the point of postponing what was inevitable?

"I'm sure you know why I'm calling," Moore said. He didn't seem surprised to find Keegan in his office on a weekend.

"I give up," Keegan said. "Why are you calling?" For no reason he could name, he thought again of Lusk's tank crowded with goldfish.

"That gun you gave me."

"What about it?"

"It isn't yours."

"Sure, it is," Keegan said. He looked at the shadows the

venetian blind made on the lacquered oak of his door. "What do you mean it's not mine?"

"I mean the serial numbers don't match," Moore said. His voice sounded weary. "Don't play stupid."

"What the hell are you talking about?" Keegan said, but his voice came out too flat. He wished he could take the line back and try it again.

"Jimmy," the lieutenant said. "I don't know what you're up to, but this is serious business. It's a homicide case. I can't just look the other way because it's you."

"I don't know what you're going on about," Keegan said. "You wanted my gun. I gave you my gun."

Keegan heard a couple of hot breaths on the other end of the phone line. "She's not worth it, Jimmy," the lieutenant said. "Whatever she did to get you into this can't be worth the trouble."

"Maybe your paperwork is screwy," Keegan said. "I mean any idiot can pass the civil servant exam."

There were a few seconds of silence on the other end. "I don't think you actually killed the man," Moore finally plowed on. "I don't think you're that stupid. But she's got you involved, and this isn't going to end well for either of you."

"Or maybe my gun got swapped when I was at that range up in Glendale," Keegan said. "I'll bet that's what happened. Those old revolvers are a dime a dozen, and they all look alike. I must have picked up the wrong one when I was packing up."

"That girl's going to get you killed," Moore said. "There's plenty you don't know, Jimmy. Trust me. She's playing you like a Steinway."

Keegan leaned forward and put his elbows on the desk. "When do I get my gun back, Lieutenant?" he said.

"You don't know what you're doing. She's got you all—"

"See, I'm a little on edge," Keegan spoke over him. "I don't know if you heard, but a guy got murdered right down the hill from me, and the perp's still at large. The cops don't seem to know their dicks from their derringers." He kept speaking, though he knew the lieutenant had already hung up.

ALL HE ASKED was that the car have air conditioning. The guy at the Thrifty Rent-a-Car counter—who had seen Keegan pull up in an MG convertible—tried to sell him on a red Mustang, but Keegan didn't want anything conspicuous. He finally got the keys to a nondescript black Fairlane that might as well have been invisible. It was big and boxy and it handled like a speedboat, but it wouldn't turn any heads.

Keegan headed over to the address for the funeral listed in Ormsby's *Times* obituary. He cranked the AC up as far as it would go. The car's big vinyl interior smelled of Pine-Sol and cigarettes, and someone had set all the radio buttons to pop music, but at least it was cold inside.

Keegan parked down the street from Knox Presbyterian, on the opposite side of the road, and left the engine running. He'd be able to see anyone who came and went. He settled in and tuned the car radio to the news on KNX. The Dodgers had won over Cincinnati, and the Angels had taken both games of a double-header. The county coroner officially ruled Marilyn's death a suicide. There was no cooling trend on the horizon.

Keegan had expected a pack of reporters waiting on the church steps, but all he saw was a lone photographer—perhaps Ormsby was not quite the celebrity Keegan assumed him to be. Maybe the widow had been telling the truth: Nigel Ormsby wasn't even a Joseph Cotten. The one photographer waited in front of the church, wilting, in the shade of a ficus tree. His boxy Hasselblad dangled around his neck on a lanyard. Freelance, maybe. Keegan couldn't see a press pass.

The other car—the one Keegan had been expecting to find—was parked in the shade of a palm tree about a half-block ahead of him on the other side of the street, a dark blue Chevy Impala. It was in a good position to pull out and follow anyone who left the church. Two men sat in it—at least, from this distance, Keegan thought they were men. Keegan owned a good pair of binoculars for when he was out on a divorce case, but he hadn't thought to bring them along. They were in his apartment's hall closet. His Nikon, with its big telephoto lens, was locked up back in his office.

When the mourners began to arrive, they also were fewer than Keegan would have expected. A handful of cars pulled in, disgorged their passengers and drove away. Keegan thought he recognized a few of them, the usual semi-familiar, too-beautiful faces of Hollywood's supporting ranks. Still, they were of the tribe who never had to wait for a table, who never entered a restaurant through the front door. He thought of Marilyn behind the Formosa Café, that quick glimpse of her smile before she turned away and ducked inside.

Well past the time listed in the obituary, a final car came by, and a man and a woman got out of the back seat. The photographer perked up, jogged over, and snapped pictures as they climbed the steps. Keegan couldn't be sure, but it might have been William Holden dressed in a trim charcoal suit. The woman with him might have been his wife. What was her name? Brenda something.

Keegan didn't see Eve or Ormsby's widow. They were no doubt already inside when he'd arrived. He could picture Eve's bright eyes glimmering behind a dark veil. *There's plenty you don't know, Jimmy.*

Keegan turned up the radio and let his head fall back on the headrest. He guessed he had an hour to kill, but he couldn't afford to fall asleep.

After a while, the sun came out from behind the trees, and Keegan folded down the sun visor to cut the glare. The Impala's two occupants sat looking straight ahead through the windshield. Both wore sunglasses. But whose men were they? They might be Catling's. They might be Louis Moore's. Tough guys either way. The thugs on either side of the law were more or less interchangeable when you got right down to it. Whoever they'd be reporting to, Keegan didn't want them to see him.

A scant half-hour later, a black limo pulled up and idled in front of the church. A few other cars came in behind it. The chapel doors opened, and mourners began to file out. Eve and Ormsby's widow were ushered down the front steps and into the limo. A hearse eased around to the front of the church and took the front spot in the line of cars. More cars pulled up and joined the queue.

Keegan kept an eye on the Impala across the way as a couple of motorcycle cops led the processions away. The car pulled away from the curb and joined the file, keeping well back from the last car. Keegan got a quick glance of the driver's profile as the Impala passed—a craggy man of about fifty. Who knew? Maybe it was the same guy who'd smoked cigarettes behind Ormsby's back gate. That would mean Catling had found his quarry even before Ormsby died.

Keegan turned off the radio and put the Fairlane in gear; it would take all his concentration to keep up with the processional without giving himself away.

The motorcycle cops herded the funeral procession along back roads, and Keegan cut an oblique path through parallel streets, crisscrossing and shortcutting, always staying a stone's throw from the line of cars but out of the Impala's rearview mirror. He had to slip in a couple of thread-the-needle left turns that could have been disastrous. He ran a light on West Puente and heard some angry horns behind him. Still, he'd be off the other car's radar.

On Verdugo Road, he screwed up and ended up directly behind the Impala. The rearview mirror framed a pair of dark glasses. Maybe the driver saw Keegan. Maybe not. The entrance to Forest Lawn was just a few blocks ahead, so Keegan pulled in at a Texaco station. He waited a minute or two, watching traffic go by, and then headed up the street after them, through the cemetery's grand wrought-iron gates.

It didn't take him long to find the gravesite, the white awning, the floral displays, the cluster of dark suits and dresses. He stopped a good distance away, and let the car idle with the AC blowing. He couldn't see the Impala anywhere. Even at this distance, he could pick Eve out of the crowd by her slight figure and her lissome movements among the others.

After twenty minutes, the distant knot of people unraveled.

The orderly line of parked cars began to dissolve as mourners here and there cruised back down the hill towards the gate and the busy, sun-drenched lives that awaited them. Eventually, the limo pulled away, too, and Keegan sat forward to watch. The Impala had to be somewhere, but he didn't see it—just the long black car Eve was in, slipping along the lush green landscape.

He waited until Eve's limo was almost at the cemetery gates before he put his car in gear and followed. He fell in behind the limo on the 2 through Eagle Rock and Hollywood. When the limo turned up into the hills, Keegan pulled over to the curb and waited to see if the Impala would pass him.

He waited half an hour, seeing nothing suspicious, and then he drove back to the Thrifty lot to pick up his MG.

AFTER NINE, SOMEONE knocked on the kitchen's screen door at the back of the cottage. Nora leaped down from the sofa to investigate. She barked twice as she darted through the doorway and into the dark kitchen. Then she started whimpering excitedly. It wasn't the lieutenant; Keegan hadn't heard a car come up the hill. Who but Eve would arrive at the back door like that? What was she thinking, coming up to see him when she'd barely buried her uncle? What would Moore think if he found them together?

Eve stood in the glow of the back porchlight, on the other side of the screen door's mesh. Her stance in that feeble light— arms crossed, head stooped—made her look impossibly small, like something seen through inverted binoculars. She wore a linen blouse and a wrinkled pair of slacks. No makeup. Her hair was mussed.

Keegan didn't turn on the kitchen's overhead light. He didn't want to draw any more attention to her presence than she'd already drawn herself. "What are you *doing*?" he said. His voice came out more sternly than he'd intended, and he saw the reaction in her face. "We shouldn't be seen together."

Eve seemed to shrink yet smaller, wretched and frightened against the mansion's garden lights below. "Please," she said, "can I come in?" Her voice was breathy and uncertain. "I just need to see you."

"Jesus," Keegan said. "You know they're probably watching us." He unlatched the screen door. "Get in here. Did your aunt see you leave?"

Eve came in the kitchen, head ducked low. Her face looked pale and gaunt, but her eyes were fiery raw — and swollen. "No," she said. She seemed unwilling to look at him. "She's asleep. At least, I think she is. And I was quiet." She leaned with her back against the kitchen counter.

"Stay away from the window," Keegan said, again more gruffly than he'd meant to.

She jerked away from the tile counter as if she'd brushed a hot stove, and then looked at Keegan imploringly — as if she just wanted him to tell her what to do. It was hard not to feel a pang of pity.

"Come in the living room," he said. "But let me turn off some lights first."

Keegan glanced out the kitchen window, though he couldn't see Ormsby's back drive from there. Then he went ahead of her into the other room. He switched off the table lamp he'd been reading by and then the floor lamp by the bedroom doorway. He tried to imagine how the cottage must look from outside through a pair of binoculars. He drew the scalloped drapes but left the lamp burning. No one would be able to see in that way, and neither he nor Eve would cast shadows on the curtains. He closed the front door.

Eve came in the room when he gestured to her. She sat in the big armchair again. She leaned so far forward — elbows on knees, face in her hands — she looked like she might topple onto the rug. "I'm sorry," she said again. "Of course, they're probably watching. I'm so stupid sometimes."

She's smarter than you and me put together, Jimmy. "What's done is done," Keegan told her. He tried to smooth out his voice for her. "Don't worry about it." He sat down on the sofa but left a little space between him and the chair

Eve sat in. He wasn't sure why preserving that small distance seemed important right then. Certainly no one could see them.

Eve rubbed the back of her neck, head still bent low. She didn't seem able to look at him. "Oh, God, what have we done?" she said.

We? Keegan thought.

"It's a nightmare," she said. "I just keep thinking—" She shook her head. Another entry in her growing catalogue of unfinished thoughts.

Keegan had never seen a woman so distraught, and he felt his irritation drain away. It was replaced with a surge of sympathy. This girl was so young and guileless, a novice swimmer dragged out of her depth by an unseen current. Despite what Moore kept saying, she clearly wasn't cut out for the situation she found herself in.

"Look, we're going to be okay," he assured her. "I got rid of the gun. It's the only thing that ties us to the—" He caught himself up, midsentence, unsure of the correct term to use. What was the proper word for this mess they were in? "*Death*," he said—though his writer's ear told him it didn't ring true. *Killing* stayed closer to the plain facts of the case, but it was a word he wouldn't allow himself to say aloud.

"What if they find it?"

"The gun?" He shook his head. "They won't."

"But where is it?" she said. She held up a hand between them and shook her head. "No, don't tell me." She knotted her fingers together in front of her and stared, pale-faced, into the middle distance. A pair of perfect tears dribbled down her cheeks, as if on cue. "Oh, God," she said. "How did all this happen?"

Keegan slid off the sofa and kneeled in front of her, forcing her to look him in the eyes. "Look, we're going to be fine," he said. "I know what I'm doing. But you're going to have to hold yourself together. For me. For us. Just trust me."

Eve nodded and drew a damp, ragged breath. She wiped

her cheeks with the linen cuff of her blouse. "It's just I'm afraid," she said. "I think I was followed."

Shit. "You mean just now?" He looked at the kitchen door.

"No. No," she said. "Earlier. The funeral. There was a car behind us." Her damp eyes wandered the dimly lit room.

Keegan spoke loudly to hold her attention. "Was it an *Impala*?" he said.

She looked at him and shook her head. "No," she said. "Oh, I don't know. I don't think so."

"What color was it?"

"A big black sedan. Maybe a Ford. I don't know." A shiver went through her as she spoke. "It followed us all the way from the cemetery," she said. "I lost sight of it on Fairfax."

Keegan barked a laugh and stood up, relieved. "Oh, sweetheart," he said. "That was just *me*." He laughed again, but more gently. "I guess I got made. I'm getting rusty in my old age."

Eve gaped up at him. "*You*?" she said. She seemed relieved—and then confused, perhaps even angry. "Wait," she said. "Why were you following us?"

Keegan took a deep breath. He should probably have told her already, but now he had no excuse to keep the whole story to himself. He sat back down on the sofa, but close enough now to take both her hands. "There's something I haven't told you," he said, measuring his words. "It's nothing for you to worry about."

He told her all about Catling and the ten thousand dollars and the set of black-and-white photos. He told her about the car parked at her back gate, and the other car waiting outside the church today. He watched her eyes as he told her the details, and she seemed to teeter between annoyance and bewilderment.

When Keegan was done with the whole sordid story, Eve pulled her hands away from him. "Why didn't you tell me all this before?"

It was the obvious question, and Keegan had no ready

answer. He shrugged helplessly. "I wasn't sure it was you in the photos," he said. "I still can't be sure. I only saw them for a few seconds." He backpedaled, lamely. "I wasn't going to take the job. So, it didn't seem—" He shook his head hopelessly. Why did he feel the need to excuse himself? Hadn't he only tried to protect her? "I gave you the gun on the off-chance you were really in some kind of danger." It had gotten so complicated so fast, and now he was too exhausted to think the whole thing through—his reasons and calculations—and put them into words. "I didn't want to frighten you when I wasn't sure."

Eve's face was a tear-streaked, befuddled mess. "But why would anyone want to find *me*?" she said. "Let alone be willing to pay a fortune to do it? It makes no sense."

He shook his head. "I have no idea," he said. "I just wanted to make sure you were safe."

Eve gave him a bitter laugh, her eyes still glassy but with an anger ember in them now. "*By giving me a loaded gun?*" she said.

Put that way, in retrospect, it *did* sound absurd. Keegan leaned back against the sofa, anger rising. "Don't try to make this my fault," he said. "I didn't shoot anyone."

"No, you didn't. But you wouldn't let me just go to the police," she said. "You're the one who turned this into some big... ordeal. We could have just told the truth in the first place."

"Look, *you* came to *me*," he said. "You could have called the police from the house. I thought you wanted my help."

Her face changed. The anger in her seemed smothered by a wave of something like remorse. She shook her head forlornly. "Oh, Jim," she said. "Isn't it possible I didn't need you to rescue me? I just needed you to hold me."

They fell into a silence. Keegan watched her watch the coffee table. Her gaze grew blank and aloof. He sighed. It was a grand, unholy mess, and he couldn't think his way to the bottom of it. It was the kiss in the brick entryway—the confusion and the sleeplessness and this goddamned skin-prickling heat. *This town is one big bar brawl waiting to happen.* "I could use a drink," Keegan said. "Want me to pour you one?"

Eve's answer was inaudible, but Keegan thought he'd pour her two fingers of the lieutenant's Old Fitzgerald, whether she wanted it or not. It would do them both some good.

He came back from the kitchen and set her glass on the table in front of her before he sat back down on the sofa. He took a sip from his own glass and let the smoky flavor coat his tongue. It somehow tasted better now than it had when he was drinking it with Louis Moore.

Eve picked fretfully at the skin around her fingernails. The clock ticked on the mantle. The whiskey was a pleasant scalding going down. Keegan took another large swallow and set his glass on the table.

When their silence showed no sign of coming to an end, Keegan cleared his throat. "Lieutenant Moore thinks you're playing me," he said

"Who's that?" Eve said.

"The detective," he told her. "The black one."

She looked at him and looked away. "I barely spoke to the man."

"He told me that your mother is very sick," Keegan went on. "He said she's probably going to die soon."

Eve bit her lip and nodded, not looking at him, like he'd added yet another bitter weight to her immeasurable burden. "It's true," she said. "Liver cancer. They say she's got a few months."

Keegan picked up his glass and took another swig. "He says the whole family fortune will come to you the minute she dies." He set the glass down again and watched her.

Eve looked at him finally—a fiery flash of a glance that took him by surprise. "He thinks I killed Uncle Nigel so I would get his share?" she said. "What kind of a ghoul thinks like that?"

"But is he right?" Keegan said. "It'll all come to you?"

"*Yes*, he's right. What of it?" she said. "Does he think I *want* my mother to die? Does he think I even *care* about the money?" She shook her head and turned away from him, but then she turned back and there was new hardness in her eyes. "Did *you*?"

"Did I what?"

"Did *you* think he was right—that I killed Uncle Nigel on purpose?"

"Of course not," Keegan said—but his answer came a beat too late. He knew it lacked the ring of certitude. "Of course not," he said again. He picked up the glass, but Eve's eyes flooded, and he put it back down, feeling like a fool.

"I can't believe this," Eve said. "*You* of all people."

"I'm sorry," he said. "That just came out wrong." He nudged her glass of whiskey closer to her.

She waved his words away with a quick flick of her hand. "You just lost your own mother," she said. "And I'd guess this house is quite a windfall for you." She gestured angrily around the room—at the doilies and figurines and the tarnished spoons lined up in their rack. "Did *you* want your mother to die?" Hot tears ran down her cheeks. "What a horrible, horrible thing to say about a person."

Keegan leaned forward and pushed his nearly empty glass to one side. "It was just something the lieutenant said," he told her. "I just thought you should know." Keegan reached across the table and took Eve's hands again, and she didn't resist. "I'm sorry," he told her. "I didn't mean to upset you."

She looked at him, searching his eyes. "You've got to believe me, Jim."

"I believe you," he said. "Of course, I do. We've both got to trust each other. We won't stand a chance if we don't."

Again, she regarded him steadily with her red-rimmed eyes. "I'm sick all this happened," she said. And then, in a softer voice: "And I'm sick I got you tangled up in it. You don't deserve any of this."

"It's all right," Keegan said. "We're going to be all right." He nudged the glass closer to her again. "Go on," he said. "Drink a little. It'll make you feel better."

She picked up the glass, sniffed at it with her damp nose and raised it to her lips.

SHE STAYED ANOTHER hour. Maybe it was the bourbon he had given her, but she had come to sit next to him, and now she was nestled against him, diagonally, with his arm drawn around her.

"When this is all over, can we go away somewhere?" she asked him after a long silence. "Just the two of us?"

Keegan smiled. For him, *getting away* might mean a summer boat ride to Catalina or a winter's drive to Palm Springs, the kind of thing you could do with twenty bucks and an overnight bag. He doubted that was what she had in mind. "Sure, we can," he said.

She sunk a little lower, so she could look up at his face. "Promise?"

Keegan nodded. "We'll drive down to Julian for some apple pie," he said. "We'll make a day of it."

"Don't make fun, Jim," she said, pulling his arm against her. "I'm serious."

"What's this about?" he said, looking down at her. Those wide eyes. That broad smooth brow. It would be so easy to let himself fall for her.

"I just want to get to know you," she said. "*Normally.*" She shook her head as if the words weren't coming out right. "Not like *this*," she said, waving a hand around the room. He knew what she meant: not with a gun and a corpse and cars in the rearview mirror. It was hard to get your footing in a situation like this.

"Sure," he told her, with little conviction but with a glimmer of hope, nonetheless. "Sure, we can."

FROM BEHIND THE kitchen's screen door, he watched her leave. He stood well back, so he wouldn't be seen. He watched until a new light came on downstairs in Ormsby's place. Eve was home. She was safe. And if anyone were watching, they'd at least know she hadn't spent the night with him.

CHAPTER SEVEN

Sunday, August 19, 1962

THAT NIGHT, HE slept a fitful hour or two while it was dark, and with sunrise he'd pulled himself up from the settee to let Nora out before she scratched away the white paint on the inside of the kitchen door. Still groggy from the limited amount of sleep he did manage to get, he stood on the top back step with a hand on the doorknob to steady himself. The dog did her business over by the rosemary bushes, which seemed to be her preferred spot, and then jogged around in a big circle inspecting the garden's perimeter. She took up sniffing at the far corner of the picket fence. A rabbit maybe, or a coyote that had come by in the night.

Once again, Keegan saw the cars before he heard them. On the road below Ormsby's place, an unmarked black sedan came around the bend, followed by a squad car. Both cars passed the turn to Ormsby's place and kept coming. The only place left to go was his cottage. At least the squad car didn't have its lights flashing—perhaps a small good omen. Then, a hundred yards behind the two cars, a large green truck lumbered slowly around the bend, laboring in low gear to climb the steep grade.

Keegan closed the kitchen door and came down the back steps, now jarringly awake. He walked around to the front of the cottage and watched the two front vehicles approach up the last stretch of hill. The unmarked car, a Crown Vic, pulled over outside his front gate, and the squad car pulled in behind it.

The lieutenant got out of the front car's driver's seat. He was clearly on duty, driving a company sedan. He held a Manila envelope in one hand and his Panama hat in the other. He put the hat on and adjusted it, looking back at the squad car. He tucked the big envelope under his arm.

The door of the squad car opened, and the young cop from a few days ago unfolded himself to his full height and pulled on his blue uniform cap. The kid still looked ill at ease, towed into the great lieutenant's orbit. He trudged over to Moore and ducked his head low when the older man spoke in his ear. Keegan stood inside the fence, arms folded, watching them. Apparently, there was a game plan. Both men walked over to the fence where Keegan stood waiting.

Keegan had an idea what was in Moore's envelope, but, as he saw it, there was nothing to worry about. The gun was miles away under thirty feet of seawater. Even Eve's wine bottle was long gone. They could toss the place. They could unscrew every vent cover and pry up every loose floorboard. They weren't going to find anything. Keegan had been too careful. He went to the front gate and stood behind it, but he made no move to open it. The lieutenant approached him, holding out the brown envelope.

"I don't need to see the paperwork," Keegan told him. "Though it's a thoughtful gesture."

"It's a warrant," the lieutenant said. He spoke louder now, because the big diesel engine was huffing up around the last bend in the road, engine complaining. "You might want to look it over."

"I know what it is," Keegan told him, "and you're wasting your time." He opened the gate in the picket fence and stepped back like a gracious host. "Come on in, boys," he said. "Take the place apart with my blessing. Maybe you'll find my good fountain pen. I have no idea where it got to."

The lieutenant shook his head. "It's not for the house, Jimmy." He was almost shouting to be heard. The big truck was close enough now that Keegan could feel its rumble underfoot. "It's for the property."

The loud truck grumbled past the other two cars and wheezed to a stop farther up the hill, near the wooden barrier at the end of the road. The side door bore a county seal. A large cable winch was mounted on the rear. The engine dropped to an idle, and the exhaust pipe belched a cloud of blue smoke into the already smoggy air.

"We're here for a tree stump," Moore said. He held the envelope out between them again and shook it. "It's all in the warrant. We're going to rip it out and take it with us."

Keegan looked down at the envelope. He couldn't make sense of what the lieutenant was saying. "Stump?"

"I'm sure you remember Officer Tate," the lieutenant said. He gestured to his right, but the kid cop had drifted backwards a yard or two, so Moore had to turn to find him.

Officer Tate, looking self-conscious, dug his hands into his pockets and stepped up to take his place beside the lieutenant.

"Tate here says you told him you were using an old tree stump for target practice that morning he came up here," the lieutenant said.

In that instant, it dawned on Keegan where this was going, and the realization hit him like a gut punch.

"We're going to see if we can dig out a bullet and get it to ballistics," Moore said. "Who knows what we'll find out? Maybe it'll look like the slug we pulled out of Ormsby." He smiled that easy, ingratiating smile of his. "At any rate, I'll bet it won't match that old wheel gun you tried to palm off on me the other night."

Moore waited a beat to see if Keegan had any response, and then he turned to the kid cop and nodded for him to scram. The kid legged it up the hill in the direction of the idling truck. He seemed happy to be leaving the lieutenant's shadow, a nervous kid let loose from the principal's office.

When Moore and Keegan were alone, the lieutenant stepped closer, keeping the fence between them.

"Tate's never going to make detective," Moore said, the truck engine still rumbling behind him. "But the kid's not entirely stupid, either. He's got a good head for details."

Keegan's fingers felt bloodless, but he kept his eyes locked on Moore's. It was what an innocent man would do.

Moore looked away, down the road towards the first hairpin turn. "The morning you were out there shooting," Moore said. "The kid said there was a lawnmower making a hell of a racket. Said the two of you had to shout to hear each other."

"So?"

"I called Ormsby's landscape company," he said. "They said they were running the mower all morning."

"And?"

Moore shrugged. "Makes me wonder how anyone could have heard you popping off your .38 up there all the way over the hill." He looked up the street at the truck and then back at Keegan. "If I didn't know better, I'd think somebody set the whole thing up," he said. "You know, told someone to report gunshots, so we'd be sure to roll up here and see you dicking around with your Smith and Wesson." He stood watching Keegan, gauging the effects of his words. "It was just a thought I had," he said. "I'm not really expecting you to answer." He touched the brim of his Panama hat. "Say hello to Eve for me the next time you talk to her." The lieutenant turned and headed up the last stretch of hill to the waiting truck.

Keagan watched the man's slow and easy stride as he walked away and tried to regather his own scattered thoughts, which seemed to have fled in every direction like pigeons from a pit bull.

SINCE HIS MOTHER'S funeral, Keegan had been spending most of his time at the cottage, but all his clothes were still in his apartment, along with his shaving kit and shampoo and his stock of canned groceries. On some deep level, he still felt like an interloper camping out up here among his mother's belongings. He still found himself placing pillows on the chairs and arranging the shelves the way she had always favored them—as if, when she returned home, she might scold him if he disrupted her brass-bound routines. It was foolishness, he knew. For better or worse, this was Keegan's cottage now. Nora was his dog.

At some point, things would get back to normal, but for now he needed to lay low awhile until he figured out what to do next, and this was the place to do it. Here he could keep an eye on things. He'd be close to Eve. He could keep track of the lieutenant's comings and goings.

That afternoon, once Moore had carted off the old tree stump and the big truck rumbled back down the hill, Keegan drove down to Frager's, a little mom and pop grocery on Sunset, and tied Nora's leash to the row of newspaper machines outside. He'd get some soap and razors, a toothbrush, a few TV dinners and some more food for the dog. Later, he'd maybe swing by his apartment and pack up enough clothes for the new week. He took a small cart from the rack inside the door and started up the first aisle.

He wondered if fetching a week's worth of clean shirts might be a bit too optimistic. Where would he be a week from now? What would it mean if the lieutenant could link the bullets in the tree trunk to the one in Nigel Ormsby? Keegan would have to come up with a plausible way to explain it—a way that didn't put the gun in his own hand. Or in Eve's.

He'd walked right by the toiletries section like a blind man and had to retrace his steps. It was pure paranoia to let himself get so far ahead of the facts. He'd come down here to the grocery for a reason. There were things he needed. Things he needed today. He had to focus on the immediate. The ballistics report was at least a few days away, even if Moore leaned on the lab to get it done. And how pristine could a bullet be once it had slammed into solid oak at seven hundred feet per second? Maybe he'd get lucky for once. Either way, Keegan had a little time to plan his next move.

It dawned on him that he had been standing in front of the razorblades, staring blankly, looking shell-shocked to anyone who might be paying attention. He grabbed a box of Gillette Double-Edges, dropped it into his basket and glanced around. There was only one other shopper in the place, a stooped old woman with her hair in a scarf all the way over by the detergents. She was too immersed in trying to read her shopping list to have noticed him. He grabbed a toothbrush, some soap and a small bottle of Prell.

The air inside the grocery store was cool, and when he pulled open the glass door in the freezer section, he could feel the icy air pour down from the case and around his shins. He stacked one of each kind of Swanson's dinner in his basket. Two aisles over, he picked up a couple of boxes of Gravy Train dog food and then got a six-pack of Olympia beer from the back cooler.

The squat, gray-haired man behind the front counter rang up and bagged his purchases. A small black-and-white television was balanced on top of the cigarette rack behind him. It was tuned to the Dodgers game with the sound turned down. The picture was snowy, despite the tinfoil flags on the antenna's prongs. Cincinnati was leading one to nothing. It was the top of the sixth, with Drysdale on the mound.

While the old man worked, Keegan watched a lazy pop fly end the top half of the inning. The TV cut to a Chevy commercial. Keegan made out a check and gave the old man his driver's license.

On the television, a man's hand plucked a Sucrets lozenge from a tin that was beaded with rainwater. A fisherman in a rain slicker unwrapped the tablet and slipped it in his mouth on the deck of a storm-swept trawler. Just as the face vanished from the screen, Keegan felt the shock of recognition. But it was too late. The image was gone. There was no way to be sure. But could it really have been Simon Catling?

NEAR MIDNIGHT, KEEGAN stood at the kitchen window in the dark cottage, absently looking out, slowly turning his glass of bourbon in heedless hands. The scorched kitchen air still smelled of burned Swanson turkey and apple-cranberry cobbler. He jumped when the wall phone rang. It was Lieutenant Moore.

When Keegan heard Moore's voice on the phone, he almost hung up, but the lieutenant talked fast. He wanted an off-the-record meeting. There were some things Keegan needed to know, but they shouldn't be seen talking, not with the investigation hanging over both of them. His words were too quick, his voice too insistent, for Keegan to interrupt, let along hang up on the man. The lieutenant would be at the wishing wells in New Chinatown at noon. If Keegan had half a brain in his head, he'd be there, too.

The phone clicked and fell into silence.

Keegan hung the handset back in its cradle and went over to the kitchen's screen door. He took another sip of whiskey and looked out. A few lights were still on in the downstairs at Ormsby's place. Eve, it seemed, was also still awake, or maybe it was just the widow, sitting and fretting in the big room. He watched for movement, but the lamps were close to the windows, so there were no shadows.

It occurred to him then that this was the first day all week in which he hadn't laid eyes on Eve. He had no idea what that might mean.

CHAPTER EIGHT

Monday, August 20, 1962

KEEGAN PARKED DOWN Broadway and walked. Despite the heat, the streets of New Chinatown were bustling. Keegan felt very tall and very conspicuous, though none of the locals who passed by gave him so much as a look.

He turned and walked through the grand archway into the Central Plaza. He glanced around the deserted courtyard—the tiled roofs with their upturned corners, the goldenrod walls with scarlet trim, the English signs in kitschy Chinese lettering. This little neighborhood was purely for the tourists. He hadn't been here for years, but little had changed that he could see. The wrought-iron benches—painted glossy crimson, like nail polish—were all empty, baking in the sun. No sightseer with any sense would be outside on a day like this. The once-red paper lanterns, strung along dipping wires that crisscrossed overhead, had long ago faded to pink. Their round shadows swept like stepping stones across the sizzling concrete. The wishing well was tucked behind a shop on the courtyard's northwest corner. When it came into sight, the lieutenant was already there, waiting.

Keegan slowed. Moore watched him approach across the deserted quad. The man's face was drawn and neutral. He stood in the full sun, leaning back against the wishing well's iron railing. Even from a distance, he looked tired—as if, for once, he hadn't gotten his eight hours. Despite the ruthless sun, Moore wasn't wearing his Panama hat. No tie or jacket, either. He wore a plain white shirt, open at the collar, sleeves rolled up above his elbows. Maybe the other outfit was all for show, hung up in the closet when the cameras were packed away. Or maybe he just didn't want to be recognized today, as the local celebrity he was—but then a tall black man wasn't likely to go unnoticed in this neighborhood.

When Keegan neared him, Moore turned his back and faced the fountain. He gripped the iron rail with his broad brown hands and scowled down at the running waters.

Keegan took his place beside him, leaning his elbows on the warm iron railing.

Keegan's feet ached, and the heat radiating up through the soles of his shoes was anything but soothing. His back had been thrumming with a dull pain since he'd climbed out of his car. His shirt clung across his shoulders now and heat prickled around the collar. Keegan yawned in the smothering warmth and looked down at the running waters, wishing he was close enough to feel their spray.

The wishing well wasn't really a well, and it wasn't a fountain. It was more an ivy-draped Himalayan mountainscape, dotted with fake trees and gold-painted Buddhas. Water ran in bright rivulets around stones and gathered in glimmering, coin-dotted pools. Here and there, a sign above a brimming tin bowl promised HAPPINESS or FORTUNE or PROSPERITY to those with loose change whose aim was true. The sun reflected hard off the glimmering water.

When the lieutenant finally spoke, his voice was flat— slack and lifeless as the window awnings in this windless courtyard. "Anyone know you're here?" His words were barely audible over the sibilant rush of water.

By *anyone*, Keegan assumed he meant Eve. In fact, Keegan hadn't told her, but that was none of the lieutenant's business. He had no idea what this meeting was about, so it was best to be cagey if he could manage it. "You told me to keep it mum," he said, an answer that wasn't an answer. "A big secret meeting." He grinned and gestured around them both. "And yet you chose the one place in town where the two of us stand out like missionaries."

"This is as anonymous as we're going to get," the lieutenant said, his voice a little louder. "Nobody here knows us. Nobody here cares what we're doing." He shrugged. "Hell, most of them wouldn't understand what we're saying."

The sun on the water was giving Keegan a headache, so he turned and leaned his back against the fence. A shopkeeper, broom in hand, stood watching them from the doorway of a gift shop. When he saw Keegan notice him, he backed into the shadows without turning away.

Keegan looked over at the lieutenant's profile. "Ever hear of Nystrom and Day?" he said. "They were the jacks assigned to Chinatown at the tail end of the war."

The lieutenant shrugged. "I've heard of them," he said. "They were before my time."

Keegan nodded. "They took retirement before you were in the academy." Keegan hadn't set eyes on them in decades, but he could still picture both men's faces, their matching lantern jaws, the gap in Nystrom's teeth. He sighed. "Hell, both of them are no doubt dead by now." He smiled ruefully and turned to face the water again. "Anyway, those two had a name for the natives around here. Called them all '*cue-balls*'."

Moore was still gazing down at the water, but he straightened up a bit, curious. "'Cue-balls'?" he said.

"Yeah," Keegan told him. He turned his head to catch Moore's reaction. "'The harder you hit 'em, the better their English gets.'"

The lieutenant glanced over at him and then away. His expression was hard to decipher, but he certainly wasn't amused.

"Their words, not mine," Keegan reminded him. "LA's finest." He glanced back over his shoulder. "But there *is* a guy watching us from inside that store, unless I'm being paranoid. I don't know what this meeting is about, but *he's* definitely paying attention."

The lieutenant glanced over at the shop, Sincere Imports, and then back at the fountain. "We're fine right here," he said. "There's nothing to see. Just two old friends having a chat." He gripped the wrought-iron fencing with both hands and shook it a little. "Besides, a little paranoia would do you some good, Jimmy."

Keegan leaned his weight on the fence, trying to rest his back. Water burbled. Nickels gleamed. Leaves collected into damp thatch in the foamy edges of the pools. He looked at the rock formations with their tin bowls. WEALTH. WISDOM. LOVE. SERENITY. And all they cost was a penny. It was far too hot to linger out here in the sun. "So, what's this big secret meeting about, anyway?" Keegan asked.

The lieutenant sucked in a long breath and nodded. He turned and looked at Keegan squarely. "I just want you to listen to me for a minute, Jimmy," he said. "Friend to friend."

Friend. The lieutenant seemed to be leaning hard on the buddy angle. He'd dropped the term twice in the last minute. Keegan didn't know what to make of it, but, as an omen, it wasn't good.

"The thing is," Moore said, "I don't really think you shot the old man." His voice sounded tinny and thin against the background hiss of rushing water. The week seemed to have aged him, or maybe the tie and the Panama hat made him look younger. "I don't think you did it," he went on, "but you're making it pretty easy for someone to convince a jury that you did."

"I'm not worried," Keegan said. "You can't have much of a case against me, if you think I didn't do it."

Moore sighed and raised a thumb. "One. The bullet in the dead man is going to match the ones we pulled out of the tree trunk," the lieutenant said. He raised his index finger. "Two. We've got you taking target practice a few hours before the deed." He raised another finger. "Then we've got you trying to pass off someone else's gun as your own." He shook his head and gave up, letting his hand drop to his side. Three fingers would be enough to make his point, though it was clear he could keep counting off digits if Keegan insisted. "Wise up," he said. "Your jury's going to be back out on Temple Street before rush hour."

Keegan was about to answer, but he caught himself and bit his tongue. Speaking was the mistake men always made in the interrogation room downtown. He thought of the countless hapless characters he'd watched being grilled from the other side of a two-way mirror—all the notes he'd jotted, all the stories he'd filed. Talk was what always got them in the end— all those panicked, careless sentences expertly braided into a noose. Most of those guys might have been okay, if they'd only kept their mouths shut. Guilt or innocence had little to do with it, once they started talking.

A house sparrow flitted down from somewhere overhead into the wishing well. It perched on the edge of a bowl that spilled over with foamy water—WISDOM. The bird hopped down into the water, and Keegan watched, with a measure of envy, as it splashed about and ruffled its feathers.

He turned from the well again and leaned back on the rail. The iron fencing pressed against the small of his back. It was hot, and it felt perversely good against his thrumming muscles. The shopkeeper still stood watching them from his store's dark interior. He held the broom with both hands but didn't move it. It was just a prop. Keegan's head was starting to swim. "So, what is it you want from me?" he asked the lieutenant. "Am I supposed to break down and confess?"

"I just want you to open your eyes, Jimmy," Moore said. "It isn't like you to let your guard down like this. I don't know what that girl has over you, but you're not thinking straight."

Eve again. What was Moore's obsession with her, with him? Jealousy, maybe?

The sparrow flew up from the fountain and darted away

over Keegan's head. "You don't know what you're talking about," Keegan said.

"That girl is leading you down a dark alley," the lieutenant said, "and you don't have the good sense to strike a match."

"I've only talked to her a couple of times," Keegan said. "We're just acquaintances." The sentences came out sounding hollow, pro forma—even in his own ears. The hot railing was beginning to burn his back now, but he didn't move. Again, he thought of the wary, hunted faces he'd watched from the other side of the interrogation-room mirror. The poor dopes never knew when to shut the hell up. "I barely know her," Keegan said, even as he warned himself not to speak.

Moore let loose a quick, hard laugh. "*That* much I believe," he said. "If you *did* know her, you wouldn't go near her. That girl is strychnine." He shook the fence again; the iron trembled against the small of Keegan's back. The lieutenant pressed on: "Did she tell you about that other acquaintance of hers? The one who ended up off Pier 12 with four bullets in him?"

Keegan straightened up and took his back away from the railing. He turned to look at Moore. "What the hell are you talking about?"

The lieutenant seemed to be studying his face, trying to discern what Keegan knew and what he didn't—a hard poker-table gaze. "Some insurance appraiser," Moore said, eyes still on Keegan's face, scrutinizing his reaction. "The family hires him to catalog the jewelry at the mother's place in Pacific Heights. He and your girlfriend get chummy. Start seeing each other after hours. Spending a lot of secret time together."

Keegan thought of Eve sitting across from him at the Regency—that frightened, trusting face. Even in memory, he could feel the pull it had on him.

The lieutenant's face was pinched up now, like maybe he, too, was fighting off a headache. Light from the moving water glimmered across his face. "The appraiser in question stops showing up for work. A few days later, some crabbers haul his body out of the Bay. Tied to a cinder block with baling twine."

Keegan turned to face the water and steadied himself on the iron rail. "Where'd you get all that?"

"Frisco's finest," Moore said. "They're sending me the full report."

Keegan's head was so light now, he felt as though his knees might buckle. "You sure they got their facts straight?"

"Gospel," Moore said. "I got it straight from the Central District Captain. They were looking at your girlfriend for it, but the brass waved them off." Moore looked down at the water again and shook his head. "Money sure as hell makes the world go 'round," he said. "Wish I had me a little."

Keegan rubbed the knot at the back of his neck. His legs prickled under his linen trousers. He leaned more heavily against the iron rail. What he wouldn't give for a few hours' shut-eye in a cool, dark place. He tried to formulate a response, but the sun beat down on him, and his thoughts burned away to nothing. Better not to talk anyway.

"Here's what I think happened that night at Ormsby's place," the lieutenant said. "The girl gave you some story about being afraid, and you saddled up and rode in to save the day with your .38 Special."

The cowboy hero image stung. It felt a little too close to the truth, and it didn't sit well with Keegan. Sweat trickled down his sides.

Moore seemed to pick up on Keegan's discomfort and pressed his advantage. "Don't get me wrong. I think *she's* the one who killed the old man, but somehow she conned you into covering it up." There was a sheen of sweat on Moore's forehead now. He looked at Keegan, and Keegan looked away. "I don't know what she has on you," the lieutenant pressed on, "but it was enough to get you to stick your neck out, and now you can't seem to pull it back in." He shrugged and gave the railing another shake. "Maybe she's blackmailing you. Maybe she batted her eyes and told you she loved you."

Keegan bristled with hot anger. He began to speak, but the lieutenant just held up a hand and talked over him.

"*Don't say anything*," Moore told him. The full resonance of authority was back in his voice now. "Don't make it any worse than it is, Jimmy. There's no way you're getting out of this without a scratch. It's way too late for that. I gave you all the breaks I could." He shook his head wearily. "Hell, I shouldn't even be talking to you now," he said, "but I feel like I owe it to you." He turned to face Keegan squarely, leaning one elbow on the railing, no two-way mirror between them. "Here's the deal," the lieutenant said. "If you don't come clean today, it's over between us. I'm no longer looking out for you. Tomorrow, you're just another perp, and I'm going to put you away." His face was gray and stern and humorless.

Keegan looked down at the fountain's water. He gathered what saliva he could and spat into it.

The lieutenant took that as the sign it was. He drew himself up to his full height and gripped the railing with both hands for a final parting shot: "And after I put you away, Jimmy?" he said. "I'm going to sleep like a drunk baby." He gave the railing one final shake. "You've got until I clock out tonight," he said. "I'll be waiting by the office phone."

KEEGAN PUT IN a few hours at the office for show and slept a bit with his head on the desk while the air conditioning ran, but the sleep was fleeting and shallow, haunted by bloated corpses pulled out of San Francisco Bay.

In a way, the lieutenant was right. He didn't owe Eve a thing. He could cut her loose and cut his losses, come clean before Moore's deadline, watch it all play out from the sidelines. What was she to him anyway? But any time her face came to mind—her wide, haunted eyes and the way they seemed to search his own—he knew he couldn't turn his back on her. She was no killer. That much he knew.

Mrs. Dodd, seeing the state he was in, answered the phones all afternoon but didn't put a single call through. He left before five and waited out the afternoon in his hot apartment. He kept the windows closed and latched, and he tried not to move around much. It would be best not to make a sound, best if Mr. Soto didn't even know he was home. Keegan could hear the little man fussing about in his kitchen, the clatter of dishes, the sound of water hissing in the pipes, voices from a radio—the sounds of a petty, cloistered life lived out without consequence behind drawn blinds.

When the sun went down, Keegan left the lights off and sat very still in the dark—a lit lamp would give him away. He'd planned to call Eve at around seven-thirty, but he nodded off on the love seat despite the clinging heat, his head lolled back against the wall. Exhaustion taking over. He dreamed he had gone to the Alpha Beta near his apartment for groceries, but the shelves were full of odd things he had no need for—doorknobs and basketballs and rows of polished teakettles. He became convinced that he might starve if he didn't find food soon, but there was no one at the store to help him. He wandered, pushing his empty cart, past displays of television tubes and bins full of roadmaps. Then a boy sat, slumped in the middle of the aisle, crying uncontrollably, making it impossible to pass.

Keegan woke with a start, damp and cranky, with a stiff neck—somehow less rested than before he'd slept. A numbing sweat had collected where his body touched the upholstery. He stood and stretched and tried to work out his body's kinks without making any noise that would register next door. He worked his head from side to side and felt the cracking in his neck. His whole body was a hot jumble of aches and fizzling electrical pulses. He reminded himself that fall would arrive, that by Halloween he'd be wearing a light jacket. By Thanksgiving he'd be cranking up the heat in his apartment. But it was no good. It felt like another lie. It was hard to imagine he'd ever feel rested again. And where would he be by the time Thanksgiving came around?

He had no idea what time it was, so he went to the refrigerator and opened the door a crack. He angled his wristwatch to the dim sliver of light that leaked out with the cold, heavy air. It was just after eight. The lieutenant would have gone home by now, Keegan's deadline lapsed. How long would it be before they came for him and hauled him away? If the ballistics report had come in that afternoon, Keegan would already be in cuffs. Tomorrow at the soonest.

The phone was on the side table right next to the love seat, so he went and sat back down in the warm, moist aura he'd left there. He rested his hand on the receiver a few seconds before he picked it up.

"We need to talk," he said when Eve answered.

He could hear her cautious breathing. "I'll come up in a few minutes," she said. "I'll tell my aunt I'm going to bed."

"I'm not there," Keegan said. "I'm in town." The heat felt like ants crawling on him under his shirt. "Listen to me," he said. "I need you to do exactly what I say. When you hang up, call a taxi. Have him take you to a payphone."

"What's this about, Jim?"

"Not on the phone," he said. "Not now. Please. I just need you to go to a payphone."

Eve was silent a few seconds. "I can go down to the—"

"No," Keegan cut her off. "Don't tell me where you're going. Do you have pen and paper?"

"Yes."

"Write this down," he said. He dictated his apartment's unlisted number. "Call from a payphone as soon as you can. Ask the taxi driver to wait."

Eve's voice became quiet, as though she was afraid of being overheard. He could picture her in her bedroom, sitting on the bed—but she might have been in the kitchen or in the living room. The images of the big house got all jumbled in his head.

"What's happening, Jim?" she said. "What's going on?"

"We just need to talk," he said. "We can't do it at the cottage. And we can't do it on the phone."

"Why not?"

Keegan sighed and squeezed his eyes shut. She was so

naïve, so sheltered—sealed off and protected from the bruising world by all that money. In some ways, she was younger than her years. How could she possibly be the woman Moore made her out to be? "Because they're probably watching us." He let his head fall back on the love seat, eyes still closed. Colors pulsed and swam on the insides of his eyelids. "They're probably tapping your phone," he told her. "That's why you need to call from a payphone."

"You *can't* be serious," she said, her voice dismissive, imperious, too loud.

"Look," he said, his voice hardening. "You're going to have to humor me. Hang up now and call a taxi. Call me back at that number. You've got it, right? Better if I don't repeat it."

"I have it," she told him.

He opened his eyes to the dark, hot room and put the phone back on its cradle. He massaged his temples and rubbed a gluey substance from his eyes. He needed Eve to take him seriously, but she would do what she would do— the heiress's prerogative. He stretched his legs out in front of him, heels on the living-room floor. It would be best if he didn't fall asleep again. He needed his head clear when she called back, if she ever did. He closed his eyes again and tried to focus on the situation, but the yellow flashes of light that darted across the inside of his eyelids made him think of Kipper Lusk's goldfish—waiting, doomed, oblivious.

He jolted awake when the phone rang, heart hammering. He took a deep breath and gathered himself together before he picked up.

"Were you followed?" he asked her.

"Of course not." Her voice was altogether too glib.

He sighed into the phone. She still didn't get it. She didn't appreciate how dire things had become. She had no idea what Moore was thinking. "Listen to me," he said. "They're better at tailing you than I was. They're not going to be so easy to see. Are you on the street?"

"Yes, I'm at an Esso station."

"Look around," he said. "But don't be obvious about it. There's going to be a car somewhere in sight. Something drab and gray. There'll be two men in it. Do you see it?"

Again, there was a silence on the other end. "No," she said. "There's noth—"

The silence hung on for too many seconds. "What kind of car is it?" Keegan said. "Is it a Crown Vic?"

"I don't know," she told him. Her voice was distant, like the reality of the situation was only now beginning to dawn on her, and she was forgetting to talk into the phone's mouthpiece. "It's just an average sedan," her breathless voice came in more loudly. "Black—or dark gray—I can't tell."

"Two men?"

"Just one. He's parked in front of a carpet store," she said. "But at the curb. He's not in the parking lot."

"Okay, so listen," he said. "That's your tail. He's parked that way so he can get out faster. Get back in the taxi. Tell the driver you want to go to the Biltmore. But ask him to take you to the rear entrance. It's on South Grand. Got that?"

"Yes."

"Don't keep looking back to see if the car is there," he told her. "It will be. If you have to look, use your makeup mirror. Keep facing forward. When you get to the Biltmore, walk straight inside the back entrance. Take the hallway to the left. Go right on through the kitchen and the dining room and out to the front lobby. Walk fast, and don't look back. Nobody's going to stop you if you just keep moving. Head out the front doors. There'll be a row of yellow cabs waiting. Get the one at the front of the queue and come here."

Keegan gave her the address to his apartment, and they both rang off, without saying more. Fully awake now, he sat in the dark, listening to the mumble of Mr. Soto's radio on the other side of the wall.

WHEN HE FINALLY opened his apartment door to her, Eve stood before him in a gray dress with a red belt. Her face was drawn and pale, but her curly hair was brushed out impeccably. Her pale hands, linked in front of her, held a silver lamé clutch. Keegan hadn't expected her to look so well appointed at this hour. Had she actually stopped to think of what to wear? Again, he was struck by how little she seemed to fathom the treacherous waters they were treading. But then Moore's voice nagged at the back of his mind: *That girl is strychnine.* Was it possible? Could he, Keegan, be the one swept out of his depth?

There were no hellos, no small talk. Keegan took her arm and pulled her in through the door and closed it quietly. He put a finger to his lips—warning her to be quiet—but the gesture wasn't needed. Eve walked past him as if in a daze. She seemed to float through Keegan's modest living room without seeing it and sat down on the love seat that must have still been radiating Keegan's body heat.

She finally turned her head to look at him. "Can we maybe turn on a light?" she asked, her voice too loud.

"Shhhh," Keegan hissed. "Keep your voice down. I'd rather no one knew we were here." He thought of Mr. Soto in the next apartment. Had things suddenly fallen silent over there? Had he turned off the radio when he heard Eve arrive? Keegan held up a hand, to keep Eve silent. He looked at the wall and listened hard. After a beat, tinny orchestra music started up on the radio again. A little dead air, was all. He was just being paranoid. He let go the breath he'd been holding. "We should probably go back to the bedroom," he whispered.

Eve shot him a hard look he couldn't interpret.

He shook his head. "I've got a very nosy neighbor," he said by way of explanation, his voice as quiet as he could make it. "That's the only reason." He nodded at the wall. "The guy's probably got his ear pressed to a juice glass right now." He gestured at the open doorway to his bedroom. "Please," he said. "This end of the apartment will be safer. We can talk more easily."

Eve stood warily, still holding the silver clutch in front

of her. She walked past Keegan to the bedroom doorway. She leaned in before crossing the threshold, as if the room might be filled with snakes. Satisfied, she entered and, seeing nowhere else to sit, perched stiffly on the corner of Keegan's unmade bed. She looked at him primly as he came through the doorway, hands folded in her lap. In that staid pose, she might have been the widow Ormsby, presiding over her silver tea set.

Keegan pulled the bedroom door shut behind them. The air was stale and sluggish, tinged with the odor of old laundry. He wished he could open a window, but then they might be heard out on the courtyard. Every window in the quad would be open tonight, every neighbor courting every breeze. "Sorry for all the cloak and dagger," he told Eve. "I'm just getting a little paranoid."

Eve nodded noncommittally. "What's all this about?" she asked.

Keegan stood looking down at her. "I'm going to get arrested any minute," Keegan said. "So, I'm a little on edge."

Eve's eyes went wide. "*What*?" she said. She caught herself and lowered her voice. "You're joking," she said in a whisper.

Not joking. Not really. Exaggerating, perhaps—but not by much. He thought of Moore standing at the Chinatown wishing well, counting off the prosecution's evidence on his fingers. How long would it take to match the bullets dug out of the tree trunk with the one dug out of Uncle Nigel? He thought of the lieutenant's grim look when they parted. Just as Moore had warned him, at this point Keegan was just another perp.

Keegan shook his head to scatter the plague of thoughts swarming there. "There's a good chance we don't have much time," he told her. "We've got to figure out a plan. I'd like us to have our stories straight before they drag us into separate rooms."

Eve looked at him, still agape. "Ar*rest*ed?" she said.

"Tonight?" It was like she was lagging a sentence or two behind his words, trying to keep up.

Keegan shrugged. "Tomorrow probably," he admitted. "I don't know. Maybe I've got a few days. A week at most." He thought of the old oak trunk tied down to the city truck as it rumbled past the cottage and down the hill. He thought of Lieutenant Moore rising from his desk and pulling on his jacket, never taking his eyes off the silent phone. He'd probably given Keegan a little extra time, arriving home a half-hour late to a cooling dinner, all for old times' sake. Again, he shook his head to clear it of the thoughts that crowded in on him like the press of hot strangers in a packed elevator.

"Why?" she asked him. "What happened?"

"The cops," he said. "They took the tree stump we were shooting at. Sawed it off at the ground and hauled it away. The bullets they pull out of it are going to match the one that killed your uncle. When the ballistics report comes back, I get hauled in. Tag, I'm it."

Again, it seemed to take a beat or two for the words to sink in, then Eve's eyes went wider. "Oh, God," she said. "Of course. The stump. What can we do?"

Keegan didn't respond. There was no clear answer to her question, and his mind was swarmed with a million other nagging questions of his own. He squeezed his hands into fists. Goddammit. Goddamn Louis Moore and his goddamn theories. Keegan glanced at the drawn curtains a few seconds and then looked back at Eve. "That morning we went shooting," he said. "Who do you figure called the cops on us?"

Eve's eyes were still wide, glimmering in what little light that made it past the curtains from the quad outside. Her brow furrowed, as if his question made no sense to her. "I have no idea," she said. "I don't really know any of the neighbors. I just stay in the house. Why? Who do *you* think it was?"

He thought of how she'd looked that morning in the wonderful slant of early light, the sharp scent of gunpowder in the air. *So innocent—yet so lethal.* "I'm just wondering how anyone could have heard gunshots with all that noise down at your place," Keegan said. "That mower was making a hell of a racket."

Eve looked bewildered. She shook her head. "I don't understand," she told him. "I don't know what you're asking."

Down a dark alley, the lieutenant had said, *and you don't have the good sense to strike a match.* Goddamn him.

"Because that was one hell of a bad hop," Keegan went on. "If that patrol car hadn't come up the hill, there'd be no way to link my old .38 to the crime. I'd be safe as houses right now. Nobody would give me a second look. That was some damned bad luck for me." And *only* for him.

"*Crime*?" Eve said, as though that single word had been the only one she'd heard. Again, she seemed to be struggling to keep up. "I don't understand what you're saying."

Keegan went to the dim penumbra of light at the curtain's edge. He put his eye to the gap and looked out on the quad with its shimmering pool and its floodlit palms. All those neighbors behind their lit curtains were going about their business. It was just a hot night in August, with TV shows and TV dinners, and maybe a cold bottle of Schlitz to unwind. In another hour, they'd call it a day with a cool shower and go off to bed with a fan spinning in the window. What workaday bliss they were living, and they didn't even know it.

Keegan turned from the window and found Eve watching him from where she sat on the corner of his mattress. Her face was blank and blameless, her wide eyes clear of any trace of cynicism. What did Moore see in that face that Keegan was blind to? She was as unworldly as a cloistered child. It couldn't be an act—though, to be fair, good actors *were* a dime a dozen in this town.

"I think I saw Simon Catling on TV," he told her. Of all the notions churning in his mind, how was *that* the one that bubbled to the surface? "I'm beginning to think he's just some two-bit actor hired to string me along." He thought of the plump envelope riding on the limo seat beside him. Was it just a prop? If he'd torn it open, would he have found stacks of paper cut from some old phone book?

Eve watched him from where she sat, but she didn't speak. There was a trace of pity in her expression now. He must sound like a raving nutjob. She nodded for him to come over and patted the mattress beside her. Her dark eyes glimmered in her blanched face. "Come sit down, Jim," she said. Her voice was calm but pleading. "*Please*. You're scaring me. You're not making sense."

Maybe he was, maybe he wasn't. It didn't help that, in this closed-off room, he felt like he was being smothered with an electric blanket.

Keegan remained where he stood near the window. "I've been talking to Lieutenant Moore," he said. He thought of the blinding ripple of sunlight coming off the water at the wishing well, and felt the same headache gathering behind his eyes. WEALTH. WISDOM. LOVE. SERENITY. "He's got me half convinced you set me up."

Eve's expression went blank, like, again, she needed a beat or two for his meaning to sink in. And then her mouth dropped open. "Wait, *what*?" she said. Exasperation seemed to crowd out whatever sympathy she'd been feeling a few seconds ago.

"Not so *loud*," Keegan hissed at her. "Everybody's got their windows open. No one can know you're here."

Eve waved his warning away and made no effort to lower her voice. "What are you saying? Are you starting to agree with him?"

Keegan squeezed his temples with the span of his right hand. Damn this headache. Damn Lieutenant Moore. "He keeps hinting that you're not what you pretend to be."

Eve shook her head, mouth open. "Jim, this isn't fair," she said. Her voice seemed tired, worn down, nearing surrender. "I don't know what that man's been telling you. Please just come and sit down." With one small hand, she patted the empty bedspread beside her.

Keegan stood studying her. His sweat-sodden shirt clung to him like a steamed towel, and the sensation made his skin crawl.

Eve sat looking back at him, her unsullied brow furrowed now. How could it be an act? Goddamn Louis Moore.

Keegan had to press on. It was the only way to get past this, to get to the truth, to formulate a plan. "Guns don't just go off," he said, lamely. "You had to have pulled the trigger."

Eve's shoulders slumped a little and then rose back up. She shook her head, but the hopeless gesture turned into a nod. "I *did* pull the trigger." Her voice was strangely steady now. "When have I ever denied it?" she said. "Come. Please. Sit." Again, her hand patted the empty space next to her.

Again, like it was a trap he wouldn't be lured into, Keegan kept his distance. He stood by the curtains and tried to force his wheeling thoughts into words. "Looked at a certain way, it seems like everything you've done since the moment we met was designed to suck me into this chaos."

Eve shook her head again, wretchedly, her patience wearing thin. "What does that even mean?" she said. "That I'm some kind of evil genius? That I planned this whole sordid fiasco out, like some B-movie *femme fatale*?"

Since the Chinatown wishing well that thought had never been far from Keegan's mind. "Moore thinks you seduced me," he said. "He thinks I helped you kill your uncle." He spoke as though the notion was an obvious lie — but from one angle, that's just what had happened, wasn't it? He'd handed a stranger a loaded gun and taught her to use it. He'd sent her back to that big, dark house with six live rounds and a jumble of nerves. If that wasn't actually complicit, it was in the neighborhood — maybe even adjacent property. Goddamn Louis Moore. "The lieutenant thinks you're grooming me to take the fall," Keegan said.

Eve considered him silently from where she sat, her face prim and inscrutable. If she was still angry or upset with him, she was hiding it well. She turned her face up to him and looked from one of his eyes to the other, as if searching him for something. "And what do *you* think, Jim?" she said at last. "Do *you* think I did it on purpose? Do *you* think I murdered my uncle?"

She spoke as though the answer should be obvious, but it wasn't. Not to Keegan. Not right now. Somewhere in this labyrinthine script, Keegan was being played—by Catling or Moore or Eve. He was somebody's patsy; he was fortune's fool.

"I don't know what I think," he said.

Eve took a couple of deep breaths and pulled back her shoulders. Her face darkened. "I am *not* going to sit here and listen to this," she said. "You got me to come all the way here just so you could—"

Another unfinished sentence to file away with the others. Another thought left hanging. She stood, gathered her clutch under one arm, and strode to the closed bedroom door.

"Wait," Keegan told her.

She paused with her back to him and her small, pale hand on the doorknob. Her narrow shoulders looked rigid under the tailored gray fabric of her dress.

"Before you go," he said, "fill me in on a few things. If I'm going to get hauled in and interrogated, it's the least you can do."

She turned back to him and took a single, grudging step in his direction, arms folded. Her chin was set and her lips pressed together. Rather than speak, she just glowered at him with that brand of haughty, self-righteous scorn only money can buy.

Keegan watched her face closely. "Let's start with something else I learned from Lieutenant Moore," he said. "Let's talk about that friend of yours they fished out of San Francisco Bay."

Eve's entire bearing crumbled in a thunderstruck instant. She took a graceless step backwards, hitting the closed bedroom door as though Keegan had physically pushed her. She pressed her back against the door then, like she needed it to keep her footing. "What did you say?" she said, her heartbeat somehow sounding in her voice.

Keegan crossed his arms and willed himself cold. "Judging by your reaction, you heard me just fine," he said. There was ice in his voice, and he didn't much like it—but what did tone matter now? What did anything matter?

Eve felt her way over to the bed like a blind woman. She sat down hard, inelegantly, knees buckling. She began to sob, hard and heedlessly, gulping for air.

Keegan, still by the window, was caught up short. How could this be an act? For a few paralyzed seconds, he watched her sob convulsively. It was raw and unflattering, utterly convincing. Her emotion seemed to surge up from some deep, secret fissure inside her.

Warily, Keegan went over and sat beside her on the bed. He took one of her hands from her lap and squeezed it. It was cooler and drier than Keegan's own. She fell against him, her head on his shoulder, shuddering. Keegan felt called upon to do something, but what? This was the kind of fraught moment that required a finesse Keegan simply lacked. It was the kind of moment that had doomed his brief marriage. He put his arm around her shoulder, clumsily, and felt her small body heave against him.

He sat with Eve that way a few long minutes until her crying subsided, and she took a few steadying gulps of air. He got up and fetched her a couple of white handkerchiefs from the top drawer of his dresser and sat beside her again while she used them. When she was done, she leaned against him and pressed her damp face to his shoulder. He put his arm around her again.

"Oh, Jim," she said. "I try to hold myself together, but you have no idea what an unholy mess I am."

"Tell me," he said. He pulled her closer and put both his arms around her.

She pressed the side of her head against his chest. He could smell that lavender shampoo again.

"The man they found in the Bay was my lover," she said. Her voice cracking on that final word, as though saying it tore something out of her. "His name was Merrill. Merrill Newsome." She sagged against him, and he held her tighter. "We were going to marry," she said. "But we had to keep it a secret. I suppose I didn't want to upset my mother, sick as she was." She sighed. "It sounds ghoulish, but it was only a matter of time before she'd be gone, and we'd be free to do as we pleased."

"Why would she be upset?" Keegan asked. The way he held her now, he could feel her heartbeat in his arms. "I'd think your mother would be happy you'd found someone before she—you know. Before she was gone."

Eve turned her damp face up to him. Whatever makeup she was wearing was streaked down her cheeks now. "You don't know?" she said. "Your Lieutenant Moore didn't tell you?"

"Tell me what?"

She pressed herself to him again, like she couldn't bear to look in his eyes, didn't want to see his reaction. "Merrill was a black man," she said simply. "I loved him more than anyone—but it would have killed my mother. She has very strong opinions about such things."

Eve was right: the lieutenant *hadn't* mentioned that detail. Moore's omission seemed significant in some way, but, in this moment, Keegan couldn't fathom what it meant or what difference it could make. "How did the two of you fall in love?"

"Merrill was an appraiser," she said. "For the insurance company. He came to the house after my grandfather died to sort through the family's assets. Granda was an avid collector—of just about everything. Rare books. Jewelry. Old maps. But he was alone in his passions. None of us had the remotest idea what he'd left behind."

The side of her face was pressed to his chest again. He could feel her voice while he listened to it.

"At first, my mother wanted to send Merrill away," she

said. "She said she didn't want a colored man in the house. She wanted me to call the insurance company to have them send someone more appropriate—which would have been mortifying. I had to convince her to let him do his job. I promised her I'd stay with him every minute." Without lifting her head, she laughed—a small, bitter sound. "And I did," she said. "Every single minute. If she only knew."

Keegan could imagine it: Eve following the man through the vast, echoing rooms, listening to him talk about topaz and Tamerlane, while she brought him tea and pastries on a silver tray. "And one thing led to another," he said. "That's the way these stories always go."

"Don't make fun of me," she said. She lifted her head to look at him and then rested her cheek against his chest again. "He was a lot like *you*, Merrill was," she said. "He was smart and witty and confident."

He could feel her fingers gather the fabric of his shirtfront as she spoke.

"I couldn't help but be smitten," she said. "I especially loved the way he didn't let the family's money push him around. He was no one's sycophant."

As she spoke, Keegan again felt an irrational pang of jealousy for a dead man. "A pair of star-crossed lovers," he said. But what he was feeling, listening to her speak, wasn't mere envy. Keegan felt displaced in some intangible but significant way. What if he, Keegan, were just a bit player—a Simon Catling—in Eve's real story? What if he were just an unbilled player with a single line in some grander, tragic story he'd been blind to? Doesn't every guard and footman think of himself as Romeo?

"We started seeing one another," Eve went on. "In secret, of course. Or at least where we wouldn't run into my late grandfather's cronies. But it was hard. Even in Dog Patch or Hunter's Point, we turned heads. We spent most of our time at a restaurant in Fillmore, down among the jazz clubs. Merrill knew the owner, and we could have dinner and drinks there without it being a fuss."

Secret love and hidden trysts. Keegan was all too familiar with that sad plotline—he'd watched it play out too many times through his telephoto lens.

"Merrill got hired by a woman to sort out a warehouse in North Beach," Eve went on. "Her husband had been killed, and she wanted Merrill to go through his belongings. It would keep him busy for weeks, and she offered to pay him well." She pressed her hand to Keegan's shirt. "Whatever was in the warehouse, Merrill got sucked in. He thought he'd found something, but he couldn't be sure. Something to do with the Hesse family after the war." She glanced up at him. "I remember because I had a German tutor with that name."

It was the name—*Hesse*—that stirred something in Keegan. Some old story he'd filed. It had been just after the war, he seemed to remember. In '47, he'd guess. American officers billeted in a German castle had dug up the family treasures. It was a screwball-comedy heist, doomed from its half-assed inception—Preston Sturges meets *Public Enemy*. Or was all that the plot of a TV movie he'd seen? Keegan ransacked his aching head. Most of the story had come over the wire, he seemed to remember. But hadn't he made a few phone calls to a friend at the *Chicago Trib* for some local color?

The memory was there, a vague outline in the darkness, just out of reach, like an elusive word on the tip of his tongue. But, hell, 1947 was the year of the Black Dahlia and Bugsy Siegel. There was so much happening right here in LA, who could spare column space for some European royals' petty woes?

"He wouldn't tell me what it was about," Eve was saying, "but he thought something was fishy. That he'd stumbled onto something big. It was something he couldn't ignore. Anyway, I showed up at the restaurant one Tuesday. It was the day before my birthday, and we were going to have lunch to celebrate," she said. "But Merrill didn't show. Walt—that was the restaurant's owner—told me he'd stopped by that morning. Said he'd be back for lunch and to make sure there were fresh crabs at hand." She pressed her palm to Keegan's chest. "Merrill wouldn't miss my birthday."

Holding her like that, Keegan could feel her shallow, even breathing, and, despite her sadness—or, perhaps, because of it—the moment held a curious allure. He ran his palm along the silk blouse at the back of her shoulders.

"I went over to Merrill's apartment," Eve continued, her small voice resonating through him now. "The place was locked up tight. No sign of him. So, I went back home and waited by the phone. By dinner time, I was frantic. When mother went up for the night, I headed over to Merrill's place again. The door was ajar. He wasn't there, but the apartment had been ransacked. I didn't know what to do. I ran back to the restaurant. It was closed, but Walt came to the window and let me in. He hadn't seen Merrill since that morning, but he told me he had left something for safekeeping."

In some niggling depth, Keegan felt the need to distrust her words, to hold her story up to scrutiny—but here she was, in his arms, and he could conjure up no doubts.

"Walt went in the back room and brought out a padded envelope," she said. "We opened it. It was a necklace. Merrill must have gotten it for my birthday. I've worn it ever since." She gathered the collar of her blouse with one hand. "I never saw Merrill again," she said. "You know the rest."

She lifted her head to look at him, and the shattered expression on her face caught Keegan off guard.

"When they found his body," she said, "my whole life fell to pieces." Again, she looked from one of his eyes to the other. "Don't you see, Jim?" she said. "That's why I was staying at Uncle Nigel's. That's why I've been such a wreck." She pressed her palm to his chest again. "Maybe I've clung to you too closely," she said. "And I'm sorry if I did. But in all my confusion and loneliness, I fell for you."

He held her for a while as she wept again, and for a long time after she'd stopped. He held her until her breathing grew shallow and even, then he laid her down gently without waking her. He stretched out on his side next to her scorching body until he too slept.

AT ONE POINT during the long night, he woke and turned and found Eve awake. She was staring up at the ceiling. Her small body, so close to him, radiated warmth. He watched her as she breathed, her eyes glistening. She seemed unaware he was watching her.

And there was Merrill's teardrop rhinestone, dangling on its gold chain. It had settled on the pillow in the hollow above her shoulder. Keegan reached out to touch it, but Eve started. She rolled away from him, as if protecting herself. She lay with her back to him in the darkness until sleep pulled him down again.

CHAPTER NINE

Tuesday, August 21, 1962

KEEGAN WOKE WITH a start. He sat up, not sure where he was. The sun glowered from behind the drawn blinds in his apartment's bedroom window. The night before came flooding back to him. Eve was gone.

He propped himself on one elbow and looked at the empty space beside him. The counterpane was smooth, like she had tugged the wrinkles out of it, careful to erase every trace of evidence that she had been there. Was it possible she had even plumped the hollow out of the pillow next to him too? He rolled over and breathed in the pillowcase. It confided only the faintest hint of lavender.

He got up and quietly slid the window open a few inches, but the air outside seemed no cooler than it was inside. He lay back down on the bed and looked up at the ceiling, feeling oddly bereft to be here alone—though, since he'd moved here years ago, no one had ever shared his bed.

He thought of Nora, truly abandoned up in the cottage. He'd slip out quietly and head on up there to feed her and let her out in the yard. He'd shower when he got to the cottage, so Mr. Soto wouldn't hear the water running. But first he'd see if he could just eke out a few more minutes of sleep before the temperature stole every possibility of rest.

NORA'S FRENZY AT seeing him come through the door only heightened Keegan's sense of guilt for leaving her alone all night. But, for her part, all seemed forgiven the moment he bent down and patted her on the head. She jumped up on him and tugged at his trouser cuffs and bolted around the coffee table, as if he might be willing to chase her—a writhing bundle of joy and energy barely contained by fur. At least some aspects of life could be uncomplicated. He let her out into the yard and fed her and refreshed the water in her kitchen bowl. Then he showered and put on clean clothes.

The dog now lay, flopped on her side and panting, under the kitchen table at his feet. Keegan sat bent over a mug of bad instant coffee, wondering if there were any point in going into the office today. It wasn't like he would get any work done. And if the ballistics report was complete, he'd be arrested. He imagined the LAPD parading him, handcuffed, past Mrs. Dodd's desk, and out along the hallway to the elevators. He thought of all the strangers in the lobby turning to gape at him as they marched him through, arms pinioned behind him. And then there would be all the foot traffic on Sixth Street, passers-by stopping to watch him get shoved into the back of a police cruiser.

No, if it was going to happen today, it would be best if he holed up in the cottage, where only Nora—simple, forgiving Nora—would witness his humiliation.

As if on cue, the sound of a car in low gear, climbing the hill, made Keegan push himself up from the kitchen table. It sounded nearby, and if it had passed the turnoff to Ormsby's front gate, it was coming his way.

He dragged himself to the sink, his clean clothes already beginning to stick to his limbs. From the kitchen window, he saw a black sedan round the last bend. It would be Lieutenant Moore. Keegan felt something close to gratitude. At least he'd come alone in an unmarked car. Despite Moore's little speech at the Chinatown wishing well, the man was giving Keegan a break, like the old friend he was. No sirens. No handcuffs. No news crew in tow. Their history still counted for something.

He ran the cold tap into the kitchen sink. He tested it with his fingers. It was warm at first but then ran tepid. He cupped his hands and splashed water in his face. He did it once more and then wiped his face with a paper towel. He went into the living room and looked around. The car was pulling up outside now. He put on his wristwatch. He slipped his wallet into the back pocket of his trousers; they'd want his driver's license at booking.

Nora jumped up on the settee, tail wagging. What would happen to her? Would they send someone up here to get her? Maybe Mrs. Dodd would be willing to take her in. The poor thing had no idea what was coming. Another master vanishing from her life.

He went over to the front screen door and looked out. The sedan idled a few seconds, as if the lieutenant hadn't finished listening to a song on the radio, and then the engine cut. Moore opened the driver-side door and slammed it behind him. He straightened up and pressed the Panama hat onto his head. This was official business.

Nora, now at Keegan's feet, pawed at the screen door and took up barking.

Moore closed the garden gate behind him. He wore a seersucker suit today, along with the hat—like a proper Englishman abroad, Keegan thought. His luminous white shirt was unbuttoned at the collar. He was camera-ready. Perhaps the press was waiting for them downtown, a convenient photo op that didn't require them to traipse up into the hills in scalding weather.

When Moore started up the front porch steps, Nora backed away from the screen, still barking. Now on the porch, the lieutenant looked at ease and well rested. His suit slacks had a nice crease running from his knees to the tops of his black penny loafers. "Don't act like you're surprised to see me," he said. At the sound of his voice, Nora scuttled back into the kitchen.

Keegan stood a few inches behind the mesh of the screen door. "Neither surprised nor pleased," he said.

The lieutenant doffed his Panama hat as if he expected Keegan to invite him inside. The hat left an indentation in his dense black hair above his ears. He looked down along the road he'd just driven up and fanned himself. "You're not going to ask me in?" He turned the hat by the brim in his hands and waited for an answer.

"I don't think I will," Keegan said. The latch on the screen door was locked, not that it mattered. It could easily be broken—though the lieutenant was not the sort of man to do such things. He had a whole precinct of shirtsleeve thugs down at Parker Center who were happy to do the rough stuff. He could afford to keep his hands clean. "Unless," Keegan said, "you have a warrant for my arrest."

The lieutenant tipped his head to one side, like he was trying to see past Keegan into the cottage. He fanned himself with his hat again, but it seemed more pantomime than purposeful. He looked maddeningly relaxed and self-possessed, untroubled by the heat. "No warrant yet," Moore admitted. "Still waiting to hear from ballistics. I was just hoping we could have a chat."

"We already had a chat," Keegan said. "I'm just another perp now, remember? Any chatting we do now is going to be through my lawyer."

The lieutenant made a face, a little put out by Keegan's lack of graciousness. "Now what would you need with a lawyer, Jimmy?" he said. "Innocent guy like you?"

Keegan tugged the front of his shirt away from his sweat-slick body. "Arrest me or leave me alone, Lieutenant," he said. "I've got things to do."

The lieutenant's smile faded, but he nodded again. He held the hat by his side with one hand and dug the other hand into the pocket of his slacks. He jingled the coins there absentmindedly. "I'm just wondering," the lieutenant said, "if you know where your girlfriend went last night."

"What Eve does is her business," Keegan said. "Maybe she's the one you should be asking." He grinned. "Say, I'll bet *she* can afford some pretty good lawyers."

Moore jingled the coins in his pocket again. It was playacting, Keegan sensed—a gesture designed to look casual, unconcerned—but it grated on his nerves nonetheless.

"She left her place before ten last night," the lieutenant said. "We've had a man watching the house—but I'm sure you already guessed that."

Keegan just stared at him.

"Your girlfriend called a yellow cab, and our man tailed her in an unmarked car," Moore said. "She didn't have any luggage, so she wasn't skipping town." Moore paused a few seconds, as if waiting for Keegan's reaction.

"I'm on the edge of my seat," Keegan said.

The lieutenant smiled at Keegan's tone. "Larry Darnell—I don't think you know him—he just got bumped up to homicide. He drew the short straw for the overnight shift. He followed her to a gas station phone booth and then to the Biltmore Hotel," he said. "She went in the back way, by the Grand Street parking garage."

"If you know where she went, why are you bothering me?"

"Well, this is where Darnell really pissed in the pudding," the lieutenant said. "Your girl didn't check in at the Biltmore. But our guy should have guessed that, since she hadn't packed any bags." Moore looked back down the hill again. "Our best guess is that she walked straight through, came out on Olive and caught another taxi to a destination unknown."

Keegan allowed himself a sly smile. It has been that easy. LA's finest. "That Darnell's a bright one," he said.

"Tell me about it," Moore said. "Fifteen watts on his best day." The lieutenant held his hat in front of him now and worked it with his hands, as if trying to adjust its shape. "So, Darnell waits out back, trying to think of what to do.

178

He parks in the garage and asks some questions at the front desk." Moore shook his head. "Then, instead of calling me, the dumbass heads back to the barn and writes up his report. 'Subject's whereabouts unknown.' His exact words. Ran out the rest of his shift with his feet up by the coffee urn chatting up the night dispatcher."

"Well, that there's some damn good police work," Keegan said.

The lieutenant smiled ruefully. "The guy's worthless, but he's somebody's son-in-law. So—" He shrugged. What was he to do? He might end up with his own brainless son-in-law someday.

"So, you don't have any idea where she went?" Keegan asked.

The lieutenant shook his head. "Nor where she is now," he admitted. "I have a theory, though."

"And what's that?"

"I think she was with you." He paused a beat to let the accusation breathe. "I think she spent the night in your apartment."

"Afraid you're wrong there, chief," Keegan said. "It's a tiny place. I would have noticed if there was a woman in there with me."

The lieutenant grinned. "If Darnell had called me at home—like any jack with half a brain would have done—I'd have told him to cruise by St. Andrews Place and see if your lights were on."

"You know where I live," Keegan said, "and yet you never stop by."

"Oh, I've stopped by," the lieutenant said softly. "Been there a couple of times this week. You're never in."

Keegan felt caught off guard—but of course Moore would have gone by the apartment. This was a murder investigation.

The lieutenant looked up the road to where it dead-ended at the wooden barrier and smiled, still working the brim of his hat. "I'll tell you what," the lieutenant said. "That guy in the apartment next to yours is a real ride-along." He didn't look at Keegan as he spoke. "I don't know how you put up with him."

Keegan thought of the trembling blinds, the bobbleheaded little man spying on the quad. He could picture Mr. Soto talking to the lieutenant breathlessly, staring at the stitching of his seersucker jacket.

"What's his name?" the lieutenant said. "Your neighbor? Lopez? Garcia?"

Keegan hissed through his teeth. He moved an inch closer to the screen. "Don't play stupid," he said. "It doesn't suit you. You know the man's name."

The lieutenant shrugged and smiled. "I gave Soto my card last week when I went by to look at your place. I told him to call me if he saw anything I might find interesting." He looked Keegan in the eye and smiled. "The guy's been calling in twice a day to tell me you haven't been home. He seems to have an unnatural interest in the goings-on at Casa Keegan. I was starting to regret giving him my direct number."

The lieutenant rocked back on his heels a little. He seemed to be having a good time spinning his story, drawing the moment out, making Keegan sweat. It was like a high-stakes poker hand—all bluff and braggadocio until somebody got a case of nerves and moved too fast. It wouldn't be Keegan. He bit the inside of his lip and waited.

"But then the guy phoned me this morning," Moore finally said. "First thing. I hadn't even hung my hat." Another pause; another aggravating smile. "He said you had a woman in your apartment last night, Jimmy." The lieutenant searched Keegan's face. "Said he heard you two talking, but he couldn't make out any words. Said she sounded angry, then she started crying, then everything went silent. Said it's the first time he's ever heard you with company over there—except for an illegal dog." Moore glanced past Keegan, as if he was looking for Nora. "He said your visitor left around five this morning. She slipped out real quiet. He could hear you still snoring."

Keegan said nothing.

The lieutenant waited. A plane droned somewhere far overhead. "Come on, Jimmy," Moore said. "At least play along."

Keegan worked his jaw from side to side, but he didn't speak.

"Say you went down to your place to get some clothes," Moore said. "Tell me you drank a little. Turned on the TV a little too loud." The smile faded from his face. "Tell me it was some late show melodrama—one of those weepies with Joan Crawford and all that crying. Tell me your neighbor's mistaken. It's all a big misunderstanding. Your Mr. Soto got it all wrong."

Keegan closed his eyes and took a few breaths. He felt bone-tired and emptied, and he knew there was no hope of sleep or solace any time soon. "Sure. Okay," Keegan said. His tone was flat, resigned. "Let's go with that. It was the TV."

The lieutenant stepped closer to the screen. "Here's what probably happened," he said. "You got her to pull that trick at the Biltmore and come over to your place." He smiled easily. "You needed to get your stories straight, because we *all* know what news I'm going to get from ballistics." He jingled the coins in his pocket again. "So, she came over, and you asked her some questions. You wanted it to be all business, but she got teary-eyed and turned you around again." A lewd smile played across the lieutenant's face. "I'm guessing it ended with a roll in the hay, and you all starry-eyed," he said. "Am I close?"

"Fuck you," Keegan said.

The lieutenant grinned. "It won't hold up in court," the lieutenant said, "but I'll take that as a yes."

The lieutenant stepped back again and looked at Keegan through the screen a long few seconds without speaking. When he did speak, it was like the will had gone out of him. Whatever game he was playing by coming up here had lost its flavor for him. "You're not good at this, Jimmy," he said. "You're good at a lot of things, but this isn't one of them."

Keegan thought of the tank of doomed goldfish.

"I love my job," Moore said, "but I'm not enjoying this, Jimmy." His voice was quiet now, the dramatic flair long gone. He put his hat back on his head and pressed it down. "My heart's not in it," he said. "I don't like taking a good man down—and I *still* think you're a good man." He turned and went down the porch steps. As he closed the gate behind him, he paused with both hands on the wood, facing Keegan. "You think you know what you're doing, Jimmy," he said. "But you don't."

Keegan watched him walk around the car and open the driver's-side door. The lieutenant stood there, looking over the car. *She's leading you down a dark alley, and you don't have the good sense to strike a match.*

"Pick up the phone when it rings, Jimmy," the lieutenant said. "Save me the trip out here. I'll let you know when I hear from ballistics."

When Keegan looked down, Nora was back at his side, watching the lieutenant's car pull away. "You good, brave girl," he said. "It was just a false alarm." He stooped down and scratched the dog behind her ear. "Don't you worry," he said. "I'll get us through this. I'll think of something."

NORA SQUIRMED TO be set down the minute she saw Mrs. Dodd behind her desk. Keegan set her on the desk blotter and headed to his inner office. Mrs. Dodd didn't say a word. She seemed to intuit that something was up. Had Lieutenant Moore talked to her as well? "Hold my calls," Keegan told her. "I'm going to put my head down for a while."

"Hungover?"

"I wish," he said and closed the inner office door behind him.

He sat down behind his desk and put his feet up. He felt his body slacken in the cool office air. He could sleep awhile, just like this, and that would be good for him—but first there was something he needed to do.

The name Eve had said had been nagging at him. *Hesse.* He knew there was a story there—one he had typed up himself. The pieces he filed had been strictly for laughs. Dimwit GIs—wasn't their ringleader a woman?—miscasting themselves as jewel thieves. Dumbasses miscast as badasses. Sure, he remembered it, now that he put his mind to it. Or was his overheated brain just grasping at straws? Was this some desperate attempt to find Eve innocent? Hell, he could barely remember his own middle name in this heat.

He dropped his feet back to the floor and reached for his Rolodex. He flipped through the cards until he found the number he wanted. When the newspaper archive room picked up, he asked for Judy. He waited on the line, basking in the air conditioning, and tried to collect his thoughts—about Eve and Merrill and the story she'd spun for him. If she'd made the whole thing up as she went along, she was a natural. It read like a B-movie script—something with low-key lighting and venetian-blind shadows, something Uncle Nigel might have acted in, as a cut-rate Sydney Greenstreet.

Judy, when her voice came over the phone, seemed happy to hear from him. "Just glad to hear you're still alive," she said. "It's been a while, and you still owe me some drinks."

"I'm good for them," Keegan said. "I'm just hoping I can add a couple to my tab." He listened for any sigh or groan or hint of grievance, but none came. This was Judy—long-suffering, chain-smoking Judy. She'd always had a thing for Keegan, and she'd made no effort to hide the fact. Keegan moved the phone to his other ear and propped his elbows on his desk. "Look, I need another favor," he said. "How busy are things today?"

"City room's kinda quiet," Judy said. "Now that John and Jackie left town, everyone's stopped falling all over themselves trying to get assignments." A phone rang somewhere in the archives room, but she seemed to ignore it. "Big earthquake in Italy," she said. "But that's going to be wire service."

"Think you could pull me some clips?"

"Unless Air Force One crashes, I'll have plenty of time on my hands," she said. "What do you need?"

"I'm not really sure," he said. "I mean I don't know if the story's even real, but it kind of rings a bell." How much did he really have to go on? He rubbed his forehead with his free hand. "Something right after the war. A blue-blood family, name of Hesse. American soldiers looting the family silver. Everything backfired. Something like that." It was just a jumble of ideas, a tangled junk drawer of memories he hadn't, for some reason, discarded. "Think that's enough to go on?"

"Actually, it *does* sound familiar," Judy said after a beat. He could hear pencil scribbling on paper. "Might have been around the time I got hired on. Let me see what I can dig up. You still have the same numbers?"

"You have my home and office," he said. "Let me give you my mom's cottage. If you don't find me at the other two, try me there."

THE BUZZ OF the intercom plucked Keegan from a nervy, shallow dream about being in a barber's chair. Marilyn had been giving him a manicure while he got his hair cut. She had prattled on and on about her plans for Christmas, but he'd sat there knowing he'd once again spend that day alone in his apartment.

He lifted his head from the desktop, and the room seemed to spin around him.

"Phone call," Mrs. Dodd's voice crackled over the intercom's speaker.

The inner office door was closed, but rather than push the intercom button, he just shouted to her. "I said to hold my calls."

Mrs. Dodd's voice came over the intercom again. "You're going to want this one, boss."

She put the call through.

"We shouldn't be talking on the phone," Keegan told Eve when he heard her small voice on the other end.

"Don't worry," she told him. "I'm calling from a booth." She was telling the truth. Keegan could hear the hum of a crowd and an echoing loudspeaker in the background—some kind of announcement. Was she at Union Station?

"You didn't go home," he told her. The room was still slowly pivoting around him, so he let his head fall back against his leather chair and looked up at the ceiling tiles. There was nothing he found more disorienting than being plucked from a deep sleep. "Where did you go after you left my place?"

"I couldn't go home," she said. "I couldn't just leave things the way they were, with you thinking—" She sighed into the mouthpiece and once again didn't finish her thought. The tone of her voice changed. "My aunt is probably frantic, wondering where I am," she said.

"Not as frantic as Lieutenant Moore," Keegan told her. "He came by the cottage for a chat. Wanted to know if I knew where you were." The fluorescent lights that were set into the ceiling had a wicked flicker to them—or was that pulsing just in his head?

"Look, Jim," Eve said. "I think I can fix this whole mess. One little bit at a time. I'm going to talk to a lawyer."

Keegan sat straighter in his chair. That one small, sudden movement made his eyes ache. He pressed his palm to his forehead. "*Wait*," he said. "No. You can't do that. That'll just—"

"No, no," Eve said. She laughed anxiously. "Not like that. Not a defense lawyer. Not about—you know—Uncle Nigel."

A man's voice on some loudspeaker drowned out the next few words Eve said, then: "He knew Merrill. He can clear all that up. He's eager to meet you. And once all that's straightened out, we can talk to him about going to the police and explaining everything that happened."

"It's too late for that."

Eve's voice grew firm. "Nobody murdered anyone," she told him. "They'll believe us if we lay it all out for them. There might be some consequences—like, I don't know, interfering with evidence, or one of those kinds of things." She paused, and he could hear a rumble of noises in the background, a jumble of voices and machinery. When she spoke again, her voice was solemn. "We're not murderers, Jim. And we need to stop acting like we are. We're not going to end up in prison over this. I can afford some very good counsel."

"But you can't just—"

"Don't worry, Jim," she spoke over him. "I won't do anything without talking to you first. I've got to go. I've got a train to catch. Stay near a phone."

There was another loudspeaker voice, a woman this time, but it was cut off when Eve hung up.

Keegan blew out a puff of air and hung the phone back in its cradle. At least the room had stopped moving, though the pressure behind his eyes was gaining ground. He got up and went to the door and leaned out. "If anyone asks—" he said.

"She didn't call," Mrs. Dodd finished the sentence for him. "I know. I know."

IT WAS DARK out by the time Eve called again. He'd dozed off in the cottage with the side of his face on the kitchen table, a restless, dreamless patch of sleep. He woke with a heart-thudding start when the phone rang, to a dark, still kitchen and a sleeping dog. He stood unsteadily, crossed to the wall phone and picked up the receiver. He slumped back down at the kitchen table before he put the phone to his ear. He didn't bother to turn on the light.

"It's me," she said. "Don't worry. I'm at a phone booth."

Keegan listened hard, but he couldn't hear any background noise. She could be calling from anywhere. He rubbed his itching eyes. How were they so dry when every other part of him was slick with sweat?

"I've been thinking," she said. "What if they've got your phone tapped?"

The phone's coiled chord sagged, full of knots, in the space between the table and the wall. If the ballistics report had come back, there'd definitely be enough for a phone tap warrant, Keegan reasoned. But there'd also be enough for an arrest—yet here he sat, a free man in his mother's kitchen. "Maybe they have," Keegan said. "Maybe they haven't.

There's nothing we can do about it right now." He turned the phone and pressed it to his other ear. "So, what's the story? Please tell me you haven't told this lawyer anything."

"I haven't," she said, sounding a little offended by his question. "And I'm not going to say anything to anyone unless you're there to do it with me." Her voice warmed noticeably. "We're in this together, Jim," she said, "hell or high water."

For richer or poorer. All or nothing. A man or a mouse. Keegan's heat-addled brain rattled off conditionals, until he caught himself doing it and forced it to stop. He pressed a damp palm to the tabletop. "So where did you go today?"

"Santa Barbara," she said. "It's all set up. He can help us. We just all need to meet."

"Who is he?"

She paused a beat, considering. "I probably shouldn't say on the phone," she told him. "It's complicated. But I promise it'll all make sense. You'll see. He'll explain it all. He knew all about Merrill, apparently, and what he'd found in that North Beach warehouse. But we need to meet him in secret."

A stab of wariness cut through Keegan's exhaustion, and he pulled himself straighter in his chair. "Why in secret?"

"Jim, please," she said. "Just trust me."

"When is this meeting supposed to take place?"

"Tonight," she said. "Midnight. By that old amusement pier. You know the one."

"Pacific Park?" he said. "You're joking." He thought of the old gun arching out across the black water and splashing up a white plume. He thought of the ramshackle silhouette of the pier's old roller coasters on the north horizon. She couldn't have known he'd got rid of it there. He hadn't let it slip, had he?

"It was the only place I could think of," she said. "It had to be a place he could find, but where no one would be around. He said he knew where it was. We can talk there in private."

You don't have the good sense to strike a match. "I don't

know," Keegan said. "We should probably make it somewhere else. Somewhere with people around."

"I'm sorry," she said. "I didn't think it would be a problem. There's no way to change it. I can't reach him between now and then."

Keegan breathed into the phone. It felt like the chair he was sitting in was drifting under him somehow. He rubbed his dry eyes again. The ache in his head seemed to be gathering at the front of his brain. He'd give a year of his life for a cool breeze through a window and a sound night's sleep.

"Please come," Eve said. Her voice was pleading now. "I want to make things all right," she said. "I want you to hold me and tell me you forgive me for getting you into all this. I want us to go back to the way things were before."

IT WOULD TAKE a half-hour to get to the pier without traffic—and there wouldn't be much traffic at this hour. He'd have to leave soon, but he was in no hurry to get out the door. He found a ballpoint and a sheet of his mother's best powder-blue stationery and sat down at the kitchen table to write a note. If he disappeared tonight, it would have to tell the whole story for whoever found it. He scribbled with the pen to get the ink flowing and then wrote as it came to him. Six pages. Everything he could remember.

When he was done, he looked down at it. His handwriting had taken on the spindly look of an old man's. The message was disjointed and jumbled, a tangle of errant thoughts and memories—but he was too tired to worry about the *five Ws*—it would have to do.

He left Nora asleep in the cottage with the doors and windows open. He filled a couple of pots with fresh water, and another with kitchen scraps, in case she was stuck in the cottage a few days and no one could hear her barking. Surely, if Keegan didn't return, Moore or his minions would find her here in a day or two.

He got his keys from the entry table and looked around

the place one last time. He patted the snoring dog on its head and slipped out the door without waking her. He crossed to the carport, leaving the front door open and the screen door unlatched.

By the time he crossed Sunset Boulevard, he had only ten minutes to make the midnight meeting. That fact didn't make him pick up his pace.

CHAPTER TEN

Wednesday, August 22, 1962

THE DASHBOARD CLOCK said it was midnight as Keegan drove past the Beverly Hilton. He should have set out sooner— he was still a good twenty minutes from the old pier—but what did it matter? Whatever was waiting for him down there at the old pier could cool its heels and wait for him. He'd arrive when he arrived.

Tall, venerable palm trees lined both side of Santa Monica Boulevard, disappearing, at a quarter their height, into the streetlamps' spidery glare. As he neared Pacific Coast Highway, the blockish, concrete offices gave way to squat, sunbaked clapboard buildings—pastel-painted tattoo parlors, dive bars, seedy diners, taquerias—all of them dark and shuttered. He yawned and rubbed his prickling eyes with the hand not on the wheel. The warm wind in his face, coming through his car's rolled-down windows, was the only thing keeping him awake.

As a kid, this part of town had always held a heady sense of promise for Keegan. This was where, from the back seat of his grandfather's Chrysler, he'd begin to notice gulls circling in the sky and catch the first whiff of salt breeze coming in off the Pacific. He'd built a kite one summer, using plans from a

Boys' Life magazine. It was a boxy thing built of newspaper and balsa, too heavy to be—

The passenger-side front wheel hit the curb with a jolt and glanced the car sideways. Keegan, jerked awake, braked and swerved back into the center of the road, where he stopped, stalled, angled across the boulevard's centerline. His heart thudded in his chest.

He gripped the steering wheel with both hands and tried to slow his breathing. He glanced behind him in the rearview mirror. He'd missed a parked Volkswagen by a couple of yards. He looked up and down the street for witnesses. The only headlights were a block behind him, idling at a red light. He started up the car again, giving it as little gas as he could while he turned the key, so as not to make much noise or draw attention. He slipped it into gear and let out the clutch, adrenaline still reaming his veins. He leaned forward and peered through the windshield, forcing his bleary eyes wide. He signaled and turned left on South Bundy. That would take him to Venice Boulevard.

There were worse ways to die than dozing off at the wheel, he reasoned. He thought of his own father climbing the safety wall with the Point Fermin lighthouse at his back. He imagined the long, sickening fall to the rocks below. He thought of Ormsby, eyes agog, bleeding out on the kitchen floor, pressing his hand to his throat and feeling the hot, slick pulse of life spewing between his fingers. Had the man looked down the dimly lit hallway and seen Eve cowering at the far end, white-faced with the realization of what she'd done? Or had he looked up to see her standing over him, smoking gun in hand, peering down at him dispassionately, waiting to make sure the wound was fatal? Yes, there were worse ways to die.

He imagined Eve now in the looming shadows of the pier's great pylons, her back pressed against the tarry wood, watching for him. Whose gun would she be holding tonight? What new patsy had she seduced to help her? He saw shadows and broad-shouldered figures and the glint of gunmetal in the moonlight. He smelled the dank, waterlogged air—

At first, he thought a low-flying plane was crossing overhead, but the red lights sweeping down at him from the sky were on the descending arm of a railroad crossing. He hit the brakes hard but could feel that it was too late, so he gunned the engine and felt the rear wheels of his car fishtail to the right.

The descending arm bounced across the ragtop roof as he sped under it. His wheels clattered across the rails, and he felt a hot light, like a spotlight, bearing down on him from the passenger side. Once he was clear of the tracks, he braked, nearly stalling the car again. Heart hammering, he watched the hulking engine and the first freight cars hurtle past from right to left in the rearview mirror. The ground beneath him trembled up through the car's undercarriage. He laughed bitterly, still catching his breath. It would be just his luck to cheat the hangman, to die, inanely, on the way to the noose, tripping and breaking his neck on the gallows steps.

He put on his turn signal, though the street was empty in all directions, and headed west down Venice Boulevard. A few blocks ahead of him, the row of streetlights ended abruptly in a black abyss where the Pacific waited.

A half-block from PCH, Keegan coasted over to the side of the road, until his hubcap scraped the high curb. He braked to a stop. The block was posted for no overnight parking, so the curb was empty. He set the parking brake. A parking ticket was the least of his worries—and at least someone would notice if he didn't come back for his car. They'd run his plates. Trace who he was. Find the note on his kitchen table. Nora would be fine.

He tilted the rearview mirror to look at his face in the streetlight that came down through the windshield. His eyes looked hollow now, nearly lifeless. He thought again of Ormsby's face gazing up empty-eyed from the kitchen doorway. Was death really anything to fear?

He slipped the car into neutral, cut the motor, killed the headlights, and sat looking out through the windshield as the hot engine ticked. Up ahead, he could hear the breakers in the darkness. He gripped the steering wheel with both hands and looked at his own two fists. His knuckles were bone-white against the wheel's leather grip.

The irony was not lost on him: Keegan had spent the last decade teaching others the art of distrust, ushering them, client by client, into the cold world of betrayal—unmasking the philanderer, the double-crosser, the liar, the cheat. Secretly, he had always felt superior to those credulous souls who came to him for help. They were dupes. They ignored all those blatant cues that should have tipped them off.

But if Lieutenant Moore was right, he'd joined their ranks, hadn't he? Eve had played him for a fool. At this moment, he felt gut-shot by the notion that he could be anyone's patsy, especially hers. He'd give everything he owned for Eve to be the woman she claimed to be. He remembered her holding the old revolver with both hands and the smell of gunpowder in the dry morning air. *So innocent—yet so lethal*, she'd said. Truer words.

He opened the car door and got out. The balmy wind coming in off the ocean rippled at his damp shirt. He was half a block from the waterfront. No one waiting for him down by the pier would have seen him yet. There was plenty of time to turn back, to start up the car and drive away, to leave Eve and her accomplices, if they existed, in the shadows.

There was a gash in his car's ragtop roof now from the railroad crossing gate, an eight-inch tear on the passenger side. He ran his hand along the slit. A few days ago, he would have been furious, but tonight it was hard to care.

He straightened up and saw that he'd parked in front of a camera shop. He could see his reflection in the plate-glass window under the red-and-white awning. He was stooped and old, a broken-down, shot-to-hell human being. Why would any woman give him a second look?

He closed the car door and tossed his keys through the open window into the driver's seat. They'd be waiting there for whoever needed them. The gesture gave him a peculiar sense of freedom. If this was the end, he'd leave few loose ends for whoever—Mrs. Dodd?—had to clean up after him: a car, a cottage, a dog. The thought of Nora made him wish he'd mentioned her in the note he'd left on the kitchen table. What would become of her?

He trudged up the empty sidewalk past an ice cream shop that was padlocked behind a steel security grate. He chastised himself for every slow step he took. He'd always fancied himself fearless. But here he was, ransacking his mind for any excuse to linger, to stall, to turn around and go back. He passed a drugstore, straw hats and suntan lotion arranged in the dark front window. Plastic buckets and spades. Beach umbrellas. Coleman coolers.

At the corner, he paused in the entrance of a penny arcade. Somehow, the breeze coming off the ocean failed to swirl through the alcove he stood in. The stale air there reeked of bubblegum and saltwater taffy. The tiles beneath his feet were sticky and sand-strewn. He ran his fingers back through his hair. He needed a haircut, he thought—and then he allowed himself a grim laugh at that ridiculous notion.

The old Pacific Park pier, a block to the north, was boarded up now, awaiting demolition. In daylight, the chain-link fencing was festooned with yellow caution tape, like a tawdry crime scene. He remembered the ticket booth there in his boyhood, the turnstile, the high arching entryway that seemed a threshold to wonder. It was all rust and splinters and shattered glass now. The years had not been kind to either of them.

He stared at the darkness under the pier, looking for any movement—a glimmer, a shadow, a struck match. The hot wind was coming in gusts now, lofting the salt spray. Up above his head, a flock of moths battered themselves against the flickering neon sign above the darkened arcade: PACIFIC PARK.

He knew the longer he stood in the safety of this alcove,

the harder it would be to take that next step into the darkness. Maybe Eve was watching out there with proof that would clear her good name, clear a pathway back to that night of Bordeaux wine and blithe banter in the hilltop cottage. But maybe Louis Moore was right, and some other fate awaited him. There was no way to learn the truth from a safe distance—no way to see the human heart through a telephoto lens. That much he knew to be true. That much his history had taught him.

He tried to bring Eve's face to mind—her looking up at him, searching his eyes in that way of hers. But instead he kept picturing Marilyn—the peaked brows, those heavy-lidded eyes, the beauty spot, her fleshy lips. He could hear her breathy voice. He could see the vampish way she smoothed down her dress at her hips. He saw that sad, shattered look in her eyes that the soft-focus lens tried to hide.

He shook his head. He was hopeless. His was a soul lost. He couldn't at this moment conjure up the slightest shred of faith—even for a woman like Eve, a woman he thought he could fall for.

For a few seconds he stood with his eyes closed, listening to the sound of the breakers, inhaling the salty air—and then he cursed himself and slipped back up the street the way he'd come.

THE PARKING ATTENDANT rapped on the driver's-side window with the butt of his silver flashlight. "Hey, boss," the man said. "You're not supposed to be here. You have to pay."

Keegan pulled himself up behind the wheel and fumbled to pull out his wallet. He cranked down the window and passed the man a twenty-dollar bill. "Here," he said. "This will cover it. Keep the change."

The attendant tipped his Dodgers cap back a little on his head, wary of this windfall. He looked down at the money a second or two before he folded it and slipped it into the pocket of his shirt. "Sure thing, boss," he said. "Sorry to wake you."

Keegan began to crank the window back up, but he stopped. "Oh, and do me a favor, buddy," he said. "Wake me up in an hour?"

"Will do," the man said. He tapped the bill of his cap with his flashlight, a kind of salute, and whistled some tune as he headed over to his shack.

WHEN KEEGAN GOT to Pershing Square, Lusk's truck was already parked with two wheels up on the sidewalk and the tailgate open. Lusk had his leather work gloves on and was lifting stacks of papers and magazines down to the sidewalk by their twine bindings. The sky farther down Hill Street was edging towards a lighter shade of gray. It would be another half-hour before the streetlamps flickered off, and the morning rush of commuters began.

Keegan paused in the alcove of the Owl drugstore. Someone must have slept there; the space smelled of liquor and urine. He stood watching a minute or two to make sure the coast was clear. His good Nikon camera, the one he kept locked in the office, the one with the expensive telephoto lens, dangled from the leather strap wrapped around his fist.

When Lusk saw Keegan crossing the street, he straightened up and grinned. "If you're here for a refund," he said. "I'm afraid all sales are final." He tugged at the fingers of one leather glove with his teeth and then pulled both off and stuffed them in his back pocket. "Or do you want me to find you the matching hat and spurs?"

"I need help," Keegan said when he was close enough to talk softly. "It's a bit of an emergency."

Lusk held out his hand for a perfunctory shake and then frowned and looked around at the empty street. "I'm doing my best to eke out an honest living here," he said, loudly, as if he thought Keegan might be wearing a microphone. And then, more softly: "What is it you need?" He grinned. It was all part of the gag.

Keegan was about to speak, but he fell quiet as a

Plymouth Belvedere pulled to a stop at the corner and idled there waiting for the light to change. The windows were rolled down and a Dinah Shore song played on the radio. Neither passenger—two men in matching white uniforms—glanced in Keegan's direction. The light changed, and the car pulled ahead.

"You said you had a gun," Keegan said. "Remember? Last time I was here. You said you could get it fast."

Lusk, untroubled, dug at something between his teeth with his thumbnail, but then his eyebrows jerked upward. "Oh, yeah," he said brightly. "The Colt. But you wanted a snub nose. That thing's got a barrel like a broom handle."

"Can you still get it for me?"

Lusk crossed his arms and tucked his chin. "What did you do with the gun I just gave you?" he said. "Don't tell me the big kids took it away."

Keegan balled his hands into fists. He wasn't in the mood for banter. "I'm not kidding, Kip," he said. He winced at the peevish tinge in his own voice. He took a deep breath and tried to settle himself. "I really need protection," he said. "I think someone's going to come for me. Can you get the gun? Please?"

"Who's coming for you?"

Keegan laughed bitterly. "I wish I knew," he said. "Just tell me. Can you get the gun?"

Lusk gave him an exasperated look, which might have been droll if it hadn't been on an unshaven middle-aged face. "Yeah," he said. "I'm pretty sure the guy's still got it, though for what he's asking, someone might have snapped it up."

"Can you check?" Keegan said.

Lusk shrugged and then nodded, noncommittally. He reached for the gloves in his back pocket.

"Now?" Keegan said. "I mean *right* now."

Lusk left the gloves where they were and looked at his wristwatch. "If he's still got it," he huffed. "I can have it here in half an hour." He glanced around at the dark plaza and then back at Keegan. "Maybe more like an hour," he said. "I might have to wake him up."

"Great," Keegan said. "That's great. Thank you."

"I can't promise the gun is clean, you know," Lusk said. "When someone offers a Caddie for the price of a Studebaker, there's probably a body in the trunk." He shrugged and rubbed the thinning hair at the back of his head. "*Caveat emptor*," he said, "with a capital *M*."

"How much will it cost?"

"A hundred. Two hundred," Lusk said. "Depends on what mood I find him in." He glanced at his watch again. "My guess is he's not much of a morning person," he said. "I'll talk him down as much as I can, but, believe me—you'll be getting a bargain in any case."

Keegan forced his numb face into his best approximation of an ingratiating smile. "The thing is, I'm short on cash right now," he said. "And I don't want to go around town cashing more checks while certain parties might be watching." He held out the Nikon camera. "I can give you this."

Lusk looked down at the camera dubiously. He didn't reach for it.

Keegan shook it. "Take a look," he said. "Please." He pressed the camera on Lusk, who finally sighed and took it from him. "Cost me nearly four hundred bucks last fall," Keegan said. "And that lens was another two hundred. Best telephoto on the market." Without the weight of the camera, he suddenly didn't know what to do with his hands, so he burrowed them deep into his pockets. "That camera should cover the price of the Colt, easy," he said.

Lusk turned the camera in his hand; it might have been a cantaloupe for all he seemed to care about it. "What the hell am I supposed to do with a camera?" Lusk said. "The people I'm dealing with are not eager to have their pictures taken." He shrugged and tried to give the camera back. "I might as well offer them tickets to the Policemen's Ball."

Keegan took a half step back, hands still in his pockets.

"Just hold onto it as collateral until I can get you the cash," Keegan said. "A couple of days, tops. You could pawn that thing anywhere in town for more than two hundred."

Lusk didn't seem pleased with the offer. He weighed the camera in his hand and shook his head ruefully. But when he looked up again, Keegan knew he was going to accept.

"It is not good business to extend such favors to friends," Lusk said, "but you seem as if you're in a predicament. So, okay, I will take your Jap camera as collateral, against my better judgment—though it does feel like you're taking unfair advantage of our camaraderie."

Keegan felt a surge of relief. He jerked his hands out of his pockets and patted both of Lusk's shoulders. "Thanks, Kip," he said. "I owe you big time."

"Indeed, you do," Lusk said, but rather than get on his way, he just looked up at Keegan. "I worry about you, Jimmy," he said. "You have the stink of desperation about you these days. How deep is this shit you're in?"

Keegan thought of Ormsby's ashen-white face against the crimson pool of blood. He thought of the darkness under the pier. He thought of Lieutenant Moore's stern face sizing him up.

He sighed and shook his head. "As shit goes, it's pretty damn deep," he admitted. "I thought I could still touch bottom, but right now I'm not so sure."

Lusk nodded knowingly—he'd been there a time or two himself. "Oh, what a tangled web we weave," he said.

As if on cue, a siren started up a block or two to the north, in the direction of the public library. Keegan went stiff. The siren cycled twice and then fell silent again. In the quiet that followed, Keegan could feel the adrenaline pulsing through his veins.

Lusk grinned at him. "Ideally, a man who carries a gun should not be so jumpy," he said. "Remember that a bullet travels faster than good judgment."

Keegan shook his head. "Don't I know it," he said.

THE BROWN PAPER bag Lusk gave him smelled like onions. Keegan didn't look in it until he was back in his car with the windows cracked and the doors locked and the Dodger-capped parking attendant safely in his shed.

The gun was wrapped in—of all things—the City section of *The Times*. SUSPECT HELD IN ROBBERY. In a parallel life, that would have been Keegan's byline. But it didn't pay to think of parallel lives.

Lusk had told the truth; the pistol was almost new, a much better specimen than the beat-up revolver he'd flung off the pier. The barrel was eight inches long and uniformly blued. He felt the heft of it in his palm, still swaddled in newsprint. If Moore ran the serial numbers on this revolver, what would he find?

Keegan pressed the newspaper around it again and slid it under the driver's seat. He'd ditch it as soon as he felt safe. But safe from what? From whom?

BACK IN THE cottage, the note Keegan had written lay untouched on the kitchen table. He'd left it thinking he'd never see it again. But he hadn't even made it to the pier. Now, that failure felt like a rebuke. He dropped down into a chair and looked the note over. It was disjointed and nearly illegible, a mishmash of facts and feverish conjecture, scrawled with a trembling hand.

He lit a burner on the stove, held the blue paper over it, and then watched it flare down to ash in the kitchen sink. He turned on the faucet and let the water flush away all evidence of his cowardice. If only everything else were so easy to erase.

He left the kitchen door open, so Nora could come and go as she pleased. If anyone came near the cottage, he wanted to hear her barking.

In the living room, he loaded the big gun from the box of .357 cartridges he'd picked up at the sporting goods place on Highland. Six brass rounds. Full metal jacket. He closed the cylinder and set the gun at one end of the coffee table, atop the Shakespeare book, grip towards him, where he could still reach it when he lay down on the sofa.

Exhaustion strummed through him like electricity. How long could a body keep going without real sleep? He had to stay vigilant, but it wouldn't hurt to nap a few minutes, just to rest his bones. Nora would wake him if anyone came up the road.

He stretched out with his head braced against the cushioned arm, shoes still on. He slipped under right away, a sleep that was weighty and lightless, a dreamless black abyss.

WHEN THE PHONE rang, Keegan jerked awake and grabbed for the gun on the coffee table next to him, but he only managed to send it, and the book it was on, clattering to the hardwood floor on the far side of the table. The phone rang again, and he pulled himself up from the sofa, cursing himself. It was just a ringing phone, for God's sake. What might he have done if he'd managed to get his finger on the trigger?

He left the gun where it lay and shuffled groggily into the kitchen, both knees aching. He expected to hear Eve's voice when he picked up, angry at him for not showing up where they'd agreed to meet—but it was just Judy from *The Times*.

She seemed happy to have news for him. "We ran about a dozen pieces on the crown jewels," she told him. "They're all your byline. Want me to keep them out for you?"

"Wait," he said, "the what?"

"They all add up to just a few inches," she said. "But it's pretty good stuff. You were having a good time with it."

"Did you say *crown jewels*?"

"Well, not the Tower of London ones," she said. "The *Hesse* jewels. That's what you wanted me to find, right?"

Keegan pinched the bridge of his nose. "These were actual *crown* jewels?" It was like he was translating the words in his head as she spoke them, and he was having trouble keeping up.

"I'm looking at a half-tone photo of some lady wearing a

crown right now," she said. There was a playful impatience in her voice now. "That's the story we were talking about, right?"

"So, remind me what I wrote."

Judy paused, and he could hear the old familiar clatter of typewriters in the background. He pictured her arranging the clips on her cluttered desk. "Bunch of GIs billeted in a big German castle—Kronberg—at the end of the war," she said. "A WAC officer—let's see…" Keegan heard the sound of papers being shuffled about. "Captain Kathleen *Nash*," she read off one of the clippings. "She finds some fresh concrete in the basement and decides to chisel it up. She and a couple other officers find buried treasure. Old family fortune hidden from the Nazis. European royalty."

It was true, he remembered now. It was no movie. "And the GIs made off with it, right?" he said. "But they were idiots."

Judy snorted a laugh. "*Were* they!" she said. "Rank amateurs. They packed it up and mailed most of it to her sister stateside. Took them weeks to wrap it all up. They even pried the jewels out of the royal tiaras, put them in a shoebox and sent them parcel post. Didn't take much to track down the thieves once the royals came home to find the basement all dug up."

"Did they get the stuff all back?"

Again, papers shuffling, typewriters clacking. "'Half of Hesse Jewels Missing, Says Princess'," Judy said, clearly reading him one of his own headlines. Her voice fell into a more natural rhythm. "A lot of the family silver and rare coins disappeared into the Chicago underground, along with the jewels," she said. "Our girl gets convicted. Five years. Millions in treasure still out there somewhere. That's the last clip we have. You want to come see them?"

Keegan stared blankly at the kitchen screen door, trying to gather in what all this meant. How would Eve have known about the theft unless her story was true? Some deep well of hope wanted him to take it all at face value—but reason wouldn't allow it. *Of course*, she'd have known about the

Hesse family fortune. That kind of news would be hot gossip in her old-money crowd. Her grandfather probably sent a condolence card to the castle, registered mail. *So sorry for your loss.*

"Some of the big jewels even had *names*," Judy went on. "*Der Alte Saphir. Der Leiningen Rubin.*" She was having fun with it. "You find them or something?"

"What?"

"Because if you're sitting on the Hope Diamond, a few drinks isn't going to cut it," Judy said. "I've got the right complexion for crown jewels."

"Sorry, girl," he said. "The best I can get you is Bombay Sapphire."

She laughed, a throaty, masculine guffaw. "I suppose," she said with mock disappointment. "Thursday, maybe?"

Keegan smiled sourly. It was funny from a certain angle. If he was still alive on Thursday, he'd likely be locked up in a cell. If Eve didn't get him, Louis Moore surely would. "Perfect," he said. "Thursday it is."

He was just hanging up the phone when Nora bolted out from under the table, barking at the kitchen's screen door. There was a shadow and a splintering sound. He was thrust forward and taken down hard, his knees buckling under some great hot weight. His cheek was pressed hard against the gritty kitchen tile. Beyond all the cussing, he could hear the phone's receiver thunk-thunking against the wall as it bounced and swung on its coiled cord. He felt a hard knee on his back and his arms wrenched behind him.

The men—six or seven in uniform—worked now in silence. Even Keegan, the wind knocked out of him, could only grunt. He could hear the dog yelping somewhere out of his line of vision and feel his heart thumping against the floor tiles. At least they were cops, he told himself. They had come to take him in alive. He wouldn't be fished out of the brine knotted to a cinder block.

He felt the cold pinch of handcuffs ratcheted around his

wrists. He turned his head so his other cheek was resting on the floor, and saw just boots, the legs of a kitchen chair knocked on its side and the bottom of a cupboard door. There, in the gap under the cabinet, lay the puce-stained cork from a wine bottle. He couldn't help but laugh.

Keegan was hoisted to his feet by the armpits and shoved forward against the sink. Out the kitchen window, a cluster of squad cars crowded the gravel drive to Ormsby's back gate. They must have assembled there while he was still asleep, crept up on the house and waited there for a signal. Judy's phone call was just the opportunity they needed.

Keegan didn't bother to put up a fight. He knew better. When he asked if he could change his shirt or comfort the whimpering dog before they took him away, it was as if he hadn't spoken. Two cops, big ones, dragged him by the arms to the front door, his feet dragging and tripping across the hardwood floor. Behind him, he heard Nora scamper after him. Then a man cursed, and Nora yelped, and he heard her run away to hide somewhere at the back of the cottage.

Outside the cottage, another group of men—all in plain clothes—waited by the front porch to be let in. The higher echelons of law enforcement—the ones who wore suit coats and didn't get their hands dirty. None of them looked him in the eye as he was heaved past them, down the steps and along the front path to the gate. He didn't see the lieutenant.

The back of the police cruiser was sticky and airless, and it was hard to get comfortable with his arms cinched so tightly behind him. The car smelled for some ungodly reason like a barbershop, all Brylcreem and ethyl alcohol— or whatever it was they used to scrub out the piss and vomit. He leaned with one shoulder against the seat's back and watched what was happening at the cottage. It didn't take long for a fat man with a stubby red tie to come out the front screen door with the Colt pistol in a clear plastic evidence bag. The man's stomach swayed from side to side as he trotted down the porch steps.

Keegan finally noticed the kid cop on the scene again. He hovered lankily on the edge of the scrum, an unhappy spectator, his arms folded across his chest at the front of the car Keegan was in. It was *his* car Keegan was in, he realized—a nice touch of irony on Moore's part, if it weren't just a coincidence.

HARSH FLUORESCENT LIGHT flickered down on him from ice-cube-tray fixtures in the hallway ceiling. The subterranean holding cell was so cold, Keegan's ears ached. He'd rolled down his shirtsleeves and buttoned them at the wrist. He'd turned up his collar and scrunched down his neck to cover as much skin as he could, but it did little to protect him from the raw cold. Up on the street, it must have been a hundred degrees. Down here was another world.

Keegan was alone, in the last cell in a long row, butted up against a pockmarked cinder-block wall. The steel bars and every metal fixture were painted the pale green of pistachio ice cream. A worn wooden bench, deep-etched with graffiti, ran along the back three sides of his enclosure. That's where he'd fallen asleep after about the first hour, curled up on his side like a dog, hugging his knees against the chill.

But now he was awake, and even with his eyes squeezed shut, the flickering artificial light made him edgy. He lay with his back pressed against the bars that separated him from the empty cell next door. In all his years as a cop-house reporter, he had never made it down here to the holding cells, but they were pretty much what he'd have expected: dank and comfortless, hard stone and battered steel, the smell of disinfectant powerless to overcome the stench of urine.

Raucous voices echoed from somewhere down along the row of cells, but another blind wall on the far side of the empty cell next to him kept him from seeing who else was in lockup. Was he being kept down here on his own to protect him from the others? Or was it to shield those garden-variety drunks and shoplifters from the likes of him—a man who likely stood accused of murder? He thought of Lusk's partitioned fish tanks, the doomed and oblivious feeder fish. *Nothing gets past you.*

Despite the noise and the chill, Keegan had slept deeply —for a few hours at least, maybe the better part of a day. With no visible windows or clocks, it was impossible to tell what time it might be. They'd taken his watch along with his belt and wallet when they'd booked him. All he knew was that he felt alert now, more clear-headed than he'd been in days.

He pulled himself to a sitting position on the bench. His shoes—they'd taken his laces, too—felt loose on his feet as he lowered them to the sticky concrete floor. Now that he sat upright, his shoulder and hip felt bruised from their hours spent pressed against the hard bench.

Keegan looked down at his mottled hands: ten ink-blackened fingertips—whorls and ridges that might link him to anything he'd touched in the past week. What other notes and photographs and statements were right now being assembled and scrutinized and filed away in Louis Moore's case against him?

He'd be taken to an interrogation room and questioned soon—that much was certain—but at least now he had his wits about him. He'd be able to hold his own. And what could they really have on him? A ballistics report and a lot of circumstantial hooey—nothing he couldn't talk his way out of now that he'd got some decent sleep and could think straight. If it got sticky, he'd clam up and ask for a lawyer. At least a couple he could think of still owed him favors.

But then the idea struck him: What if they were holding Eve in another cell somewhere? He felt his confidence crumble. Of course, they had her; it was standard procedure when there was an accomplice. And what would her version of events sound like? He'd wanted them to get their stories straight, but a lot had happened since the night in his apartment. What version of the last week would Eve be weaving in the interview room? He'd have to wait and see. What point was there in getting worked up about it now? It couldn't take much longer for them to come and get him.

He got up and limped to the front bars, testing the pain in his back and hipbone. He pressed his face into the gap between two cold bars. "Hey," he called out to anyone who might hear. "Can I get a blanket? It's freezing in here."

"This ain't the Ambassador," a voice shouted back from the far end of the hallway. There was no way to know if it was a cop or some drunk sobering up from a Boyle Heights bender. "No room service here, bub," the voice said. "This is where you freeze your ass and think about your misdeeds." Someone farther down the row laughed at this.

Keegan strode a couple of laps around the cell, swinging his arms to get the blood flowing. He pressed his face to the bars again, but he couldn't see far down the hall, just a series of notices stenciled on the whitewashed brickwork in English and Spanish.

NO LOUD OR PROFANE LANGUAGE. NO SMOKING. NO GRITAR O DECIR PALABROTAS. NO FUMAR.

"Can someone put in a call to Lieutenant Moore," he shouted. "I need to talk to him."

"Sure thing," the same voice called back. "He's been sitting by the phone, hoping you'd call."

More laughter echoed down to him from the far end of the hall.

Keegan went back to the bench and sat down. It was clear he'd just have to wait.

WHEN THEY FINALLY came to get him, Keegan had no idea if it was night or day. A sallow-faced cop led him by the elbow down the corridor and up the echoing back staircase with his wrists cuffed behind him. Without laces, Keegan had to curl his toes to keep his shoes from falling off as he walked, but the cop pulled him along anyway. His beltless trousers hung loose on his hipbones.

"What time is it?" he asked the cop.

"Thursday," the cop informed him.

THE COP SAT Keegan in a steel chair at a steel table in a cinder-block room that was painted the color of a sardine. He left him there alone, still cuffed.

Keegan looked around. A large tape recorder was bolted down to one edge of the table. The wide, scuffed mirror mounted along one side of the room was obviously two-way, but it was impossible to know if anyone was behind it now, watching Keegan wait. He'd seen this very room before, no doubt, but it was a whole different world on this side of the mirror.

Waiting, Keegan had long ago learned, was part of their game. He was supposed to sit here and think too much. He was supposed to fidget and bite his thumb. He was supposed to rehearse his story in his mind, and then second-guess, and then guess again, until the whole thing unraveled before the first question was even asked.

The chair he sat on was bolted to the ground, with heavy metal rings welded to the sides in case there were chains. The seat of the chair was slotted steel, and the back seemed set at a ninety-degree angle, as if it were carefully engineered to deny comfort. With his arms still pinioned behind him, he had to lean forward, his ribs pressed against the table's metal edge. At least this room wasn't as freezing as the holding cell or as hot as it must be outside—it was a lukewarm limbo, free of sensory distractions.

On the other side of the closed door behind him, he could hear muffled voices; ringing phones; passing footsteps; the slow, hunt-and-peck clicking of typewriter keys. Water hissed in pipes somewhere overhead. For everyone on that side of the door, this was just a day at the office. Make some phone calls, file some paperwork, gossip a bit at the coffee urn and keep an eye on the clock. He knew the workaday world of the cop house. He'd been there himself, cooling his heels, sipping weak Folgers, waiting for the show to start.

At last, the heavy door opened, and Keegan strained to look over his shoulder. Lieutenant Moore stepped into the room, followed by a plump, florid man in an ill-fitting brown suit. It might have been the harsh fluorescent lighting, but Moore looked tinged with gray now—his face, not so much his hair—like he'd aged a few years since Keegan had seen him yesterday morning at the cottage. Moore held an evidence folder in one hand. He pushed the door shut behind them.

It was the other man who sat down in the chair opposite Keegan. His big red face looked Keegan over. Moore set the folder on the table in front of this man and took his place a few feet behind him and off to one side. Moore folded his arms across his chest and stood with his feet apart. Maybe, given their long acquaintance, the lieutenant had recused himself from doing the actual questioning. Or maybe the red-faced man was the titular lead detective on the Ormsby case. Either way, the man seemed flustered to find himself playing the lead with Moore in the room, hovering behind him. He twisted a knob on the tape recorder, and the reels started turning. He cleared his throat to get Keegan's attention. "Mr. Keegan…"

Keegan ignored him. "What's the idea with the handcuffs, Lou?" he asked the lieutenant. "You know I'm not going anywhere."

The man in the chair across from Keegan glanced back at the lieutenant. Moore gave him a nod, and the man sighed and got to his feet. He hiked up his pants and came around behind Keegan to remove the cuffs. He went back around the table, slipped the cuffs into the pocket of his rumpled suit coat, and took his seat again.

Keegan rubbed the red lines that were bitten into the skin of his wrists. He opened and closed his hands to get the blood flowing. Oh, for some soap and hot water to scrub the damn ink stains off his fingers.

Moore watched Keegan silently, his face expressionless as a mugshot.

The nameless man sitting across the table cleared his

throat again. "We're hoping you'd be willing to answer a few questions," he said. "And this recording is just to make sure everything is on the up-and-up." His voice was unsure, wobbly. "Is it all right with you if we record this interview?"

"Are you serious?" Keegan said, addressing the lieutenant again and not the man who had spoken to him. "This whole bringing-me-in-for-questioning isn't scaring me. It's just getting my Irish up."

"I just need it for the recording, Mr. Keegan," the other man said, raising his voice feebly. "All you have to do is answer yes or no."

"*Mister* Keegan?" Keegan said, still talking to Moore. "Lou, come off it."

The other man tapped the tabletop with a plump index finger to draw Keegan's attention back to him. "Sir?"

"Yes, I know my rights," Keegan told the man. "And the recording is okay with me. But, as your boss can tell you, I'm not the type to sit by and let you railroad me. I didn't shoot Ormsby."

The other man pressed his palms down on the steel table. "So, just to be clear, you're aware that we're recording the interview. Is that correct, Mr. Keegan?"

"I've got the Fifth Amendment memorized," Keegan said. He was no rube when it came to procedure. "I'm willing to talk to you for now. But I'll clam up the moment the mood strikes me."

The man glanced over his shoulder, got another nod from the lieutenant, and turned back to Keegan. "Where were you last night between the hours of ten in the evening and six this morning?"

"*Last* night?"

The man nodded. "Last night," he said.

"I was in my mother's cottage, trying to get some sleep," Keegan said. "Where were *you*?"

The man blinked twice but didn't otherwise respond. "Did you leave your home at any time?" he asked.

"No," Keegan lied. "I was there all night."

Behind the florid man, the lieutenant worked his jaw from side to side, glowering silently. He clearly hadn't liked Keegan's answer.

The nameless man folded his plump, pink hands atop the Manila folder. His fingers were short and thick, and they had a tremble to them. He seemed skittish to have the lieutenant looming, just out of sight. His eyes kept darting to one side. "Did you drive to Santa Monica last night?" the man asked.

Keegan shook his head, disgusted with himself, with the entire hopeless mess he'd allowed himself to get mired in. "Shit," he said, looking at the lieutenant. "You were having me tailed?"

The lieutenant seemed to rise up an inch or two where he stood, his arms still folded. "Did you or did you *not* drive to the beach last night, Jimmy?" he said, his voice cool and smooth as a glassy ocean.

A look of something like panic came over the florid man's face. He was being bypassed, and he seemed to know that wasn't a good thing, career-wise. He sat straighter in his chair. Keegan ignored him.

"If you had someone following me," Keegan told Moore, "then you know where I was."

"Again, Mr. Keegan," the other man said, "we ask you to answer the question put before you." He was trying hard to pull himself back into the loop, but Keegan wasn't having it.

Keegan pivoted on the hard chair a little so he was squarely facing Moore. "You *know* I drove to the beach," he told the lieutenant. "And you also know I turned around and went right back home." He looked from Moore to the other man and back again, trying to read their faces. Something wasn't adding up. He leaned back as best he could in the hard steel chair. "If your guys were tailing me, there's no point in asking, is there?" He nodded down at the folder on the table. "You've got the details all typed up in triplicate by now."

"Don't play stupid," the lieutenant said, repeating Keegan's words from the day before. "It doesn't suit you."

Keegan sighed and put his elbows up on the steel table. "Did it ever occur to you that maybe I *am* stupid?" he said. "Think of how much that would explain."

The florid man leaned farther in and tried again to hold Keegan's gaze. "You know you slipped the tail." He seemed to be making an effort to keep his voice monotone and his face neutral. This was a man who watched *Dragnet*.

"What?" Keegan said, deigning to address the man directly. "What the hell are you talking about?"

"That little stunt at the railroad tracks," Moore said.

Keegan looked over at the lieutenant. "*Stunt?*" he said. And then—with a flush of foreboding—he understood. He remembered the descending railroad-crossing arm bouncing along the cloth roof of his convertible, slitting the black fabric. He remembered the freight train thundering by in the rearview mirror, spewing diesel fumes and hot creosote in its wake. Keegan had driven on, shaken but unscratched. He'd slipped the lieutenant's tail without even knowing it was there.

The lieutenant's face looked metallic now under the fluorescent lighting, an angry visage cast in pewter.

"Okay," Keegan said, "*that* was an accident." He splayed his hands out on the tabletop. "I was asleep at the wheel. It just *hap*pened. I'm lucky I didn't get killed." For some reason, he could feel his pulse in his wrists where the cuffs had been. He lifted his hands to find damp prints on the steel table. He opened and closed his fists again. This interview was getting away from him. "I drove another couple of blocks. I got out of the car. I got back in and drove home. End of story." He scooted forward a little on the steel chair. "Believe me, you guys didn't miss much," he said. "I wish to God you'd kept up with me."

The other man leaned farther forward into the overhead light. His ruddy cheeks were mapped with broken capillaries. A drinker, maybe. "You drove all the way to the beach for a

Lucky Strike, Mr. Keegan?" he said. He was trying to sound menacing but couldn't quite pull it off.

"I thought I was going to do something," Keegan told him. "But I changed my mind." He turned to the lieutenant. "I haven't been sleeping, Lou," he said. "It's hard to think straight in this heat."

"Where was your girlfriend that whole time?" the lieutenant asked. His voice, compared with his colleague's, was stern and commanding, too big for the small room they were gathered in.

"Eve wasn't with *me*," Keegan told the lieutenant. "At least the guys tailing me can tell you *that* much. Even your idiot Darnell couldn't miss a woman in the goddamn passenger seat of a roadster."

The other cop sucked in a breath and sat suddenly straight, looking confused. This, Keegan realized, was Darnell himself. Sure. Why wouldn't it be?

The lieutenant shook his head and shifted his jaw from side to side again. He seemed to be losing whatever composure he'd mustered before he walked in the room. "Don't try to be funny, Jimmy," he said. "Even with your train stunt, we can put you within five blocks."

"Five blocks of *what*?" Keegan said.

For a few long seconds, the lieutenant just stared at Keegan, his lips tense. It was as if he was searching Keegan's face for something—almost the way Eve did. Keegan felt a sinking sensation creep up through him, pulling him down, like a slowly descending elevator. He looked from the lieutenant to Darnell and back again and squeezed his hands into fists on the tabletop. "Why don't you ask *her* where she was?" he said to fill the uneasy silence. His mind was flailing now. "Why the hell are you talking to *me*?"

The lieutenant started to say something, and then stopped and stared at Keegan some more. The whites of his eyes seemed tinged gunmetal gray under the buzzing fluorescent lights. The man's expression made Keegan's heart stumble. Something was wrong here.

"What?" Keegan said. His voice was quieter now. "What the hell is going on here?"

Moore shook his head slowly, slightly. The tension in his features relaxed into a look of reluctant astonishment. "My God," he said. "You're not bullshitting us. You're telling the truth."

"Of course, I'm telling the truth," Keegan said. He sat back in his chair and folded his arms uncertainly. "I turned around last night and got out of there. Swear to God."

The lieutenant came over to the table and leaned on it with the fingertips of both hands. His tie dangled an inch or two above the tabletop. He gaped at Keegan a few more seconds, brow furrowed.

Keegan's stomach clenched. The air seemed to sting his face with static electricity. What was he missing?

"Jesus," Moore said. He straightened up and looked down at Keegan blankly. "Jesus, Jimmy. I'm sorry."

Keegan was about to respond, but some blunt instinct kept his tongue still. He was missing something, and he wasn't sure he wanted to find out what. He rubbed the stubble on his throat with one hand.

The lieutenant turned to the other man. "Go ahead and show him," he said. He turned his back on both of them, like he didn't want to be a witness to whatever happened next.

Darnell turned the folder to face Keegan and flipped it open. His stubby fingers arranged the photographs on the tabletop under the strident lights.

The shock hit Keegan like a sucker punch. They were crime-scene photographs. The body lying on the sand was Eve's. He felt some chasm open beneath his chair and clutched the table's edge as if it might slow his fall.

Three photographs. He stared down at them, trying to fathom their meaning. The photos showed Eve from three different angles, lying supine in the sand. Her soaked slacks and blouse clung to her limbs like cellophane. One arm was crossed over her breasts, and the other lay off to the side, palm up, fingers gently curved. In the close-up of her face, those lavender-scented curls were pasted to her forehead with saltwater. Trails of sand traced the soft lines of her face and filled the gap between her slightly parted lips.

The lieutenant, who'd been staring at the back wall, turned around, but his eyes wouldn't meet Keegan's.

Keegan looked back down at the photographs, mind reeling. They lay spread out on the table in front of him: another set of three to tally with Catling's photos from a week ago—also eight by ten, also black and white. Keegan was again in the dark, in the company of a man who held all the cards. "Are these real?" was all he could think of to say.

"They're real," the lieutenant said. His voice no longer filled the small room. "Some fishermen found her at the high tide line this morning. Venice. Just south of the pier."

Keegan moved his lips but made no sound. The blood had drained from his face and hands. Did Eve now lie on the same steel table Marilyn had occupied a couple of weeks before? "Drowned?" he said.

Moore shook his head. "Shot," he said. "Twice in the chest. Both bullets exited the body. No slugs, no cartridges. No real crime scene."

Keegan remembered the fat cop coming down the cottage's front steps with Lusk's Colt revolver in a plastic evidence bag. He understood the real reason he was here.

"Just tell me, Jimmy," the lieutenant said. "Tell me once and for all you had nothing to do with this."

The photos in front of Keegan were colorless and starkly lit in the photographer's flash—cold and still, sterile as a scalpel. He thought of Eve's scalding flesh beside him on the bed, the gentle rise and fall of her chest as she slept. "She wanted me to come to her," Keegan said, finding his mouth dry. "I was going to, but I bailed out at the last minute.

I turned around and went back home. I left her out there waiting for me in the dark."

"So, this was not your doing?" Moore asked. There was something leading about the way he asked the question—like he was pleading for Keegan to deny it. "You *didn't* kill her?"

Keegan shook his head. "Jesus," he said. "Of course not." His words were lifeless and seemed to hang in the air like a foggy breath. "Not on purpose, anyway," he said. "I didn't kill her. But maybe I could have—" He had neither the heart nor the words to finish the thought.

"Do you have any idea who would have done this?" Moore asked.

Keegan thought of the actor in the Sucrets ad on the grocery store TV. Was Simon Catling even real? A man with money and a motive? A man who had killed Eve's lover and was happy to do it again?

Keegan shook his head. "She said she wanted me to meet someone down by the old pier," Keegan said. "She didn't tell me who it was." He thought of the story Eve had told him in the furnace-heat of his bedroom. Secret trysts and crown jewels. "The man they pulled out of San Francisco Bay," Keegan said. "The one you told me about. Was he black?"

The lieutenant straightened up a little. He seemed taken aback by the pivot in Keegan's reasoning. "Yeah," Moore said. "He was. What of it?"

"Nothing," he told the lieutenant. "It was just something she said."

He bent to look closely at the photos again. He tried to avoid Eve's face. Her tasteful blouse clung close to the secret contours of her body. She wore only one shoe. A delicate watch dangled from her wrist, crusted with sand. It looked expensive, but the killer had left it behind. He looked closer, and then he looked away.

The next minutes were a mute, numb daze. Darnell and Moore talked quietly together, their voices like a distant wind scattering leaves. Eventually a uniformed cop—bald-headed,

216

slope-shouldered—came in from the hallway and told Keegan to stand.

Darnell felt about in his coat for the handcuffs, and the cop clicked them back on Keegan's wrists, more loosely than the first cop had. He took Keegan's elbow in his plump fingers. "Nice and easy," he said. "Let's get you back downstairs." He led Keegan, anesthetized, to the room's open doorway.

"Let me work on this, Jimmy," the lieutenant's voice called from behind them. "Get some sleep down there. We'll talk. We'll figure this out."

Keegan nodded without looking back. He floated past desks and doors and bulletin boards and panes of wire-mesh glass. His loose shoes shuffled far, far beneath him. She was dead. She was gone. The thought seemed to strike him again and again and again, like cold water lapping the shore. He thought of the small, searing body on the bed beside him. He thought of the way she had rolled over in the dark when he had reached for her necklace. That image—her slender back in the shadows—was the last he would ever see of her.

Keegan stopped dead and brought the cop behind him up short. *Some of those jewels even had names. Der Alte Saphir. Der Leiningen Rubin.* "No, no *wait*," he said. "Wait. Take me back." He turned to go back down the hall, but the cop's grip tightened on his arm.

"Hey, easy there," the cop said.

Keegan tried to shake his arm loose and step around the man, but the cop took hold of both his arms in some kind of wrestling hold, and then another body, also in uniform, appeared out of nowhere to block his way.

"No," Keegan said. "You don't understand. I need to talk to the lieutenant." Both his arms were wrenched back, but he kept pressing forward, back along the hall towards the open door of the interrogation room.

Down the hall, Darnell came out through the doorway with the folder under one arm, followed by Lieutenant Moore.

"*Lou*," Keegan called out. "*Lou*."

The lieutenant looked in his direction, surprised, and, just as their eyes met, the cops kicked Keegan's legs out from under him and brought him down hard to the floor. His face glanced off the tiles and then he lay with the side of his head on the floor, no longer struggling. His second takedown of the day. His bottom lip pulsed with pain.

A pair of well-polished black shoes came into view.

"What's going on?" Moore's voice said up above him. "Let him up."

Keegan was pulled roughly to his feet again. One of his shoes was missing, and his stocking foot felt cold and vulnerable on the floor tile.

"Let go of him," Moore said roughly. "It's okay."

The hands holding Keegan released him, and he took a quick sideways step to keep his balance. He rolled his shoulders away from the cops and dug his foot into the empty shoe on the hallway floor. He felt a bubble of blood at his mouth when he exhaled.

"What is it, Jimmy?" the lieutenant said.

Keegan glared at the two uniforms and then looked at Moore. "The photographs," he said. "Let me see them again."

The lieutenant regarded him evenly. "You sure?"

"Yeah, Lou, I'm sure," he said. "I think something's missing."

The lieutenant sighed. He shot Darnell a look and then nodded. "Okay," he said. "And uncuff him. He's fine."

Moore led him back towards the interrogation room, and Darnell fell in behind them.

As he walked, Keegan pulled out the front of his shirt and saw a spray of blood there. His lip pulsed numbly. He lifted his arm and wiped the blood on his sleeve. It wasn't too bad, just a trickle, really.

This time, Moore sat in the chair opposite Keegan's, so Darnell set the folder on the table and then stood with his back to the two-way mirror, self-consciously shifting his weight from foot to foot.

"What is it you want to see?" Moore asked. He set the first photo on the table face up. Eve lay on her back on the sand with her one hand beckoning the viewer closer. Keegan looked away.

"Not that one," he said. "The other. The close-up."

The lieutenant set that photo down on top of the other and leaned in, so he could watch Keegan's face.

Keegan was right. The necklace was gone. There was no sign of the chain at the back of her neck or of the large teardrop stone under her clinging damp blouse. "She had that necklace," Keegan said. "She always wore it. You had to have seen it."

The lieutenant frowned and then nodded. "Yeah," he said. "I did. A big, clunky stone—like the size of a cherry. Blue."

"She thought it was a rhinestone," Keegan said. "I don't think it was." He was assembling the puzzle together in his mind, piece by piece, as he spoke. "She always wore it. Said it had great sentimental value. I think she got it from the dead man." He tilted his head and looked at the photo again. "I've never seen her without it." Again, he thought of her scorching body rolling away from him in the dark.

The lieutenant flipped through some of the pages in the file until he found what he was looking for. He ran his finger down the page. "You're right," he said. "It's not listed. It wasn't on her when she washed up." He closed the file and looked at Keegan. "The fishermen?"

Keegan tugged the other photos from underneath and tapped one with his finger. "They left the watch." He shook his head and slumped back in his chair. He sat a moment, speechlessly smoothing down the jigsaw he'd assembled in his head. "Merrill found his proof," he said. "And he'd tried to keep it safe. He thought no one knew about the restaurant."

The lieutenant leaned in. "What are you talking about, Jimmy?" he said. "What the hell does all this mean?"

Keegan sighed and tried to find the words. It was all so complicated—yet obvious, now that he could think clearly.

"That stone was part of the Hesse crown jewels. Merrill found them, and they killed him to keep him quiet." He shook his head. Eve had told him nothing but the truth.

The lieutenant regarded him grimly and rubbed the back of his neck. "You're not making sense, Jimmy," he said. "Back up and take it slow."

"The man in San Francisco Bay was Eve's lover," Keegan said. "They were going to marry after Eve's mother died. She wouldn't condone a marriage to a black man. The guy stumbled onto war loot. Probably worth millions." He watched Moore's face, to make sure he was making enough sense. "He was going to tell the authorities, but they killed him. Eve had nothing to do with it." It was all so simple really, and she had told him everything he needed to know.

The lieutenant nodded, brow furrowed. "The stone would have proven it," he said.

"They were famous jewels," Keegan said. "They had *names*," he added, though he knew it would make no sense to Moore.

"And the gunman wanted it back."

Keegan nodded. "She thought it was a birthday present for her, Lou," he said, "but it was Merrill's evidence—and it got her killed." He found himself rubbing chills from his arms. "Call over to *The Times*. They've got the clippings all laid out for you."

The lieutenant sat back in his chair. It was clear he was giving Keegan's story some credence. "What about Ormsby?"

Ormsby. That seemed eons ago. A small, sad accident he'd managed to blow up beyond all recognition. What would have happened if they'd just done what Eve had wanted? "That was an accident," he said. "Eve thought someone was after her." He laughed bitterly. "Turns out they *were*." He could taste the blood from his lip as he spoke. "She was a bundle of nerves," he said, "and I handed her a loaded gun."

"Where is it now?"

"The ocean," Keegan said. He waved the question away. What did it matter now? "A diver could find it."

"And the break-in?"

"That was me," he said. "I was just trying to keep her out of trouble."

Moore nodded grimly. He held his tongue, and Keegan was grateful.

"Start to finish," Keegan said, "Eve didn't really do a thing."

Moore straightened up and looked at his watch. The man looked spent, vanquished. It was hard to know what he thought of the jewel story, but it was clear he'd work the whole thing through again. "You could have told me all this," he said. "You could have told me, Jimmy, and none of this would have happened." Moore slipped the photos back into the folder and closed it, and then he regarded Keegan wearily from across the table. "We're going to need to talk some more," he said. "We'll hold onto you for now while we check out the story. If what you say is true, we'll have to rethink this whole mess." The lieutenant shook his head. "Maybe you didn't kill anyone, Jimmy," he said. "But you sure as hell didn't help anybody out."

THE COP ESCORTING Keegan back to the cells paused before a set of steel doors. Keegan was in cuffs again, and the cop held him by his elbow, unnecessarily. Keegan could barely summon the will to keep breathing, let alone run. A woman behind a caged window looked them both over and pushed a button somewhere. Locks clunked open. The officer pushed Keegan through the doorway and then down a steel staircase towards the holding cells. The temperature chilled with each step they descended, and goosebumps rose along both Keegan's arms. Outside, there was relentless heat and sunshine, but it might as well have been another, distant planet.

As they descended towards the rows of cells, Keegan's heart beat faster. He thought of Marilyn, sunlit and beautiful, as she slipped into the Formosa Café. He thought of his

mother's last, lonely years—with only a dog for company—
while he frittered away his days not ten miles away. He
thought, then, of the flavor of Ormsby's wine on his tongue
and of Eve turning away from him on his dark bed.

Down the last few steps, he could hear the raucous, echoing
voices from the other cells. He understood he had descended
into a frozen hell of his own devising—and he wondered if
he would ever find his way back to sunlight.

ACKNOWLEDGMENTS

A heartfelt thanks to all those friends and family who were so generous with their time, patience and story-sense: Mel; Hedgie; Ryan; Jim Blaylock; Lyle Wiedeman, Katie Caffrey and Heidi Lup, the Thursday-night regulars; Janette Holm; Austin Holm; Steve Buchanan; Shelley Garcia; Kent Dunnington; Paige and Hannah, the fabulous Dinneny sisters; Santa-Victoria Pérez; Cameron David Quinn, Esq; and the intrepid team at Legend Press, especially my editor Lauren Parsons.